MORE PRAISE FOR RONDA THOMPSON!

PRICKLY PEAR

"A sure bet. Especially fun and engaging, this one is an unexpected surprise!"

—*Romantic Times*

"Ronda Thompson's *Prickly Pear* holds the flavor of a true western historical romance skillfully seasoned with sexual tension."

—*New York Times* bestselling author Jodi Thomas

CALL OF THE MOON

"Ms. Thompson puts a clever and intriguing new spin on werewolf mythology. Rich with ancient myths and modern-day passion, *Call of the Moon* is very satisfying reading."

—*Romantic Times*

AFTER TWILIGHT
*USA TODAY Bestseller
*Winner of the PEARL Award for Best Anthology

"Fans of werewolf romances will fall in love with [Thompson's short story] 'Midnight Serenade.' Intense emotion and sparkling dialogue make this a story you won't want to miss."

—*Romance Reviews Today*

"Ronda Thompson is a fresh new voice in the paranormal genre. . . . Simply riveting!"

—*The Belles and Beaux of Romance*

SCANDALOUS

"*Scandalous* is a wonderfully wry Regency . . . that makes you want to come back for more."

—*Romance Communications*

"Ronda Thompson is not to be missed. An innovative writer, she is not afraid to take chances. *Scandalous* is a juicy Regency which will have you smiling over the foibles and fancies of the period. Wonderful as usual."

—*Affair de Coeur*

"*Scandalous* is a fast-paced romp readers will find difficult to put down until the last page is read."

—*Under the Covers Book Reviews*

THE TEPEE HEATS UP

"Walk into the flame with me," Swift Buck whispered, his voice a husky caress against her ear. "Do not fight a battle you cannot win. You are mine. You have always been mine."

Rachel recalled what she'd been dreaming about and felt her face flush. What had she said? What had she done? What should she do now? Deciding that she needed distance between them in order to think straight, Rachel tried to move. His arms were around her and she couldn't budge.

"The others," she whispered.

"Are gone," he informed her.

"But Amoke," she tried.

"Jageitci will look after her."

"Breakfast—"

"Is prepared and waiting for us whenever we choose to rise." He pressed a heated kiss against her neck. "but I would rather nibble upon you."

RONDA THOMPSON

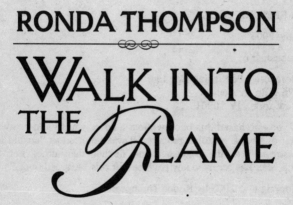

WALK INTO THE FLAME

LEISURE BOOKS NEW YORK CITY

A LEISURE BOOK®

June 2003

Published by

Dorchester Publishing Co., Inc.
276 Fifth Avenue
New York, NY 10001

ISBN 0-8439-5119-2

Printed in the United States of America.

Visit us on the web at www.dorchesterpub.com.

To Tami Sutton, a fan who once took the time to write to me about how much she enjoyed my books and became more than a fan— she's become one of my dearest friends. Thank you, Tami, for the gift of your friendship, for your moral support as well as the support you give to me by taking the time from your busy schedule as wife, mother of twins and nurse, to edit and send out my newsletters and to handle my contests. I appreciate you more than you will ever know.

WALK INTO THE FLAME

AUTHOR'S NOTE

The fort and reservation upon which I loosely based *Walk into the Flame* is the Bosque Redondo Reservation on the eastern plains of New Mexico, the site of Fort Sumner. In 1862, when Brig. General James H. Carleton ordered that all Mescaleros in the area be captured or killed, any Apaches who survived the slaughter were herded to Bosque Redondo and forced to live there. The conditions were horrible, and many Native Americans died due to disease and starvation. Three years later, the Mescalero Apaches eluded their military guards under cover of darkness and escaped. They returned to their spiritual home in the White and Sacramento Mountains and were never recaptured.

CHAPTER ONE

Rachel Morgan's first glimpse of the reservation was a sobering one. What crops managed to grow from beneath the cracked, dry soil stood frail and fruitless beneath the blazing New Mexico sun. The water used to irrigate those crops—if such a vain struggle could be called irrigation—was brown and brackish. How could the United States Army possibly believe this was a decent solution for the Mescalero Apaches?

Skin drawn tightly over bony faces, eyes without spark, souls without spirit—these were not Rachel's people . . . at least, not the ones she remembered. In the distance, children wailed, hungry because their fathers could not hunt, naked because their mothers could not sew.

"Pitiful, aren't they, Miss Morgan?"

Rachel pried her gaze from the nightmare before her and glanced at Captain Franklin Peterson. Her party had arrived at the fort that guarded the reservation two hours ago. Captain Peterson, the installation's commanding officer, had seemed less than happy to see them—Rachel and the Reverend and Mrs. Stark—and certainly not pleased about their mission. Rachel knew that the Army did not care for civilians prying into their affairs.

"Pitiful conditions produce pitiful people, Captain," she said stiffly. "I thought that the Mescaleros were to receive proper supplies to sustain them." Her gaze swept the skeletal forms slowly making their way toward them from the camps in the distance. The sight sickened her. "These people are obviously starving."

The captain shrugged. He wasn't much taller than Rachel, but he held himself ramrod straight, which gave him an appearance of height. He seemed young to be in command of a fort. A shock of pale blond hair hung across his high forehead, and his eyes were light blue. They lacked warmth— she had noticed that immediately.

"Supplies have a way of disappearing before they reach their appointed destination," he said. "We do the best we can here, Miss Morgan. Surely you understand."

She understood all too clearly. The more Apaches that died from starvation and disease on reservations, the fewer Indians the Army had to shoot.

"Of course we understand," Nelda Stark piped up. "Miss Morgan has been quite instrumental in seeing that we brought along a good number of supplies for these people, however. And the Reverend Stark and I brought Bibles. Feed sinners scripture along with their meals, and they will soon learn that it is by the grace of God they have been shown mercy."

"Amen," Nelda's husband, Reverend Roman Stark intoned. "And we are so pleased that Miss Morgan, good Christian woman that she is, has funded our journey."

Rachel felt a stab of guilt. She'd used Roman and Nelda for her own purposes. Clay, her half-brother, once known as Cougar to these Mescalero Apaches, had heard about the mistreatment of the Indians in this region through his circles in Washington. He'd been so outraged by the senseless slaughter of both Mescalero and Navaho that he'd lost his temper during a political meeting and nearly killed the general who had ordered the attacks. Clay was now cooling his heels in jail.

Rachel had felt honor-bound to see that the remaining Mescaleros were provided for. Yet, with her brother in jail . . . A proper white woman did not traipse all over the country alone. Nor could she furnish those whom most of her race viewed as the enemy with food and medical supplies without a good excuse—and not an excuse such as she'd been raised by the savages. Christian charity was the best alternative she'd come upon.

When all eyed her, Rachel whispered, "Amen," and bowed her head. Inside, however, she seethed with helpless rage. She had lived in the white world for five years. She had learned to dress properly, to speak properly, and to behave as white society expected, but beneath her pale skin, behind her blue eyes, her heart still beat with Apache pride. From what she'd seen so far, conditions at this reservation were insufferable.

"Why are they coming this way?" Mrs. Stark asked, fondling the neck of her drab, shapeless gown.

Rachel wore a similar gown, and her long, wavy hair was forced back in a prim bun. The traveling party had been escorted to the reservation by the relief guards for the fort. During the long days and nights of their journey, she hadn't wanted to appear as anything but plain and uninteresting to the men.

Captain Peterson's gaze lingered over her for too long despite her efforts. He turned his attention to Mrs. Stark. "They know it's the day we take count," he said. "See if any are missing. They also know if they show up, we'll spoon them a cup of rations."

A buckboard stopped behind the group of whites. A few soldiers scooted large soup pots to the edge of the tailgate, but the pleasant aroma of food did not fill the air. Rachel wondered what type of soup was in these pots. She longed to unload the supplies she'd brought and start handing them out, but she supposed she must bide her time, mustn't seem too suspiciously eager to help her people.

No, not *her* people, Rachel reminded herself. Her abusive father had given her to the Apaches to raise from the age of three. Her skin was white, her hair the color of the sun. She was white on the outside, but on the inside she still didn't feel as if she'd found her place. She was trying.

The Mescalero band that raised Rachel had called her Silent Wind because she did not speak. Not since her mother passed, and her father had thrust her at the Mescaleros like so much baggage. Only five years ago had she again begun to speak, and then only because the traumatic—

"You womenfolk had better stand back now!" the captain instructed, interrupting Rachel's thoughts. "You don't want to get too close. These are savages, and no doubt some of them carry some foul disease."

When Nelda Stark hurried behind the buckboard, Rachel was surprised and more than a little confused. "How are we to preach to them, to help them, if we cannot get close?" she asked.

"I'll see to that, Miss Morgan," Reverend Stark said, but he looked somewhat paler than he had upon their arrival. "Don't you worry."

Rachel *was* worried, though: fearful that her supplies and medicines would mysteriously disappear, frightened that she'd come all this way only to be swept into a corner like a cobweb and forgotten. White women, she had learned over the last five years, were not allowed the freedom that Indian women enjoyed. But Rachel refused to be swept aside as if she were nothing, the way her father had done by giving her away.

"I will ladle the soup," she insisted, moving to the wagon. "I feel a strong calling to help these . . . s-savages." She stumbled over the word. "I haven't traveled all this way to hide behind a wagon or watch from a distance."

"Headstrong," Reverend Stark commented under his breath, but Rachel heard. When she looked at the man, he cut his eyes toward the captain and admitted, "Miss Morgan did fund our mission, so the wife and I tend to humor her in these matters."

The captain's cool eyes moved over Rachel again, and she wanted to shrink away. Men were for the most part untrustworthy—all except Clay, and it had even taken him some time to win her confidence. Otherwise, the men in her past had only caused Rachel pain, shame, and sadness . . . all men but one. She shied away from thoughts of him. He was dead. He had to be. He was a warrior. He would have never surrendered to the army. Never.

"I will stand beside you, Miss Morgan, my gun at the ready," the captain announced. "I consider you under my protection." His gaze encompassed the good reverend and his squeamish wife. "All of

6

you are, of course, while you are here."

"You are too kind." Rachel forced the words from her throat. She felt certain that a kind man would not allow conditions like these to exist for animals, much less people. She lifted a lid from one large pot. Bile rose in her throat. The pot's contents looked more like pig slop than soup.

A fresh wave of anger washed over her, but Rachel fought it. Too much anger, just like too much pity, would make a man such as the captain suspicious of her—and neither he nor anyone else at the fort must ever know the truth.

Her brother, Clay, and her pretty sister-in-law, Melissa, had explained Rachel's situation clearly enough to her during the past five years. No one would believe that she had lived among Indians and not been taken as some brave's prize. She would lose all respect from those of her own race. Men would force themselves upon her, believing her to be ruined and of loose moral fiber, and women would shun her. It was simply the way of things outside the world in which she'd grown up. Thus, she had to lie about her past.

Would any of her people recognize her? Indeed, were any of them still alive? As the Mescaleros of the reservation grew nearer, Rachel had to wonder if she would recognize any of them. The tribe she'd left had been robust, healthy, and happy. These Indians shuffling toward her, heads bent, eyes downcast, were only shells, like those Rachel had seen upon the sands before the great waters: empty things that had once housed life.

"Lieutenant Chambers," the captain called, "take count of the men. Ignore the women or children . . . any missing are most likely dead."

Rachel grabbed the ladle from a pot, trying to ignore the casual way in which the captain spoke of death, and the pot's questionable contents. If any members from the band of Mescaleros she had been raised among had survived the recent campaign to wipe them out, and if they now lived on this reservation, she doubted they would recognize her.

Once, her skin had been kissed golden by the sun. She had worn soft doeskin, moccasins upon her feet, her wild hair confined in two long braids. Now she wore the trappings of a white woman.

Her whalebone corset dug into her ribs. Her kidskin boots pinched her toes. The heavy fabric of her modest gown didn't allow room for her skin to breathe, and she perspired in the afternoon heat. The pins that held her bun in place dug into her scalp. At times she wondered why any woman would want to be born white. The color of her skin brought not only restrictions, but discomfort.

As if the prisoners had practiced this ritual many times, they formed a line—a long one that Rachel feared stretched farther than the meager rations would last.

"Don't give out a full cup," the captain said beside her. "There won't be enough to go around."

Rachel chewed her bottom lip. "Perhaps we should have some of your men bring out the supplies—"

"Miss Morgan," Peterson hissed. "I understand your desire to perform your Christian duty by providing for these Indians, but we don't want the men too fat and healthy. A strong buck is harder to deal with than a weak one."

"What about the children?" Rachel's anger grew as a young mother and her starving child shuffled forward. "The *children* are no threat."

Captain Peterson adjusted his hat and squinted into the sun. "This is no place for a woman, Miss Morgan, and certainly not one of your compassionate nature. Little savages grow into big savages. It's that simple. Life is difficult here, for the Indians and for the military. It is survival of the fittest, and our job is to see that *we* are the fittest."

He glanced at her, and his light blue eyes softened. It was the first time since she'd met the captain that she saw any break in his hard demeanor. "I don't mean to be harsh, but you should have spent your money and your compassion on a worthier cause."

Rachel lifted her chin. "I have plenty of funds at my disposal, Captain. The supplies, medicines, and Bibles we brought are meant to do God's work. If we can save even one soul, the funds were well spent."

It wasn't a lie. Rachel's half-brother, Clay, had inherited his late father's shipping fortune. On top of that, he had the gold he'd stockpiled during his New Mexico trapping days. Clay Morgan was a very wealthy man, and he'd made certain that Rachel would never want for anything for the rest of her life. She was certain that her desire to use his money to help the Mescaleros would be encouraged as well.

"Some believe that Indians have no souls, Miss Morgan," the captain finally responded. "As I've said, I hope you haven't wasted both your time and your money on this venture."

Everything living had a soul, or so the Apaches had raised Rachel to believe. She declined further comment when the Mescalero woman and her child reached the buckboard, heads bent, tin cups outstretched to receive their rations. Rachel filled the child's cup to the top, regardless of the captain's instruction. The mother glanced up from beneath her lashes. That was when Rachel noticed the woman had a purple bruise on the side of her face and a split lip.

"They war amongst each other," the captain commented. "We try to stay out of it, for the most part."

"This woman should have the cut on her lip doctored," Rachel said. "Such a cut can easily become infected."

"There are no medicines . . ." Then Captain Pe-

10

terson seemed to remember that such was no longer the case. "Well, perhaps you can see to the minor injuries among the women and children, but I cannot in good conscience allow you near the men. You might prove too great a temptation for them."

The way his eyes drifted over her again left little doubt that the captain himself found her tempting. The realization shouldn't have sent a shock of distaste pulsing through her, but it did. Rachel understood she would have to overcome her distrust of men, especially if she wanted to truly meld with white society and find her place in life, but . . .

To hide her unease, she concentrated on spooning out rations, studying the Indians from beneath her lashes, and looking for familiar faces. The women and children came first. She recognized a few women, although none would raise their eyes long enough to recognize her in turn. Rachel had nearly made it through the long line before her pulses suddenly leapt.

One woman's face was wreathed in wrinkles, and her skin hung from her bones like an oversized coat, but Rachel recognized her: Laughing Stream, the woman who had taken her in and raised her like a daughter!

Rachel couldn't control the slight gasp of joy that left her lips. It caused the old woman to glance up at her, and then Laughing Stream gasped as well.

"Silent Wind? Can it be you?" she whispered in Apache.

Feeling the captain's curious regard, Rachel had no choice but to act as if she didn't understand. "I think she wants more food for the child," she explained. She turned to the toddler at Laughing Stream's side and filled the child's cup. Suddenly the container was knocked from the child's hand.

"You will not poison my child with your spoiled food!"

The words were spoken in Apache, spoken low and deep, every word heavy with hate. Rachel glanced up, but the sun silhouetted her assailant and blocked his features from her eyes. He was tall, his body strong despite the ribs she saw jutting through the bronzed muscles of his chest.

"Get back in line!"

The captain stepped forward, in front of Rachel, and struck the Apache across the face. The Apache staggered back. Without thought, Rachel rushed in front of the captain, placing herself between him and the fallen Indian. Again, her eyes sought the Apache's face. Her heart slammed against her chest. It was a face she knew, but its owner looked different. Older. Harder. Dangerous. Swift Buck. His dark gaze met hers, confusion knitting his brow.

She knew the moment he recognized her. He sucked in his breath sharply; his dark eyes widened, then quickly narrowed. He did not smile in recognition of a child raised by his own parents—a girl whose white brother had mixed blood with his to make them brothers as well—but snarled.

Hate. Why did he look at her with such hatred in his eyes?

The captain pushed Rachel aside and stormed forward. "Don't you dare look at a white woman that way, buck!" he shouted. "Or do my men have to beat some more sense into you? Starve you a little more?"

"Captain, please," Rachel said, unable to stop herself. When Peterson glanced over his shoulder, she continued. "I don't think he meant me any harm. It was the child he—"

"The child is his spawn." The captain kicked out, landing a boot in the Apache's ribs. "And if he wants to keep her alive, he'll damn well start showing some respect!"

Swift Buck's child? The captain's boot might as well have connected with Rachel's ribs. The air left her lungs in a whoosh. Swift Buck had a child? A wife?

"Soldiers!" Peterson shouted. "Get this savage out of here. He will receive no rations!"

Two burly men rushed forward and dragged the Apache to his feet. They held his arms, though he did not struggle. Instead, his eyes found Rachel again. He stared at her as if she were a stranger . . . and suddenly Rachel realized that she was. To him, she was a white woman—not the child who had grown to womanhood within his parents' lodge, not the strange girl with pale skin and a voice that had died with her white mother.

Rachel had thought that he must surely be dead, but he stood before her, refusing to look away. *Swift Buck.* God, the one man who'd been good to her was alive.

The heat suddenly felt as if it were pounding down upon her head. Her corset felt as if it were strangling the life out of her. Rachel swayed. Black dots danced before her eyes, and she collapsed.

CHAPTER TWO

"Miss Morgan? Can you hear me? Miss Morgan?"

"Try the salts," a male voice suggested.

Rachel caught a whiff of something that made her throat constrict. She coughed, struggling to expel the foul smell beneath her nose.

"There, she's coming around."

She was in a dark, cool room. Rachel made out the shape of Nelda hovering over her, and behind Nelda, the captain, standing stiffly at attention.

"What happened?" she whispered, confused by her surroundings. "Where am I?"

"The good captain has kindly allowed us the use of his private quarters during our stay," Nelda explained. "And you fainted, dear." The woman helped Rachel sit up. "Can't say as I blame you.

15

That Indian must have given you a horrible fright. I know he did me."

That Indian? *Swift Buck*. He was alive. Rachel still couldn't believe it.

"He's a troublemaker, that one," the captain commented, moving into Rachel's line of vision. "He will spend the rest of the day in chains. Now perhaps you understand the good sense of keeping your distance from the men."

"Yes," she answered. But she hated the thought of Swift Buck in chains for trying to protect his child. *His child*. Rachel would think about that later. She rose from the pretty chaise lounge where she sat. It looked out of place in a man's sleeping quarters. "But you did say that I could tend to the women and children," she reminded the captain.

"Well, all in good time." He smiled and the expression softened his severity. "Now, I think it would be best if you relax and stay out of the heat. I have ordered my cook to make us all a nice dinner. Mrs. Stark has agreed to share my quarters with you during your stay, and her husband and I will reside with the enlisted men in the barracks. I hope that meets with your satisfaction."

Rachel thought the accommodations were satisfactory, but she couldn't see why Nelda would. "A husband and wife should not be separated," she said.

"Nonsense," Mrs. Stark fussed. "The good reverend and I sleep in separate beds at home. I'm past the childbearing age, you know," she added. A second later she blushed to the roots of her graying hair. "Oh, dear, not a thing to discuss in mixed company. Not a thing to discuss at all."

"Well," the captain suggested dryly, "I will leave you ladies to your leisure. Do help yourselves to anything in my quarters that you might need." He touched the brim of his hat. "Until this evening, Miss Morgan, Mrs. Stark."

He marched from the room. Nelda stared after the captain, then turned and smiled at Rachel. "Such a gallant young man, and he clearly knows a pretty girl when he sees one. I do believe you've captured his interest."

Uncertain as to how she should react, Rachel brushed the wrinkles from her plain blue dress. "Mrs. Stark," she began hesitantly. "Earlier, you hid behind a wagon. Are you afraid of these people?"

The woman blushed again. "I did find them frightening," she admitted. "Sometimes the call to duty is more appealing than the duty itself. I'm wondering what in the world we've gotten ourselves into. Aren't you, Miss Morgan?"

Yes, Rachel did question the sense of taking on this task that her brother might have handled much better. But then, Clay would have probably just killed all of the soldiers and helped the Apaches escape. Recalling the starving people and the horrible living conditions outside, Rachel wondered if

17

her brother's method wasn't such a bad idea. Then she quickly brushed the thought aside. She'd been raised with violence—had witnessed too much of it in her lifetime.

"I find it difficult to fear people who are obviously starving and sick," she answered. "People who have been beaten. People who have had their lands and their way of life stolen. People—"

A commotion outside interrupted her. A window in the captain's bedchamber stood open, and, curious about the racket, Rachel moved to it and peered out. Four men were wrestling one Apache into chains.

Rachel's first instinct was to cry out, to tell the men to release Swift Buck, but she bit her lip and held the response in check.

He fought admirably considering his condition. Restraining him took four soldiers, and two more to slap on the irons. As her shock at seeing him again dulled somewhat, Rachel took the time to really look at Swift Buck. He was, of course, thinner than she recalled. In the past five years, the angles of his face had sharpened. The fullness of his lips contrasted with those angles and drew her gaze to his mouth.

It was an arrogant mouth, as was the look in his eyes as he stared at the soldiers subduing him. He wore a breechclout, knee-high moccasins, and nothing else. There were cuts and scrapes all over his body, but for some reason, they did not detract from his good looks; they merely added to his appeal.

His hair was long and black, and he wore it loose around his shoulders. Rachel had always envied Swift Buck his hair. Her own blond curly locks had stood out starkly from the straight black hair of the tribal members.

The soldiers secured Swift Buck's arms over his head, leaving him dangling in the hot sun by his wrists from a tree branch. His feet were also shackled. Once he was immobilized, one of the soldiers spit on him. Another kicked him in the stomach.

"Stop!" Rachel couldn't control her outburst. The soldiers' heads swung around. Spotting her standing at the window, they had the manners to blush and hurried away. Slowly, Swift Buck's head lifted. His gaze found her. Again, the hate that she saw there made her take a step back. Once, he had gazed at her with softness in those eyes. Now, there was no softness to be seen in him.

She thought that he might speak to her, but instead he glanced away, ignoring her. Nelda pulled Rachel from the window, shivering.

"That Indian frightens me. He looks so mean, so full of hate. I don't believe his is a soul we can save."

"Kick a dog enough times and he will bite you," Rachel said softly, still upset by the roughness of the soldiers and by everything she had witnessed today.

Clay, her brother, would be furious when he managed to win his release from jail and discovered she had taken matters into her own hands. Of course she hadn't told him her intentions. Clay would have forbidden her to come. But now a small part of her wished that he had found out and put a halt to her plans.

She'd been much happier remembering the Mescaleros the way they were, not as she was seeing them today. Swift Buck in particular. Although a mighty warrior, he'd had a softness about him then. He had tried to make her laugh back in those dark days when she had forgotten how. He had tried to make her speak when her voice was dead. He had been her brother's friend, and, she supposed, her own brother since his parents had raised her, but she had trouble seeing Swift Buck as a brother, then and now.

"Why don't you rest, dear?" Nelda said. "Soon we will have a nice dinner and the pleasant company of Captain Peterson to take our minds off of today's unsettling events. I could use a nap myself." The woman's gaze darted to the window. "Not that I can sleep with that savage chained only a few feet away." She rubbed her arms and moved toward the bed. "But we should try."

Her spirits sagging, Rachel settled next to Nelda. She didn't like the fact that the bed belonged to Captain Peterson; it seemed too intimate for her to be resting in the place where he slept. Still, the captain had been nothing but attentive and gentle-manly in his manners toward her since she'd arrived with the Starks that morning—other than staring at her for too long and making her nervous—and he wouldn't dare step outside the boundaries of correctness. At least, he wouldn't long as he never knew the truth.

She thought of something else. Would it be wrong for her to use the captain's interest in her for the purpose of softening him toward the Apaches' plight? She'd journeyed here to help the Mescaleros. How far should she be willing to sacrifice herself on their behalf?

The question brought a flush of guilt. The People had raised her, provided for her, and protected her. None had treated her differently from the others because her skin was white, her hair blond. They had accepted her unconditionally among them—all save one. There had been Tall Blade. But thank goodness her brother Clay had killed him.

Tall Blade had also been Rachel's father's son, a half-breed. But Rachel had not known the truth of his heritage, nor had her half-brother Clay, until the hate-filled brave had tried to kill them both. Tall Blade had resented them because they reminded him that white blood ran in his veins. Clay had nearly died in the ensuing struggle. But that was all in the past. And good had come of it.

It was during that traumatic time that Rachel had finally found her voice again. And it was then that

Swift Buck had seen Rachel, had realized that she had not been killed by Tall Blade, and he had looked at her for the first time without a mask covering his emotions. What she'd seen had frightened her, though she had been flattered as well.

Still carrying the scars of her abusive father and the shame of being abandoned by her family, Rachel hadn't been ready to lower her guard and return Swift Buck's feelings. In fact, she wasn't certain that it was her right. She wasn't a true Apache. Yet she wasn't truly a white woman, either. In her confusion, she had allowed Clay to talk her into leaving the Mescaleros. He had told her that she must be given a choice—must learn about her own people, too.

In truth, Rachel had been glad to go with him, to leave her confusing feelings for Swift Buck behind and search for a place where she felt she might belong. She had reasoned that she did not belong in Swift Buck's world because of the color of her skin, but deep down, she had gone because she was afraid to confront her feelings for him—afraid to trust him with her fragile heart.

Now it was clear to Rachel that he didn't trust her either. Considering all that he had suffered at the white man's hands, Rachel could hardly blame him. She could blame him about the child—about the wife that he must have taken to produce a daughter. . . .

Nelda snored loudly, interrupting Rachel's

thoughts. She closed her eyes and tried to rest. Lying there, Rachel thought of Laughing Stream—the joy and the sorrow of seeing the old woman again. She thought five years would have changed her, but in the second when her adoptive mother's eyes had met hers, the years had melted away. Rachel longed to feel Laughing Stream's fingers lightly combing her hair, the soft sound of her humming.

She longed to walk freely through tall, yellow grass again. To feel the sun upon her skin, the wind in her unbound hair. Once, she had sat and listened to the children laugh and play inside the camps. Today, she heard no laughter.

Would supplies and medicine be enough to heal these Apaches? Perhaps their bodies, but only freedom would heal their spirits. And freedom was the one thing that Rachel couldn't give them.

Thoughts of Swift Buck surfaced again. Outside. Chained like an animal. Starving. Perhaps dying of thirst. And Rachel herself lay inside a cool room with a promised feast ahead of her. All because her skin was white and his was not.

Later, under the cover of darkness, she would go to him. Despite the hate in his eyes, she would take him a drink of water, food if she could manage to spirit some away. But would he accept her offering?

Swift Buck's throat burned with thirst. The iron bracelets around his wrists cut into his skin. From across the darkened landscape, he heard the muted cry of a child. Was it his child crying because she was hungry?

Frustration churned his own empty belly. He could not allow his daughter to eat the rations from the soldiers. The food was spoiled and would make her sick. But he was not allowed to hunt for his family. Even the few horses the soldiers had originally allowed them to keep were now butchered for food.

For a man to watch his flesh and blood suffer and starve was no life. Especially considering he'd only been taken because of his daughter, Amoke. He had thought the soldiers would kill her, as they had killed many—man, woman, or child, it did not matter to them. While trying to protect her and his mother, he had been hit with a weapon, woken to find himself in a place worse than death.

Swift Buck was happy that his father, Crooked Nose, had not lived to see these times. Gray Wolf, his band's leader, had warned often of the dark days ahead for The People. Those days had now come.

Swift Buck hoped that somewhere in the mountains, Gray Wolf and other uncaptured braves waited, still free. The band's numbers were small now. They could not attack this fort unless they gathered warriors from other bands. Would they do that? When? And how many of their kin would die of sickness and starvation before they could be rescued?

Swift Buck's gaze swung toward the fort, hoping to see Silent Wind. She wore the trappings of a white woman now, her summer hair pulled back away from her face in a way that did not please him. Too, her words were in the white language. But they were strong now; she had found them inside herself again.

Seeing her had taken him by surprise. He thought she had gone, never to return to The People. Why had she come to this place? And why had her brother, Cougar, not come with her? And why had neither come before now?

Anger rose inside him, resentment toward the two who had abandoned The People. Silent Wind and her brother had once walked among them, had been accepted as Apache, even though their skin was pale. And Silent Wind had turned her back on him directly, on the feelings she knew he held for her. Five years ago that had been, when she had left to learn about her own people. When she had made the choice to leave him.

Where was his choice, then or now? He had watched, his heart torn out, as Cougar took Silent Wind away. For two years he had waited, watched for her return, but she did not come and he became the object of many jokes. Out of duty to his band, and to his mother, he had chosen a wife. He had tried to love that wife, but inside his mind, always,

Silent Wind had been there. White Dove had died when she gave birth to their daughter. Swift Buck had grieved for her, had missed her gentle ways, but he had never loved her. And for depriving him of that, he could not forgive Silent Wind.

A rustle in the dark drew his head up sharply. Who roamed the night? Soldiers full of firewater, with hurtful fists to torture him? Maybe their leader? That pale man had looked at Silent Wind as if he had claimed her for his own, and Swift Buck had seen them through the glowing eye of a window earlier, talking while they ate and drank, neither caring that there were people outside the walls of the fort who had no food or decent water. He hated the leader the most.

True, the man usually did not dirty his hands with wrongs committed against Swift Buck's people, but he turned his back when his men raped a woman, or when they beat a brave to death for nothing more than meeting their gaze. That made him just as bad. Or worse.

Today was the first time the leader had dirtied his hands. He had done so for Silent Wind. He had done so to show everyone that she belonged to him. Maybe he was the reason Silent Wind had come.

A scent, one Swift Buck remembered even though it had been five years, drifted to him on the night: a scent as fresh as dew in the morning, as sweet as the wildflowers that grew in the meadows of the Sacred Mountains. The smell had once tempted him in the darkest hours of the night, while Silent Wind lay sleeping across from him inside of his parents' lodge. But he had been wrong to have feelings for her. The fire inside him that burned for Silent Wind had been a terrible mistake.

"Swift Buck. I brought you water. Some bread."

He did not speak. He could not. The sight of her stepping from the darkness into the light of the moon stole his voice. She was a beautiful woman. Her hair draped over her shoulders like waves of yellow grass. She wore a long white dress that hung loose, and a coat of some sort over it. She stepped closer, lifting a tin cup to his lips.

Swift Buck would have liked to refuse what she offered, but his needs shamed him and he drank greedily. The water did not taste foul like that of the river, which his people were usually forced to drink. He drank until the cup was empty.

"I have bread," she said. "I'm sorry I couldn't bring you more."

Again he wanted to refuse, but his belly grumbled loudly at the thought of food.

He noted that she spoke to him in the white language her brother had taught him when they were boys. Long ago, she had spoken in the darkness while dreams held her. Sometimes the words were Apache, other times the language of her birth. Now, as then, the low, soft sound of her voice enveloped his senses, awakened more than his anger.

She lifted a piece of bread to his lips. He took it between his teeth, then to shock her he sucked her finger into his mouth.

CHAPTER THREE

Rachel gasped and jerked her hand away. In the darkness, Swift Buck's eyes shone with strange light. His eyes had always fascinated her, so dark compared to her own. Once, they had expressed his feelings for her; now, they were guarded. Questions tumbled through her mind. She wanted to ask him why she had seen hate for her in his expression. She wanted to know about the child and the wife he had chosen.

As in the past, when words had died for her, she couldn't force the questions past her lips. It was just as well. She should leave. What if she were discovered by one of the soldiers? Or worse, by their captain?

"I must go," she whispered. She turned to leave, but his words stopped her.

"Do you run to *him?*"

Rachel's pounding heart skipped a beat. She glanced back at Swift Buck. "Run to whom?"

"The pale one. The leader. Is he your mate? Is he the reason you came here?"

Rachel's face flamed. "I came here to help The People. I never met Captain Peterson before this morning."

"You come too late." Although he did not raise his voice, Swift Buck's eyes glittered dangerously. "Our people have been slaughtered by yours. Forced from our homes, starved, beaten, and you and your brother did nothing."

"That isn't true," Rachel protested, then glanced around because she'd forgotten to keep her voice quiet. "We didn't know. Clay—Cougar speaks on your behalf to the men who make politics in Washington, but because the whites know he sympathizes with the Apaches' plight, they keep things from him. When he learned that a general had ordered all Mescaleros captured or massacred, he nearly killed the man. They have put him in jail, or he would be here instead of me."

"You did not want to return." It was a statement, not a question.

"No," she admitted. "Not while I thought that life went on as always for you. I have a home with my brother and his wife. I make the best of what I've been given."

The hardness in his eyes did not soften. "Given? You made the choice five years ago—to turn your back on your people, to leave the mother who raised you, the father who loved you."

The brother whom I never looked upon as a brother, she mentally finished.

"Cougar wanted what was best for me," she explained. "I had to leave."

Swift Buck made a sound in his throat. "Cougar wanted what was best for Cougar, as always. He wanted a chance to erase the wrongs he had done to you. He wanted to ease his own guilt."

To argue different would be a lie. Her brother had ignored her for a long time as well, like her father. He, too, had left her with the Indians. It had taken her some time to understand why. She had forgiven him, but had he taken her back to their white heritage to ease his conscience? It was possible.

"Why are you angry with Cougar?" she asked. "He did as he promised. He's spoken many times to the lawmakers on The People's behalf."

Swift Buck glanced at the chains encircling his wrists and holding them overhead. "Words are useless. Voices do not reach ears that do not wish to hear. You should not have come. You and your brother are dead to us now."

If he wanted to hurt her, he succeeded. Although

she'd tried hard to learn the white ways and blend into their society, Rachel had always hoped that if she wished to return to the Mescaleros, they would welcome her back with open arms. She saw now that too much time had passed. Too many wrongs had been committed against The People by whites. Yet would they all feel this way toward her? Or was it Swift Buck alone?

"I will do what I can for you," she said softly, then moved away, off into the shadows. Swift Buck did not speak again.

Holding her breath, Rachel moved through the darkness. As she rounded a corner to the quarters she and Nelda shared, she froze. Captain Peterson stood smoking a cheroot, leaning against one of the posts that supported his quarters.

"Miss Morgan," he said, his voice surprised. He shoved away from the post and approached her. "What are you doing roaming around in the darkness?"

In the folds of her robe Rachel hid the tin cup, her mind frantically searching for a reasonable explanation.

"I couldn't sleep," was all she could think of. "Mrs. Stark snores something awful." Which was no lie. "I thought that the night air might help soothe this headache she's given me."

His gaze moved over her. Although she wore more clothing than she had among the Apaches, she felt exposed beneath his stare. "It's dangerous for a beautiful young woman such as yourself to leave the safety of my quarters and wander about at night."

"I assumed no one would be up," she said.

"There are guards always on duty to watch the fort." He reached out and lifted a lock of her unbound hair. "We never know if the Indians will attack us, or if renegade bands will try to rescue our prisoners. I'd hate to see this pretty hair hanging from a scalp belt." He rubbed the strands between his fingers as if absorbing their texture.

"Oh. I can't imagine the Apaches would ever be so bold." She stepped away, pulling her hair free in the process. "From what I witnessed today, they seem resigned to their life here on the reservation."

"Most are," the captain agreed. He dropped his cigar and ground the stub beneath his polished boot. "But there are some we still consider dangerous." His gaze moved past her to the darkness beyond, and she knew he meant Swift Buck. "Besides, my men are sometimes lax in their manners. We don't see white women here often, Miss Morgan. It is difficult to remain civilized while living among the uncivilized."

"I'm sure they follow your example," she said, then wished she could have kept the sarcasm from her voice. The captain's eyes narrowed. "You're clearly a gentleman," she added, hoping to remind him of the fact. "Dinner tonight was lovely."

The tension slowly ebbed from his stance. "I'm

pleased that you enjoyed it, Miss Morgan. I look forward to many nice dinners together during your stay."

Her visit to the fort was not a social call. Rachel thought it best to remind the captain of that. "I should get some sleep. Tomorrow you did promise that we could hand out provisions and evaluate the health of the women and children."

A sigh escaped him. "Yes, I did promise. I would rather you allow me and the reverend to handle all matters with the Apaches, but if you insist upon getting your lovely hands dirty, then I won't stop you. Within reason," he warned. "Good night, Miss Morgan."

He tipped his hat and walked off. As she saw his destination, the distant barracks where the enlisted men slept, it dawned on her to wonder what he'd been doing hanging around his quarters when he'd given them to her and Nelda for their stay. Probably he was only making certain that all was as it should be. Maybe he'd only come to get one of his cigars . . . but that would mean he'd gone inside. She shivered in the night air.

The captain's quarters consisted of more than the bedroom. There was his office and then a door that led to a parlor area, then another door that led to the bedroom. He wouldn't have entered where he thought she would be sleeping even if he *had* slipped inside to get a personal item. Would he? Not quite assured of the matter, Rachel entered and

34

made her way to the bedroom. Nelda still snored loudly.

Rachel placed the cup next to the basin, removed her robe, and crawled into bed. Her thoughts immediately returned to Swift Buck. She had never seen him eaten up with anger. It was a side she did not like, a side she found frightening. Once he realized that she meant to help The People, maybe his eyes would soften again when looking at her. Tomorrow, she would roll up her sleeves and get to work. The Apaches would see that she was their friend, not their enemy.

The morning sun was already warm, but Rachel felt flushed by more than the heat. The captain had erected a large tent outdoors and a soldier poured cups of strong coffee for Captain Peterson and Mr. Stark, and sweet hot chocolate for Rachel and Nelda.

Outside, those Apache men who were capable struggled to weed their sorry stands of crops. Swift Buck had not been tethered this morning. Rachel hoped they had released him. She hoped he was still alive. The women and children were being herded forward like cattle.

A portion of the food Rachel had brought was stacked in a nearby wagon. "I assumed we would give out all the supplies at once," she commented, lifting a china cup to her lips that seemed out of place at the fort.

The captain, impeccably dressed and groomed, waved a hand in the air. "Miss Morgan, if you give them all of the supplies at once, they'll only waste them. They will eat until they are sick. It is better to teach them restraint."

It was on the tip of her tongue to point out that the Mescaleros seemed to have been taught that lesson all too well already, but she resisted. Being able to again express her thoughts and feelings aloud was not always such a blessing after all.

"Well, if you'll excuse me, I need to get my medical supplies and have a look at the women and children," she said.

The captain bounded from his chair and pulled out hers. He took her arm. Rachel hoped he wouldn't be hovering over her while she tended to the Apache women and children. Laughing Stream had probably told those who hadn't recognized her yesterday of Rachel's presence among them. What would she do if they all tried to speak to her? She hadn't clearly thought this situation through, and now she realized there was even more danger than she'd suspected.

"Don't let me keep you from your duties, Captain," she said, gently tugging her arm from his grasp and moving out toward the food wagon. "Mrs. Stark will help me." She turned her head back toward the tent. "Are you coming, Nelda?"

Her snoring bed-partner pinched her lips together, then, with a sigh, she rose from the table.

"I thought we were to let the good reverend see to this nasty business," she muttered, casting a dark glance at her husband.

"I plan to distribute the Bibles to the Indians as soon as the captain gathers a proper escort for me," he assured his wife. Then he returned to his coffee.

Nelda joined Rachel beside the wagon. Captain Peterson stood beside her. There were armed guards all around. "I believe that you are to gather an escort for the reverend," Rachel reminded the officer. She nodded toward the guards. "Mrs. Stark and I are perfectly safe. Please go about your business, Captain."

His face flushed beneath the brim of his hat. "I get the feeling you're trying to rid yourself of my company, Miss Morgan. Protecting you from these heathens is my duty. I apologize if I'm bothersome in doing so."

She'd said the wrong thing. Rachel saw Nelda pinched her lips together and roll her eyes. She tried to smile at the captain, although she felt certain the expression did not reach her eyes.

"I'm sorry," she finally said. "I certainly didn't mean to imply that I find your company unwelcome. I simply realize that I am a burden on your time and your duties to the fort, and I don't wish to be. I'm afraid my words don't always come out as I intend."

His expression softened and he smiled. He had nice straight teeth. "You are rather outspoken," he said. "But I suppose you mean well. I would count it a great honor if you would call me Franklin."

His request brought a lift of Nelda's brow. Rachel choked down her first instinct to tell the captain that she would rather not, and she nodded. "Of course . . . Franklin." She wasn't without manners—or rather, without the education of them. "And you must call me Rachel."

"A beautiful name for a beautiful woman," he proclaimed. "Rachel it is." And with that, he tipped his hat and left her to her duties.

"Told you that he was interested," Nelda whispered when Peterson was gone. "A girl could do worse than that handsome officer. You aren't getting any younger," she added.

At twenty-three, Rachel was a spinster by societal standards; she knew that. She supposed if she truly wanted to fit in, she should do her best to find a husband. Yet she hadn't journeyed to New Mexico for that purpose, so Rachel turned her focus on the reason she *had* come: the Apache women and children.

As the crowd reached her, they stood staring as if unsure what to expect. Rachel wondered how she would communicate without speaking in Apache. An idea occurred to her.

"Do you know Spanish, Nelda?" she asked.

The woman shook her head. "No, I'm ashamed to say that I was never good at learning to speak Spanish."

Nelda's ignorance of the language pleased Rachel. "I learned Spanish in my studies back home," she lied. She knew it because most Apaches learned how to speak Spanish as a precautionary measure. Mexicans often took them as slaves to work in their haciendas or in the copper mines. Although Rachel had not spoken at all while growing up with the Apaches, she had listened.

"I will speak to these women in Spanish and see if they understand me," she informed Nelda. And she did. She told the women to be seated. Those who understood followed her instructions, and those who didn't were quickly corrected by the others.

Once the women were all seated, Rachel took her medicine kit and descended upon them. Nelda did not follow, but stood by the wagon as if she would bolt at the slightest provocation. The situation suited Rachel fine. She doubted that Nelda knew much about doctoring.

Rachel would be more ignorant than she was regarding the subject if not for her sister-in-law, Melissa. Clay's wife's father had been a doctor, and Melissa had inherited a natural gift for healing from the man. Rachel had watched the woman tend to sick friends and neighbors back home in Washington.

Although not as skilled as her sister-in-law, Rachel at least knew which salves to apply for which afflictions. She'd learned about healing plants from the Apaches, too, though there were no herbs growing in this arid landscape.

"I wish you no harm," she said to the Apache women. "I have brought medicines for your cuts, supplies for cooking."

There came no response. Rachel approached Laughing Stream and squatted beside her. Again, the woman had a child with her, but she did not see the mother.

"Will you tell them they can trust me?" she asked, still using Spanish, aware that her adoptive mother knew the language.

Laughing Stream would not look at her. "My son has told everyone that you are not to be trusted. He says your heart is white now. He says you are dead to us."

Pain swelled inside Rachel. She felt her eyes water but blinked back the tears. "Is . . . is he all right?"

The old woman's expression softened. "He is sore from the beating the soldiers gave him, but he is alive. He rests inside my lodge until he regains his strength. You should not have come back, Silent Wind."

First the warning from Swift Buck, and now from Laughing Stream—her mother; at least, the only mother she remembered. It was heartbreaking. "I came to help. I thought you might be happy to see me again."

Laughing Stream's eyes filled with tears as well,

but like Rachel, she blinked them back. "I have lost you twice. My heart dies at the thought of losing you again. But Swift Buck says you are dead to me, and I must honor him. He is the man of our lodge."

Rachel had lost her adoptive father, Crooked Nose, shortly before she left the Mescaleros. He had been much older than his wife, and Rachel had felt twice as bad for leaving her adoptive mother alone. She glanced at Swift Buck's child—a beautiful little girl, two and a half at the most. The child had her father's eyes, and his stubborn chin. "Where is your granddaughter's mother?"

She'd been fighting herself not to ask the question, and doing so brought a slight lift of Laughing Stream's brow.

"The one we used to call White Dove left for the spirit world after giving the child birth."

White Dove, Rachel remembered, had been a pretty young woman, her eyes always following Swift Buck around the camp. Many female eyes had followed Swift Buck, but he'd seemed not to notice.

"The one who is gone was a good choice for your son," she found herself admitting.

Again, Laughing Stream's brow lifted. "He could not wait forever, Silent Wind. You gave him no reason to believe you would return. You cannot hold anger in your heart that he chose another."

Rachel's back stiffened. "I am not angry. I am happy that Swift Buck found a woman, and sad that

41

he has lost her. I am also sad that he is full of hate for me. I was once his sister."

With a snort, Laughing Stream said, "You two were never brother and sister. Not by blood, and not by your own choosing. Do not pretend otherwise."

"Rachel, what are you saying to her for so long?"

Nelda's call saved Rachel from a response, and reminded her of her duties. "I will give you salve to treat Swift Buck's cuts," she whispered to Laughing Stream. "I will give you food to help him and his daughter grow stronger."

"And who will feed us when you are gone?" the old woman asked. "You only prolong our deaths— and in this place, death is not our enemy. If you want to help us, make the soldiers release us so we may go home."

It was the one thing Rachel couldn't do. The Indians were a threat to the settlers moving into the territory. It didn't seem to matter to anyone that the Indians had lived there first. Being able to see both sides was also not a blessing to Rachel. She couldn't understand why everyone couldn't live in peace.

"I'm explaining about the provisions," she called over her shoulder to Nelda. "Telling her and the other women not to waste them."

Nelda nodded and retreated further behind the wagon.

Glancing around, Rachel saw that the captain

had busied himself with gathering an escort for the reverend and paid her no heed. She continued; "I brought food, but The People must use sparingly what I will give them today. I am not positive how long it will last, or if the soldiers will soon claim it for themselves."

Laughing Stream nodded in understanding, but she wouldn't look up, so Rachel figured their conversation had ended. Looking down, she saw Swift Buck's child smiling shyly at her.

Rachel couldn't resist smiling back. She ran a hand over the girl's small cheek. She was beautiful, if thinner than Rachel would have liked.

Rising, Rachel moved among the other women and children, examining their bruises and cuts, doctoring those who would allow it. The woman with the split lip and bruised jaw was not someone she'd known.

"What happened?" Rachel asked in Spanish, squatting down beside her. "Did someone hit you?"

The woman's gaze moved toward a group of soldiers, but she said nothing.

Rachel sighed, rose, and went to the supply wagon. From there she distributed blankets, flour, sugar, salted pork, and cornmeal. The women all accepted the supplies. None thanked her. None even gave a smile.

"Miss Morgan . . . er, Rachel," Captain Peterson called from atop his horse. "The escort and I are taking Reverend Stark and his Bibles out into the camps. Would you care to accompany us?"

His offer surprised her. Peterson had said he didn't want her too close to the Apache men.

He seemed to read her mind. "You should be safe as long as you stay by my side," he assured her. "Do you ride?"

Rachel loved to ride, and she considered herself an accomplished horsewoman. She wanted to see conditions at the camps. Yet . . .

"I'm afraid I'm not dressed for the occasion." She glanced down at her dull gray gown. "I do have a riding outfit, if you'll allow me to change. I'll be quick about it," she added when he frowned.

The captain nodded. "Hurry, then. I'll have a horse saddled for you and brought around."

A soldier helped her and Nelda into the empty supply wagon, and they headed back for the captain's quarters. Nelda smiled at her—rather smugly, Rachel thought. Well, let her think what she wanted about the interest of Captain Peterson. Rachel only wanted to view the camps.

And, if she were honest with herself, she wanted to make certain she saw Swift Buck up and moving about.

CHAPTER FOUR

His sides hurt where the soldiers had kicked him, and his jaw was slightly swollen. Swift Buck stared up into the top of his mother's tepee, wishing for the old days when he would rise, walk outside to greet Mother Earth, then maybe catch his horse and go hunting.

Those days were lost to him, taken from him by the greedy whites. It was not right, but the white man had no sense of what was right or wrong. They pretended to, calling themselves decent and the Indians savages, but deep down, the whites had evil hearts. They did not respect Mother Earth. They ravaged the land, killed too much game—left a path of destruction and waste across The People's lands.

His mother and daughter entered. Amoke ran to him, throwing herself on him and giggling, unmindful that she made his ribs hurt more.

"We have food supplies," his mother said, laying her blanket upon the ground and exposing several burlap bags. "Silent Wind brought them."

"Then you should have refused," he scolded. "We will not eat out of the whites' hands like dogs."

Laughing Stream sighed. "Would your pride see your daughter starve? Amoke must eat. *You* must eat, and regain your strength. I will die here, but I do not wish to see you and Amoke go with me to the spirit world. You must be ready when the others come. You must have the strength to fight."

Swift Buck set Amoke aside, rose, and went to his mother. "Do not speak of the spirit world, *Shimaa*. You will not die in this horrible place." He bent beside her and took her thin shoulders between his hands. "This is a promise I make to you. When your time comes, you will be free, as we all will be."

His mother touched his cheek. "Then you must gain back the strength lost to you so you can take me from this place."

Grudgingly he nodded.

"Amoke will help me make corn cakes for our supper. Rest, my son."

"I need to walk outside," he argued. "The longer I stay still, the more I ache when I move." Swift

Buck walked to his daughter, ran his hand over her small head, and left the tepee.

Grass did not grow upon the land the soldiers forced them to occupy. There were no trees to shade him from the blazing sun. Swift Buck walked to the stands of crops the men tried to revive, but their efforts were useless. If the Apaches had to depend on these crops to feed them through the winter, they would all starve.

The rumble of a wagon and the beat of horses' hooves drew his attention. Soldiers approached the camp. Did they come for him? Or maybe a woman? The white soldiers occasionally came for one of the young pretty ones.

As the group drew closer, Swift Buck noticed in the wagon the man in dark clothing who had arrived at the fort with Silent Wind. Then the sun caught a flash of golden hair. Silent Wind rode toward the camps beside the pale leader of the fort.

Swift Buck reminded himself to no longer think of her as Silent Wind. Now, she was only a white woman. Yet her act of kindness the previous night caused him a moment of guilt. And today she had given the Mescalero women supplies and medicines.

He watched as she smiled at something the leader of the fort said to her, and jealousy suddenly engulfed him. She had never smiled for him. She had run from him, abandoned him, abandoned The People. And this man—did she flirt with him because his skin was white, the same as hers?

Once, Swift Buck had thought that this woman feared all men, and that that was the reason he could not tempt her into the flame of womanly feelings for him—but maybe it was not so. Maybe she had thought she was above him because his skin was not the same color as hers.

Even as these thoughts took shape in his mind, he saw her gaze move around the encampment—felt as if she were searching for someone. Their gazes met, held; then she quickly glanced back at the leader and spoke to him.

The joining of their eyes had been brief, but Swift Buck had seen for a moment the girl he'd known. He had seen the one who'd stared at him only when she thought he was not watching. He knew—or so he told himself—that she'd once had feelings for him, though she had been too afraid to act upon them. He'd heard his name upon her lips while she dreamed, even before she knew that words still lived inside her.

She was a woman now. Had her cold heart thawed? Had she forgotten the scars that Cougar and her father—the man called Brodie—had given her? Swift Buck watched as the leader of the fort's soldiers brushed a stray lock of hair from Silent Wind's face, and Swift Buck saw her slight flinch. No, she had not healed—she had not forgotten.

"Men, gather around," the white captain called as the wagon stopped, speaking in Spanish because he was too lazy to learn the Apache language. "A man of God brings you the Word."

Curious, Swift Buck moved forward with his fellows, the men coming from the fields. They all gathered around the wagon. The man dressed in dark clothes rose. He held up a book.

Swift Buck had seen books before. Years ago, Cougar sometimes brought them to their camp. Although Silent Wind's white half-brother had said he could not read them, he liked looking at the words.

"In this book is the word of God," the man said in poor Spanish. "I have come to save your souls so that you may learn to be civilized—and if it is the will of God, to enter His kingdom when you depart from this world."

None of the Apaches responded. Swift Buck knew they were not interested in the white man's God. They were not interested in the books the soldiers began shoving in their hands. They could not eat books. They could not drink them. But as a black book was shoved into his own hands, Swift Buck realized they did serve a purpose. He thought they might burn.

"Upon these pages"—the man held up a tome—"is the way to deviation."

Swift Buck frowned. Another man laughed.

Silent Wind urged her horse closer to the speaking white. "I think you mean salvation, Reverend, not deviation," Swift Buck heard her say softly.

The dark-clothed man's face turned red. "My Spanish is terrible at best." He glanced to the pale fort captain. "Could you instruct one of your soldiers to assist me?"

"You!" The leader pointed. "Come help the good reverend."

The chosen soldier did the leader's bidding. Swift Buck watched the leader dismount, then go to help the white woman from her horse. He held her longer than he should once her feet were on the ground. This time, she controlled her slight shudder better than before. The pair began to walk.

The dark-clothed reverend spoke, and in turn the translating soldier delivered words about the white man's God to the Indians. Swift Buck did not pay attention. He watched the leader and Silent Wind move through the camp. A pair of soldiers on horseback followed them, their hands on their weapons.

Rachel tried to hide her disgust of the camp conditions. There were no camp dogs, no women working outside, skinning or cooking, no warriors making weapons or riding off to the hunt. In the distance she saw more camps, those of other Navaho and Apache bands, and they too looked lifeless. Somberness hung in the dry, hot air. Rachel felt eyes watching her, and knew who they belonged to.

She'd been relieved to see Swift Buck among the Mescalero men, not too worse for wear after the night spent in chains. As she felt his dark gaze follow her through the camp, she tried to concentrate on Captain Peterson's remarks.

"As you can see," the captain was saying, "we allow them to live in the manner to which they are accustomed. We thought they would be more content in their tepees."

Curses screamed through Rachel's mind. This was not the way a normal Apache camp looked. She could say nothing. Tears burned the backs of her eyes. She blinked them away and swallowed the argument upon her tongue.

"I'd like to return to the fort," she said. "The heat is unbearable."

"Forgive me," the captain quickly apologized. "I've forgotten my manners. A genteel woman such as yourself would not be accustomed to such cursed conditions." He took her arm and steered her back toward their waiting horses, their escort trailing behind them.

Rachel saw the Mescaleros looking at their new black Bibles with blank expressions. They cared nothing about the word of the white God, she'd wager. All were wondering what true use the books might serve.

"Soldier, be sure to explain that if they destroy those Bibles, they will feel the lash!" the captain called to the reverend's translator. "The Reverend Stark plans to come out and preach to these people daily, until they begin to understand the word of

God. If they are capable of intelligent thought," he added to Rachel with a wink. She couldn't manage an answering smile.

When she passed Swift Buck, Rachel again felt the heat of his dark gaze.

"Does he know who you are? Does he know that you understand what I am saying to you?" he said in the Apache language.

Her heart lurched. Good Lord, Swift Buck had spoken to her. Flustered, she hastened her steps toward the waiting horses.

Captain Peterson's hand still rested upon her arm, however, and he slowed their progress. "What is that one jabbering about?" he muttered darkly. "Cursed Apache. You'd think he'd learn his lesson about being rebellious."

The captain turned toward Swift Buck, forcing Rachel to do the same. She met Swift Buck's gaze with silent appeal. He smiled slightly at her.

"He does *not* know," he answered what she could not. "He does not know that you lived among us, were one with us."

"I do not understand," Rachel replied in Spanish, feeling Captain Peterson's grip tighten upon her arm.

Swift Buck's smile stretched, and she knew it was over her obvious discomfort.

"Why in the hell is he speaking to you?" the captain snarled. "He should know better than to even look at a white woman, much less speak to her."

Rachel feared that more violence would erupt, and Swift Buck would bear the brunt of it—not that she wasn't furious with him at the moment. "I assume he's thanking me for the supplies I gave to the women," she said to the captain.

"You are welcome," she said to Swift Buck in Spanish, then tried to turn the captain toward their waiting mounts.

Peterson scowled at her. "Don't lower yourself to speaking to him," he instructed. "To do so . . . well, frankly it cheapens you, Miss—Rachel. I only tell you this for your own good. Consorting with the women and children is one thing, but the men . . ."

A blush crept into her face, but it was a blush of anger. How dare this man tell her what she could or could not do? Societal rules—how she hated them. "Of course you're right," she breathed, pulling her arm from the officer's grasp to make her way to her horse. "I told you—the heat, I'm afraid it's made me feel dizzy and confused."

Franklin's expression quickly dissolved into one of concern. "Let me help you back to the fort."

But she wanted *away* from the captain's cloying presence. "Maybe I should ride with the good reverend in the wagon," she decided. "I fear I might fall from my horse in a faint again."

Franklin's lips formed a momentary pout; then he nodded agreement. "I did enjoy riding with you," he said, "But the wagon is a wiser choice, given your frail health."

Rachel had never been sick a day in her life. She'd never fainted before yesterday, and it was only from the shock of seeing Swift Buck when she had assumed he'd been killed during the campaign to wipe out the Mescaleros. She did allow Peterson to help her up beside the reverend. As the driver turned the wagon back toward the fort, she fought herself not to turn and look again at Swift Buck.

She had to find some way to make him realize that her situation at the fort was a dangerous one. The captain and his men must never find out that she'd lived among the Mescaleros—she wasn't prepared to handle the consequences. Recalling the camps and their pitiful conditions, the starving people who'd had their way of life stolen from them, she felt another jab of conscience. What matter was her reputation compared to their suffering?

"I fear we are wasting our breath here, Miss Morgan," Reverend Stark said beside her. "I'm not sure those Indians care about salvation, or God." He sighed heavily beneath the blazing sun. "Today they stared at me with barely concealed animosity. How am I to win their trust, their respect, their souls, when they despise me?"

She softened toward the reverend. He and his wife were basically good people. They meant well. "You must give your mission time, Reverend," she said. Rachel glanced around and lowered her voice.

"The Indians have been given few reasons to trust the white man. To win their respect, you must first show them respect in return. They have had their pride stripped from them. Their lands, their way of life. To win their souls, you must first appeal to their hearts. Show them the kindness that I know lives within you. The compassion. Do not see them as Apache, or Navaho, but as people."

The reverend stared at her thoughtfully, then nodded. "You are wise beyond your years, Miss Morgan. I admire your dedication to these people, strangers to you before yesterday. My calling is weak if I'm ready to give up after only one attempt. I am humbled by your insight into these strange people. I will try to be more like you and broaden my mind."

Another hot blush stained her cheeks. She held an advantage over the reverend concerning the Indians. Her insight stemmed from having lived with them most of her life. She was almost tempted to confess as much to the preacher, but she fought the urge, as she did most of her impulses. This was a man of God, but he was still a man, subject to men's instinct to judge first and ask questions later.

"I do hope you'll be recovered from the heat in time to honor me with your presence at dinner this evening, Miss Morgan." The captain had ridden up beside them. "And of course, you and your lovely wife, Reverend," he added.

"We'll all be looking forward to it," Roman Stark

answered with a smile, and Rachel suppressed an irritated sigh. She wondered if all men thought they had to answer for their womenfolk.

Indian women were given much more freedom with their opinions, and their decision making. As if Stark's word was all that was required, the captain tipped his hat and rejoined his men riding behind the wagon.

"I think he's sweet on you," Stark whispered with a grin. "Who knows, maybe I'll get to perform a wedding before we've completed our mission."

She couldn't help herself; Rachel snorted. "I wouldn't count on it, Reverend. I'm not looking for a husband."

He frowned at her. "All single women are looking for a husband, Miss Morgan. A woman needs a man to take care of her," he explained, as if she were unaware of society's beliefs. "Although, if you had a husband already, I'm sure he would have never allowed you to journey here and mix with these Indians."

It was on the tip of her tongue to tell him that was the exact reason she didn't have a husband, but Rachel knew it would shock the man. She feared that most of her opinions would shock him, and society as a whole.

"I enjoy being independent," she explained. "Do you think that's a sin?"

The reverend's brow furrowed. "I'm nearly positive that it is," he answered.

Well, he didn't know half of her sins, Rachel decided. No one did. She wondered how long she would keep her secrets from the reverend, his wife, and the captain. Not long if Swift Buck continued to taunt her by speaking to her in Apache.

CHAPTER FIVE

Rachel honored the captain again with her presence at dinner that evening, and the next two as well. The fourth night she would have loved to beg off with a headache or some such feminine affliction, but in reality, Rachel found solitude in the captain's dark quarters depressing and lonely.

She'd love to be able to climb inside of Laughing Stream's home, make her bed in soft pelts, watch the fading embers glow from the cooking pit, hear the muted voices of old men telling stories outside around a campfire. But then, Swift Buck would also be sleeping inside that tepee. . . .

"Where do you originally hail from, Rachel?" the captain asked, breaking into her thoughts. "Were you born and reared in Washington?"

Her fork poised halfway to her lips, Rachel froze. She couldn't tell the captain she was born in New Mexico—the daughter of a crude, abusive trapper and a genteel mother forced from society when she'd gotten herself with child. She couldn't tell him how her half-brother's father had been killed at sea before a marriage could take place between him and her mother. And she certainly wouldn't tell him that her poor mother had died of neglect and sickness when Rachel was three, or that Rachel's voice had died along with her. She couldn't tell him that the Mescalero Apaches had raised her because her father had given her to them like some soiled possession he no longer wanted.

"Texas," Rachel lied. "I was born in Texas. My father was a cattle rancher. Later he took to politics, and that is how we ended up in Washington." She thought lying came sinfully easy to her, but as long as she'd gone this far, she might as well continue. "Mother and Father are both gone now."

"Then you are alone?" the captain asked softly. When she glanced at him, he had a distant look in his eyes. "Me, too," he admitted. "The war . . . well, it changed everything. My family were once one of the wealthiest families in Virginia. Now the great plantations are nothing more than burnt-out ruins, the fields desolate and empty. We lost everything. A commission as an officer in the Army was the best I could do for myself."

Silence followed his statement before Nelda said,

"There is no shame in protecting decent people from savages and the like, Captain. The Lord doesn't close a door that he doesn't open a window."

The captain smiled indulgently at the woman, and Rachel had to admit that Franklin Peterson possessed a certain amount of Southern charm at times. Ironically, the captain was very like the Apaches. He'd had his way of life taken from him, his home, his family, by the war. So why, then, did he not show people in similar circumstances more compassion?

"The Indians are starting to take an interest in my sermons," Reverend Stark proclaimed proudly. "Well, a few," he amended. "There is one fierce-looking fellow who just stands and stares at me as if he considers me some sort of demon."

The hairs on the back of Rachel's neck prickled. She suspected the Indian in question was Swift Buck.

"I believe I know which Apache you refer to," the captain muttered. "That buck reminds me of a wild mustang I once tried to break for the Army. The horse pitched every time I climbed on him. He kept throwing me, and I kept climbing right back on. I never could break that mustang's spirit." He shook his head.

Rachel rubbed the back of her neck, feeling as if eyes were boring into her from somewhere outside. "Did you set the mustang free?"

Franklin laughed, showing his small, perfect teeth. "Of course not." He took a sip of his coffee. "I shot him."

Rachel might have choked had she had anything in her mouth. "You are joking?" she asked.

Peterson shook his head. "No. You see, Rachel, the horse was worthless. He couldn't be broken to the saddle and his bloodlines were poor. He served no purpose. There was no choice but to destroy the animal."

Tears filled Rachel's eyes as she imagined the proud horse destroyed for his spirit. She'd always felt a close bond with animals. When as a child she'd run wild in the mountains surrounding their summer camps, she'd made friends with the wolves. She rose, placed her napkin on the table, and went outside.

Darkness had settled over the land, and a slight breeze played with the rebellious strands that had escaped her prim bun. She hugged herself, listening to the yips of coyotes in the distance. A door closed behind her, but she didn't turn. The captain had a particular scent—some type of tonic water. Swift Buck had always smelled of nature—horses, earth, sky.

"I've offended you again. . . ." He let the statement trail off.

"I have a fondness for animals," she said. "I believe that spirit is an admirable trait, in both man and beast."

61

She felt the heat from his body close to her back. "I must apologize for offending your feminine sensibilities. I forget at times that there is a softer side of life, that there is more than war, and hate, and survival in this world." His hands clasped her shoulders from behind. "You are like a flower blooming in a desert. You make me see that there is still beauty around me, if I but stop long enough to look."

His words held a pretty ring, but Rachel wouldn't and couldn't forget his story about the mustang. "These women and children need more supplies." She pulled away and turned to face him. "Will you allow me to work with them tomorrow?"

She felt his gaze move over her face. He sighed. "Yes, you may distribute more supplies among the women and children tomorrow. And you may ride in the wagon when the reverend goes out to preach. I, of course, will be your escort."

"Thank you," she responded, more out of social duty than gratitude. "Then good night, Ca—Franklin." But when she went to move around him, Rachel found her path blocked.

"May I speak bluntly?"

She lifted a brow.

Franklin Peterson smoothed back the sides of his pale blond hair. "I would like the opportunity to court you properly, and slowly, but our time together may be shorter than etiquette allows. May I kiss you, Rachel?"

The question so shocked her that she didn't answer. Franklin obviously took her silence for compliance. He bent forward and brushed his lips across hers. Rachel gasped, but rather than dissuade him, the reaction made Franklin pull her into his arms.

"I've wanted to do this from the first moment I saw you," he said against her mouth. "Tell me you feel the same."

She couldn't tell him that she didn't feel the same; she was speechless. His kiss didn't repulse her, really, but she felt nothing. No spark, no disgust, nothing. He pulled her closer, and panic took over. Rachel struggled from his grasp.

"Captain," she warned when he took a step after her. "I'm not used to men being so bold with me. I am shocked by your behavior."

In the light spilling from the windows of the mess hall, Franklin had the decency to blush. "Again, I must apologize for my behavior. I beg your forgiveness over my forwardness."

Adding to her discomfort, the man went down upon one knee. Rachel would have liked to plant her foot in his chest and topple him backward, but she did hope to sway the captain into showing more compassion toward the Indians. If doing so called for allowing him to slobber and fawn over her, she supposed she must suffer his attentions a bit.

"Of course I forgive you," she managed. "But if you will excuse me, I wish to retire for the evening."

"I'll escort you safely to my . . . well, currently your quarters," he finished with a flustered laugh; then he rose. "May I take your arm?"

At least he had asked her this time. They walked in silence, the moon a big white face in the sky. As they approached the captain's quarters, Rachel felt the prickly sensation of eyes watching her. A shadow moved up ahead. Or was it her imagination? The captain didn't seem to notice; at least he never broke stride or tensed in sudden apprehension of danger.

"Are you all right, Rachel?"

She hadn't realized she'd dug in her heels until she'd forced him to stop as well.

"Nelda, Mrs. Stark—I've left her behind."

Franklin Peterson laughed. "I'm sure the reverend and his wife are enjoying a time of solitude together. Besides, if you hurry to bed, you can get to sleep before Mrs. Stark starts her snoring."

His teasing helped relax her. Rachel hadn't thought he had a sense of humor. They set off again, soon arriving at Franklin's quarters. There was an awkward moment outside; then Franklin bade her good night and strode away.

Rachel wasted no time in getting ready for bed. She did in fact hope to be asleep before Nelda returned to ply her with silly questions about the captain or began snoring. She lay there in the darkness, thinking about Franklin's kiss. She knew that men and women in the white world touched mouths—

she had seen her brother and his wife do it often enough—but The People considered such a practice unclean.

Maybe that was why she hadn't responded to the surprise kiss Franklin had bestowed upon her. Or perhaps it was because she had mixed feelings toward the captain. Would she feel the same if Swift Buck pressed his lips against hers? She chided herself for even making comparisons. Swift Buck hated her; he wouldn't want to touch his mouth to hers. He considered her dead to him and his people. He had turned his back upon her, just as he claimed she had turned her back upon him and the Mescaleros.

Tomorrow she would venture out into the camps. She would distribute more food and medicines among the women and children. She would no doubt catch a glimpse of Swift Buck as the men were called to listen to Reverend Stark preach the gospel. Again she would show him that she was not his enemy but had come to help his people. Satisfied with her plan, she closed her eyes. Sleep came quickly since she'd gotten very little of it over the past few nights due to Nelda's snoring.

Within the foggy recesses of her mind, when Rachel was not fully awake but dreams had yet to claim her, she felt a presence in the room. A silent shadow moved through the darkness to stand over her. Sudden fear did not jolt her awake. She recognized the shadow's scent, and the smell of earth and sky soothed her rather than caused her alarm.

"Swift Buck," she whispered, sighing before she snuggled deeper into sleep.

Swift Buck crept into his mother's lodge. His heart pounded and he could not catch a deep breath. The soldiers would have killed him if they caught him sneaking around their camp.

Taking chances had made him feel alive again. He told himself he had gone to prove he was still a warrior, would be a warrior until he left for the spirit world. But he had not simply crept into the camp and stolen back out again. He had gone to watch Silent Wind through the eyes of the eating lodge.

She had sat there, wearing her white-woman's clothes. The leader had said words that angered her, and she had gone outside. But she had not stayed angry with the white man. She had allowed the man to touch her, to put his mouth on hers.

Swift Buck knew about the practice of kissing between whites. Silent Wind's brother, Cougar, had once been given a white captive. Cougar's woman had touched her mouth to Swift Buck's in a tactic to confuse him, to soften his heart so that he might help her escape The People. He had liked touching mouths, had touched mouths with his wife—had taught her that it was not a bad thing. He did not like to see the leader kissing Silent Wind.

Later, he had gone into the place where she slept. He did not know why he tortured himself with the sight of her, with the smell of her. Seeing her only made his suffering worse. She brought back memories of when they had both been different. When *life* had been different.

His mother coughed in her sleep, rousing him from his thoughts of Silent Wind. The cough was deep and rattled her frail bones. Swift Buck was worried. His mother was sick, would not live much longer if he did not get her away from this horrible place. She needed the fresh, cool air of the mountains to heal her.

She needed to be free, as did Amoke. His child would not grow to womanhood as a prisoner of the white man. But how would he take them from this place?

Weapons were forbidden to The People here. Swift Buck had tried many times to rally the men of the camps into action against the soldiers, but they were afraid. There were more soldiers than Apaches. The soldiers had guns, knives. The People had nothing with which to fight.

Still, he must find a way to escape the reservation and take his mother and daughter with him to the Sacred Mountains. Maybe he would find the others there—the few who had escaped. But how would he do that? And when?

His mother coughed again, her gasps for breath tugging at his heart. Swift Buck knew that whatever he decided to do, he must act very soon.

Chapter Six

The Indian women gladly accepted the food and medicines Rachel distributed, but again, there were no smiles of gratitude or words of thanks spoken to her. The women were a ragged bunch, and one in particular worried Rachel: her adoptive mother, Laughing Stream.

The old woman looked too thin, as did the other women and children, but Laughing Stream also had a pale cast to her skin and a rattling cough. Rachel wanted to ask her about the cough, and wondered how she could do so beneath the captain's watchful regard.

"Franklin," Rachel finally ventured. "The old woman with the horrible cough—I'd like to instruct her on how to prepare a poultice for her chest. She should have the correct ingredients in her tepee, and I could show her what to use."

The captain frowned. "Are you suggesting that you go inside the woman's home?"

Rachel nodded.

His nose wrinkled. He tugged at his gloves as if to make certain they were secure around his wrists. "You do realize that her lodgings are probably filthy?"

Seriously doubting that, Rachel nodded again. Franklin stared at Laughing Stream, who still stood coughing a short distance away.

"I suppose she looks harmless enough," he decided. "I'll go inside with you just to make certain, though."

Since she seemed to forever be offending Franklin, Rachel chose her words carefully. "This is an old woman, frail and sick. I won't ask you to go inside a filthy tepee when there is no reason for you to do so. I'm certain I will be safe."

He kept staring at Laughing Stream, his gaze narrowed. Finally, he nodded assent. To Rachel's surprise, he withdrew a small knife from his boot. The captain handed it to her.

"Slip that into your pocket. You might have need of it."

Stifling the urge to laugh, Rachel did as he instructed. "I will be careful," she assured him, then walked to Laughing Stream. Rachel took her by the arm and used Spanish to ask her which lodge was hers. Swift Buck's small daughter followed along, clutching at Laughing Stream's worn clothing, as they went to her tepee.

Once they entered, Rachel felt an immediate sense of homecoming. Her brother's wealth had purchased many fine things. Rachel had lived with him and his wife, Melissa, in a huge house. She had never liked that house. It was too big. A house too large allowed room for people to become separated, but in a small lodge such as this one, families had to remain close.

"I have told you before that my son does not wish for me to speak with you." Laughing Stream settled upon a threadbare blanket before a cold cooking fire. "Come, Amoke." She motioned her little granddaughter forward. As the child snuggled into her lap, the woman asked, "What do you want, Silent Wind?"

Rachel was stung by the continued rejection. But then, she'd been gone for five years and probably expected too much, even of her adoptive mother. All would not be forgiven so soon. Rachel bent beside her. "I hear the cough that rattles your bones. Why do you not make a poultice for yourself?"

Laughing Stream sighed. "My days are short. Soon I will be with my husband in the spirit world. I go to him with a happy heart that I can leave this sad place." The old woman patted Amoke's head. "This one, though, I worry about. What future does my granddaughter have in this world?"

At her adoptive mother's talk of death, Rachel's stomach twisted. She had left Laughing Stream five years ago and she had not come back, but somehow she had thought that Laughing Stream was invincible. She had thought there would be time to say the words that had been locked inside her for so long.

"You must not speak of the spirit world," Rachel scolded the woman. "You must make a poultice and sleep with it upon your chest for as many nights as it takes to cure your cough."

Laughing Stream glanced at Rachel. Her smile was sad. "I am not important. What of my granddaughter? What will become of Amoke—forced to live under the white man's thumb? It saddens me to know that she will not walk in the sunshine of our ways. Only darkness lies ahead for her."

Rachel stared at the child nestled in Laughing Stream's lap. Swift Buck's daughter was beautiful; she favored her father, but she also held a resemblance to her beautiful mother. How sad that she would be forced to grow up in such a hellish place.

"This is no place for a child," Rachel agreed with Laughing Stream. She found herself saying, "Maybe when I leave here, I can take Amoke with me." Her suggestion had been impulsive, but Rachel realized that what she suggested was not a bad idea. She couldn't save all of the children on the reservation, but maybe she could save this one— Swift Buck's child.

"You would take her from this place?" Laughing Stream whispered, hope entering her eyes.

"You will not take Amoke from me."

The sound of his voice made Rachel jump. She turned to see Swift Buck standing inside the tepee. She wondered how he'd managed to slip inside without the captain seeing him.

"You should not be here now," she told him. "If Franklin saw you—"

"Franklin," he snapped, the name sounding difficult upon his tongue, "did not see me slip away from those forced to listen to the man speak from his book. But I was watching you and I saw the pale ones' leader give you a knife."

Swift Buck's presence filled the tepee with an energy not unlike the air before a storm. Rachel's senses stirred and made her acutely aware of him as a man. His dark eyes, so intense, were focused upon her.

"Give me the knife."

The fine hairs on her arms stood on end. "Why?"

He moved toward her. "All our weapons have been taken from us. I need the knife to protect my family."

Rachel rose to meet him face to face, even if she had to look up to accomplish that. She was afraid of what would happen if the captain caught Swift Buck in the tepee with her. He might be beaten or worse.

"You should go," she warned him.

"The knife," he persisted, holding out his hand.

Unconsciously, Rachel's hand slipped into her pocket and fondled the weapon. "Frank—the captain will ask me what happened to the knife. He will want it back."

Swift Buck shrugged, calling her attention to his broad bare shoulders. "You will say you lost it." He wiggled his fingers to remind her that he waited.

Shaking her head, she took a step back. "If he finds you with a knife, if any of the soldiers see that you have a weapon—"

"Silent Wind."

He said her name in a way that she had never heard him speak it before: soft, like the light touch of a feather against her skin. His dark eyes held hers. She was mesmerized by them, flooded with sudden heat, breathless. As if she had no will of her own, Rachel pulled the knife from her pocket. With trembling hands, she extended the weapon toward him.

"Get away from her, savage!"

She jumped, the spell broken. Rachel glanced behind her. Franklin fumbled to pull his gun.

"No!" she shouted.

In the blink of an eye, Swift Buck grabbed the knife from her hand and turned. She knew that his skill at throwing a knife was unrivaled, but she also knew that a bullet could travel faster. Rachel threw herself between the men, hoping to stop either Franklin or Swift Buck from killing one another.

Swift Buck had no choice, given the circumstances. He pulled Silent Wind against him, holding the knife to her throat. He had wondered how to escape from the reservation with his mother and daughter, and the answer had been given to him.

"Lower your weapon or I will kill her," he said to the leader.

The white man's eyes widened. He had considered Swift Buck an ignorant savage, one who would not know how to speak his language. He did not follow Swift Buck's instructions.

"Let the woman go," he challenged.

"Drop the weapon," Swift Buck countered. "The woman means nothing to me. I will gladly spill her blood as a small revenge for all the blood that you have spilled."

A muscle jumped in the white man's jaw. A bead of sweat trickled down the side of his face. "The woman has nothing to do with our war," he said. "She is not your enemy. Release her, and maybe I won't kill you for touching her."

As much as Swift Buck desired hand-to-hand combat with the leader, he could not let hatred and his thirst for revenge overpower his mind.

"Her skin is white. She is my enemy. We will make a trade, but only if you drop the weapon and kick it to me. If you do not do as I say, I will take great pleasure in killing her."

The gun in the man's hand trembled, but Swift Buck knew it was not a reaction of fear but of rage.

"The minute you try to leave this tepee, you will be shot by my soldiers."

"Drop the weapon," Swift Buck repeated, and for his mother, and his daughter, he forced himself to press the knife against Silent Wind's soft throat. She gasped, and the leader, his lips tight, his eyes blazing, dropped his gun and kicked it within Swift Buck's reach.

Wrapping his hand in Silent Wind's hair, Swift Buck forced her down with him so that he could pick up the weapon. He was not ignorant about white men's armaments. He lowered his knife but pressed the long barrel of the leader's gun against Silent Wind's throat.

"What do you want?" the pale leader demanded.

"I will take my mother and my daughter from this place, and you will not stop me. If you try, I will kill the woman. Call out for your soldiers to bring three horses." To his mother, who sat clutching Amoke, Swift Buck said, "Gather what little we have, quickly."

He felt the tension of Silent Wind's body against him and sensed that she wanted to speak to him, to reason with him. But she did not want the pale man to realize that she had known the Indian long before she came to the place. Swift Buck did not want the leader to know this, either. The man might believe he would not harm a woman raised as a daughter by his mother. Swift Buck did not wish to prove otherwise.

The man called for the horses to be brought. Swift Buck would have liked to demand the release of all his people held at the reservation, but he knew the leader would not make such a trade, not even for this woman he wished to make his own.

"When I have my family safely from the camp, and I am certain that you and your soldiers will not follow, I will release the woman."

The leader narrowed his pale eyes. "How do I know you will keep your word?"

Swift Buck smiled. "You do not. But you must do as I ask or see her die now."

"If you don't release her as you promise, I will kill every man, woman, and child in the camps."

Swift Buck did not doubt the man's word. "I know that truth all too well. And you must understand that if you punish any for what I do now, I will kill the woman. Go outside in front of us," he ordered. "Command your warriors not to fire their weapons."

The leader followed orders, but Swift Buck saw the anger on his face, the violence he held inside, by the clenching and unclenching of his fists.

"I'm going to kill you for this," the leader assured Swift Buck, but he shouted the orders to his men.

Dragging Silent Wind with him, Swift Buck quickly saw his mother and daughter mounted on one horse. He threw their meager supplies over the back of a second animal, then mounted and pulled Silent Wind up before him on the third horse, careful to keep the gun pressed against her head.

To his people, who stood staring at him with the first spark of life in their eyes that he had seen in many months, he shouted, "I will return for you! Be ready!"

Motioning for his mother and daughter to go in front of him, Swift Buck backed his horse, keeping his captive and the gun pressed against her within sight of the soldiers.

"I will pray for you, Rachel!" the man in dark clothing called, waving his black book in the air. "Have faith that God will protect you!"

"No!" the pale leader shouted. "Have faith in me, Rachel!"

Swift Buck leaned forward and pressed his mouth against Silent Wind's ear. "Have faith in neither. You are now my captive."

CHAPTER SEVEN

Rachel swallowed the bitter taste of fear. She didn't fear that Swift Buck would use the weapon pressed against her temple, but that one of the soldiers would open fire and Laughing Stream and the child would be killed . . . along with herself and Swift Buck.

He was insane for taking this chance. But she couldn't blame him. Laughing Stream wouldn't have lasted much longer at the reservation. And the child? Could she blame Swift Buck for wanting a better life for his daughter? Still, as they continued to back away from the soldiers, she realized that no matter how much she wanted to rationalize Swift Buck's actions, they were suicidal.

She knew that the captain and his men would

never rest until they had hunted down Swift Buck and killed him for his daring escape. And what had Swift Buck meant that she was now his captive? He had promised to release her as soon as he and his family were safely away from the reservation.

"The soldiers will keep hunting you," she told him. "You have placed your mother and child in danger."

"And they were not in danger before?" he asked. "Be quiet. I did not give you permission to speak to me."

Rachel snapped her head toward his and became instantly pinned by his dark eyes. "I don't need your permission to speak. I was silent for most of my life. No one will tell me to be quiet again."

His gaze never wavered. "You forget yourself, woman. A captive does as she is told."

She had known him since she was a child and thought his references to her now were ridiculous. "Do not call me *woman*. You know my name."

"Which name do you claim now?"

Lifting her chin, she answered, "Rachel Morgan."

A slight smile crossed his lips. "A white woman's name. Not even the name you were born with. You take your brother's name out of shame for your own, but I think his name is no better now than that of the man who raised him."

Rachel had tried to explain the reason for her brother's absence, but Swift Buck seemed determined to think the worst of Clay. "You judge him unfairly. It is not in your nature to do so."

All traces of humor, whether his amusement had been sarcastic or not, faded from his dark eyes. "You no longer know my nature. It is time that you did. It is time for you to pay for your people's crimes against mine."

As he turned their horse and ran after his fleeing mother and daughter, a shiver raced up Rachel's spine. Once, she had feared Swift Buck, but only what he made her feel inside. She had feared giving away a heart badly battered by her abusive father, her indifferent brother. The fear she felt now was very different. She didn't know the eyes of this man, the eyes that no longer looked at her with longing or tenderness. Swift Buck had become a stranger to her, and she to him.

"It is good to breathe air that is free again," his mother called, slowing her horse so that she rode beside them, her grandchild settled before her. "My granddaughter was only a baby when we were taken to the reservation. She knows nothing beyond the stench of those camps, their foul-tasting water and the hunger that burns her belly." Laughing Stream glanced behind them, worry drawing the wrinkles deeper into her weathered face. "But the soldiers will come for us—they will come for Silent Wind. They do not know she is one of us."

Swift Buck yanked up on his horse's reins. "She is *not* one of us," he bit out. "I have told you this.

The woman is a captive, nothing more. You will not treat her as you once did . . . and neither will I. Go," he ordered, nodding ahead of them. "I will make her understand who and what she is to us now."

The fear inside Rachel grew, and the concerned look that Laughing Stream cast her son only increased her agitation.

"No, my son," the woman said. "I beg of you to treat her with kindness. She was never a sister of your blood, but she was a daughter of my heart. To disrespect her is to disrespect me."

"You will not beg for her," Swift Buck said. "A true daughter of the heart does not leave her mother to starve. Your daughter chose to abandon you, to become white. Let her suffer the way you have suffered, the way we all have suffered. Keep moving, as I have told you to do."

Laughing Stream lowered her gaze submissively, but she said, "Sometimes I believe I have not only lost a husband and a daughter, but a son as well. We have not gone far. Leave her lesson for another time."

"What I must do will not take long," he said. "Go. I will catch up with you quickly."

Heart pounding, Rachel watched the woman gently knee her horse forward, leaving them behind. "W-what are you planning to do to me?" she asked.

Swift Buck did not answer. His face a stone

mask, he searched their surroundings. The land was flat and barren, like the reservation, but bluffs rose a short distance to their left. He turned the horse in their direction.

Would he kill her? Beat her? Cut out her tongue? The anger she had sensed in him at the reservation had not slackened since his escape. If anything, Rachel felt it grow stronger in him. He prepared himself for something . . . something that had to do with her.

What he must do sickened him, but Swift Buck's anger argued that it was necessary. Silent Wind deserved this punishment, this humiliation. It was the way of his people to shame the enemy in this manner, even if it had never been his own way. His captive still believed he thought of her in the way he once had, that he was soft inside for her. He would prove otherwise. As he steered his horse toward the bluffs, he felt her trembling against him.

The woman should be afraid. She should know her place among his people. If his heart softened, he would summon the visions that haunted him, the nightmares that he lived with when darkness fell: remembrances of blood, of killing, of slain children, and of women, naked and bleeding, left to die after the soldiers had finished with them.

Silent Wind laughed and flirted with the enemy. She allowed the pale leader to touch her, to kiss her, to despoil her. A woman of The People would have spat in the man's face. She would have taken a knife and cut out his heart.

Thoughts of the leader's hands on her fueled his anger, the hatred that had taken root inside his heart and now grew there, strong, unlike the crops he had helped to plant at that barren reservation.

When he found a place where they would be hidden from view if the soldiers were foolish enough to pursue them, he stopped his horse, dismounted, reached up, and dragged Silent Wind from the animal's back.

She faced him, lower lip quivering, but a stubborn streak of defiance shining in her sky-kissed eyes. "This would be a good place to leave me until the soldiers find me," she said. "At least there is shade from the bluffs."

He took a step toward her, pleased when she retreated, even if the action seemed to be one that she did not realize she made.

"I am not going to release you. The soldiers will kill those I have left behind the moment that you are safe with them. I cannot let that happen."

Her eyes widened. "But you said—"

"I would say anything to take my mother and my daughter from that place. As long as you are my captive, the others are safe. I will find those of our band who eluded the soldiers, and we will make plans for a rescue."

"A rescue?" Silent Wind shook her head. "There cannot be many Mescaleros left. Not enough to fight those soldiers and free the others held prisoner at the reservation. To try would be foolish."

"To run away is worse. Only a coward abandons his own kind to save himself."

Pink flushed her cheeks. "And only a fool fights a battle he knows he cannot win. Take your mother and daughter and escape. Leave me here so that the soldiers won't come after you. I'll tell them you went in a different direction."

Swift Buck took another step toward her. "And you believe that I trust your word? The word of a white woman? The word of my enemy? My heart is no longer soft for you, for anyone with pale skin. I have brought you here to prove this to you, and to prove it to myself."

She stumbled back from him. Swift Buck lunged forward and grabbed her shoulders. He shoved her down to the ground, towering above her.

"Do you know what it is like to see our women dragged away in the dark of night by soldiers? To know the humiliation the white men inflict upon them, and upon the Apache men who can do nothing but wait for the women to return, bloody, beaten, their honor stolen from them as the whites steal everything else from us?"

Silent Wind shook her head. "No. You must be mistaken. The captain would never allow his men to abuse the women in such a manner. He's a gentleman, a man—"

"Who turned his eyes away from the crimes his

men committed against our women," Swift Buck interrupted. "He knew, but he did nothing. Will he do nothing when he learns that his woman has been humiliated in the same way he allowed his men to humiliate our women?"

"I am not his woman," she cried, scrambling back from him. "You cannot punish me because you want to punish him. You cannot—"

Swift Buck reached down and hauled her up against him, ending her words. "It is not your place to tell me what I can or cannot do, woman!" The fresh scent of her hair, of her skin, made his nostrils flare. The feel of her pressed against him awakened desire for her that he had tried to forget.

"Do you like it when the pale leader does this to you?" He crushed her mouth beneath his. She struggled, but Swift Buck wound his hand in her thick hair. He forced her lips apart, exploring her mouth with his tongue. The sweet taste of her, forbidden to him for so long, fired his senses and turned his blood hot in his veins.

"Do you like it when he does this?" Boldly Swift Buck splayed his hand across her breast, thinking he should have ripped the garment from her so he could feel the softness of her skin.

She gasped then tried to twist away from him. Swift Buck easily wrestled her back into his arms, his mouth claiming hers once more. He felt the wild beating of her heart against his chest. Her fear enveloped him, when it was her arms that he longed to feel wrapped around his back. How many times had he imagined holding her pressed against him? But never had she been afraid in his dreams; she had wanted him with the same fire that burned inside him for her.

He pulled back to look at her. Whatever she saw burning in his gaze did not chase the fear from her eyes or the paleness from her face. He reached to touch the smooth skin of her cheek, but she flinched, as if she thought he meant to strike her.

"Five winters have not changed you," he said. "Ice still flows in your veins instead of blood. Your mind will not forget. Your heart cannot forgive. It is good that the pale leader did not come to know you as I have known you. A man prefers a woman beneath his blankets whose touch does not freeze him like a winter wind."

Where a moment ago her skin had turned a shade lighter than her natural coloring, now bright color flooded her face.

"I know only what I have been shown," she said. "Today you did prove something to me. You proved that I am right not to trust men, regardless of the color of their skin. Five winters might not have changed me, but they have changed you! Now all you feel is hate, the need to punish, to fight, to kill, to become all that you despise in your enemies." She tilted her chin up at him. "Or can you prove me wrong?"

It was a clever tactic, to challenge him to do the

opposite of what he intended. He thought he could punish her, humiliate her as he and his people had been humiliated, but the need to use his hate against her had turned into another need—the need to make her respond to him with something other than fear.

This time when he took her lips, he did so gently. She stood very still, her eyes open. He touched her cheek, the softness of her skin warm beneath his palm. She tensed but did not struggle. Slowly he ran his tongue along the contours of her lips, tasting her, coaxing her to open willingly to him. Whether she followed his command or was simply shocked by his tactic, her reaction allowed him entrance.

Swift Buck slanted his mouth across hers, exploring the moist cavern of her mouth. She tasted as sweet as a honeycomb. Her lashes drifted down in a response of surrender, even if she did not realize they closed. He pulled her closer, the feel of her softness pressed against him, chasing thoughts of war and revenge from his mind. That was when Swift Buck realized that she had tricked him. He had forgotten for a moment that she was his enemy, his captive. He broke from her lips.

Without a word, Swift Buck dragged her to his horse, mounted, and pulled her up before him. He would quickly close the distance between himself and his mother and daughter. It had been foolish of him to stop for even a moment. The soldiers

would come after them. The pale leader would
want his woman back.

Rachel's heart pounded as she, Swift Buck, and his
family raced across the flat plains, dust rising from
their horses' hooves. Laughing Stream had refused
to look at her once they'd caught up, but the
woman's lack of attention came as a relief to Rachel; she feared the woman would assume that her
blushes of shame stemmed from reasons other than
the truth. When Swift Buck had kissed her, Rachel
had felt something other than fear. He had stirred
feelings deep within her—feelings of longing and
desire.

His kiss had drawn a different response from the
captain's. She had felt something—a spark, a
flame, a remembrance that she had once cared for
Swift Buck, and not in a sisterly way. He claimed
to be her enemy. He'd kissed her roughly. She
shouldn't have responded to him with any emotion
except resentment . . . but she had.

Rachel made out the distant shape of mountains
ahead. Those mountains had once been her home,
first with her trapper father and her ruined mother,
then with the Mescaleros. She was going home.
Only now she went as a captive, an enemy of The
People, not as Silent Wind, adopted daughter of
Laughing Stream and Crooked Nose; adoptive sister of Swift Buck, a once fierce yet gentle warrior.

Her hair, a tangled mass hanging past her shoulders, blew behind her in the wind. The sun beat down upon her, and the world passed in a blur of earth tones. For a moment, she felt free, alive, but then Rachel remembered that she was *not* free. She must talk Swift Buck out of his suicidal plans. He should take Laughing Stream and his child and hide with the others, if indeed there were others left, and not fight.

There couldn't be many Apaches who had managed to escape the recent campaign to kill or capture the Mescaleros—not enough to overpower the soldiers at the fort at any rate. To attempt a rescue would only lead to more bloodshed, both the deaths of soldiers and Apaches. The Apaches had once forced her brother to choose between his white blood and his Apache heart. Now Rachel found herself in a similar predicament.

She hated conditions at the reservation. Yet she understood that the Indians would pose a threat to the whites hoping to settle in New Mexico. The Apaches would never give up their lands without a fight, and she couldn't blame them. Like her brother, Rachel seemed trapped in a situation where there were no simple solutions.

Laughing Stream's jarring cough drew her attention. Rachel's adoptive mother tried to keep the cough hidden, but the old woman's shoulders shook. Rachel turned in the saddle to see if Swift Buck had noticed, and came face to face with him. His mouth seemed disturbingly close to hers.

His features were proud—long, straight nose, high, chiseled cheekbones, and strong jawline. His hair, dark as a raven's wing, hung past his shoulders. She had once thought that the reason he'd seemed so handsome in her memories was because she'd known few men to compare him to . . . but she had been wrong. He was a man to steal a woman's breath away.

"Your mother," she whispered. "Maybe we should stop so she can rest."

He lifted a dark brow. "And maybe you would like for us to stop so that the soldiers will catch up with us."

The last thing Rachel wanted was to witness a confrontation between the soldiers and Swift Buck. She knew that he wouldn't be recaptured without a fight, and she knew his odds for survival would not be good. Swift Buck seemed determined to think the worst of her motives.

"I care for *her*," she proclaimed. "Regardless of what you believe about me, I would never wish your mother harm."

"Yet you did not come to see her in five years. You did not waste your thoughts upon her sorrow at losing a daughter. You did not consider that she would worry about you, wonder if you were happy with your new life. Just like your brother, you think only of yourself."

His words brought guilt. She had thought of her Apache family often during the past five years.

90

When she had first left the Mescaleros and her home in the mountains, she had felt as if she'd die of homesickness. Yet Rachel had been looking for her place in life, a place where she might fit in with those around her. She'd hoped to find a home where she was wanted, instead of one that she had been thrust upon.

She and her brother were somewhat the same, even if they did have different fathers. Both had learned to shield their hearts at an early age. Hiram Brodie had mistreated both. But Clay had changed. His love for his wife Melissa had softened him, and he loved his children with all his heart.

Rachel had learned to forgive her brother for his cold treatment of her before Melissa became the light in his dark world, but she hadn't learned to love as he loved, to give as he had learned to give.

"We will stop for a short time," Swift Buck called to his mother. "Amoke is tired. She is not used to riding."

"We cannot stop, my son," Laughing Stream argued. "The soldiers will be close at our backs. Amoke is fine."

Rachel glanced back at Swift Buck, hoping he would argue. His eyes touched Rachel's face, but then he nodded, prodding his horse forward again.

"But—" she began, and his arms tightened around her.

"She has her pride," he said softly. "Say nothing."

A small shiver raced up her back at the feel of his warm breath against her ear. It took all her willpower, but she obeyed him. Laughing Stream would never allow herself to be the reason her son and granddaughter were recaptured by the soldiers.

They rode until the sun began to drop behind the still-distant mountains. Amoke had slept most of the time; now she stirred and cried softly, telling her grandmother in short words that she was hungry.

Laughing Stream looked at her son, and Rachel noticed the paleness of her skin, the thin sheen of sweat coating the woman's face.

"We will find a place to camp," Swift Buck announced, and Rachel breathed a small sigh of relief.

Only after Swift Buck found a place with a measure of cover, and the weary foursome dismounted, did it occur to her that she was once again at Swift Buck's mercy. Would he leave her alone tonight, or under a blanket of darkness did he plan to finish what he had begun earlier?

"My mother is tired," he said to her. "Prepare a meal. Fill the canteens on the horses with water from the river,"

So, he would treat her like a captive, no better than his slave? Rachel didn't argue with him, but only because she didn't want Laughing Stream to further strain herself. The woman had already removed the pack from the extra horse, and the child still cried to be fed. Rachel hurried to take the heavy pack from Laughing Stream. The old woman smiled gratefully.

"It is good that you are here to help my son," she admitted quietly, then a rattling cough wracked her reed-thin frame.

"You must rest," Rachel insisted, steering her adoptive mother to a place where Swift Buck had spread a blanket on the ground. "After I prepare a meal, I will make a poultice for you."

Laughing Stream shook her head. "It is too late for medicine." She coughed again, gasping for breath. Swift Buck appeared in an instant, pushing Rachel aside to kneel beside his mother. He clasped her thin shoulders.

"You must rest, *Shimaa*."

"I am fine," Laughing Stream insisted between gasps for breath. "I will help prepare our camp for the night."

"No," Swift Buck insisted. He nodded toward Rachel. "She must learn the ways of a captive. It is her duty to serve us." He rose and scooped his crying child into his arms. "Come, Amoke. You can help me with the horses."

Rachel bristled as he walked away, but her concern for Laughing Stream outweighed her anger toward the woman's son. "He is right," she said, once again settling beside Laughing Stream. "It is my place to care for you. Not because I have become a captive in Swift Buck's eyes, but because for many years you cared for me."

A strained smile shaped Laughing Stream's cracked lips. "Once, you were everything in his eyes. You will be again, but you must give him time to mend from the wrongs done to us, and you must free your heart so that you can walk into the flame. You cannot give a heart that does not know where it belongs."

Frowning, Rachel said, "I have heard The People speak of this, but I have never understood. What does it mean 'to walk into the flame'?"

A frail hand reached for hers. "Some mates join out of duty. Some join because they do not wish to be alone. But when two come together because it is their destiny, because one cannot be whole without the other, it is like walking into a flame. These cannot put out the fires that burn in their hearts for one another. Even death cannot damp the flame. To brave the fire, you must learn to trust—in yourself, and in the one who is your spirit mate. You must be willing to sacrifice all for him, for love. For some, for those who do not truly understand, to walk into the flame is to only give in to your desire for another—but there is more, so much more. I hope you will understand what I have told you one day, but I will be gone before then."

Again, fear rose up inside Rachel. "Do not say such things. We have many summers left together. Time to—"

"Woman!" Swift Buck snapped. "My daughter and mother are tired and hungry. Prepare them food, and fetch the water as I have told you to do."

Casting a dark glance toward Swift Buck, Rachel patted Laughing Stream's hand and rose. She found some corn cakes and dried beef and set them out; then she gathered the canteens and moved toward the river. Swift Buck followed her, no doubt to make certain that she didn't try to escape.

She felt his eyes boring into her back as she bent next to the river. The water here looked a little clearer than it had at the reservation, but not much. In the mountains, there were many clear streams where water ran down from the snowcapped peaks. Rachel hadn't tasted water as pure and sweet since she'd left the Mescaleros.

The pleasant memory was short-lived. The stifling heat brought her from thoughts of clear water and the cool breath of the mountains. Rachel pulled her thick hair to one side, cupped water in her palms, and splashed the back of her neck. She would have loved to strip off her heavy clothing and take a bath, but with Swift Buck standing guard over her, that was not an option. How did he expect to escape the soldiers, a lone man traveling with a sick old woman and a small child?

He might get them all killed. Still, Rachel couldn't blame him for wanting to spare his family from the horrible conditions at the reservation.

With time, she might have improved conditions— might have softened Franklin's view of the Indians and made life better for The People and the soldiers. By taking matters into his own hands, Swift Buck had ruined any chances for her future plans. He'd proven that the white man could not tame a warrior's heart. He'd taken a hostage and escaped the soldiers, making Franklin look the fool in front of his men. She suddenly shuddered. Franklin would kill Swift Buck for his spirit, just as he had killed the mustang he could not break. Or perhaps Franklin would meet his death at Swift Buck's hatred-filled hands.

There were no peaceful solutions to what had happened earlier today. Rachel saw her middle ground fast slipping away. Feeling Swift Buck's gaze, she finished filling the canteens. The feel of his eyes upon her was unsettling. The fine hairs on her arms prickled. Heat flooded her face at the re-membrance of what had taken place between them.

Would Swift Buck attack her again? Not with his child and Laughing Stream near, she assured her-self—but that was not to say he wouldn't drag her away from the camp. She shuddered again.

Still, his anger she could suffer; it was when he was tender that he frightened her the most.

CHAPTER EIGHT

The night surrounded them. To ensure that their location remained hidden, no fire burned to bring comfort and warmth, but Swift Buck felt as if a hundred eyes watched him in the darkness. He needed rest, but he dared not sleep. The soldiers would be trailing them. He knew that the leader would not keep his word and wait to see if Silent Wind returned to the fort.

They had a few-hours lead only because the captain would have taken time to organize. If they could only reach the mountains, Swift Buck felt confident they could elude their pursuers. The mountains were his home; he knew the land there like he knew his own heart. The soldiers would be at a disadvantage.

Silent Wind moaned softly in her sleep. His eyes strayed to her, a bundle wrapped in a blanket. A moment later, he found himself standing over her. A silver strand of her hair caught the moonlight, and unconsciously he bent and tucked it into place. His fingers brushed the smooth curve of her cheek. Her skin gleamed pearly beneath the moon's glow.

Once, she had been a silent nuisance, always under his feet; then she had grown into a beautiful woman. He had paid her little attention as a child, and when the woman took her place, he had been stunned by the transition—stunned and captivated. Stunned, captivated, and ashamed of his sudden feelings for a child raised by his father and mother. She should have been a sister to him, but he had never shared his heart with her in that way.

Her brother Cougar was like a brother to him, too. He and Cougar had mixed their blood, had taught each other their languages. They had hunted together, warred beside one another. His desire for Silent Wind soiled what he and Cougar shared. He had shamed his family and his brother, over a woman, through his desire.

Worse, she was a woman who had proven herself unworthy of his heart—of the hearts of The People who raised her. Hurt and anger rose inside him again. Swift Buck wanted to punish her for her crimes against him, her people's crimes against his. For two years he had been forced to watch the degradation of his people, of the women in the camps,

helpless to act against the soldiers who would welcome any excuse to kill him. Now he was no longer
helpless. He was free—free to lash out at his enemies. Free to seek his own justice.

His hand moved from her cheek to the soft,
warm skin of her throat. He felt her pulse beating
there, felt it speed up a measure. She was not sleeping, he realized. Her eyes remained closed tight, but
her breathing had become labored. She feared him.
Should he give her something to fear? She was his
by rights now. He had claimed her as a captive. His
mind sought excuses for his body's reaction to her
closeness, he admitted, sickened by his weakness.

He wanted more than a fast revenge, an imper-
sonal assault upon her body. He wanted the sweetest
revenge: her complete surrender.

His mother coughed, and Swift Buck jerked
his hand from Silent Wind as if he were a small
boy caught touching something forbidden. Another
wracking cough echoed off the bluffs surrounding
them. Swift Buck hurried to his mother's side.
Amoke had become used to the sound of her grandmother's sickness, and the child did not stir. Swift
Buck gently shook his mother.

"Wake, *Shimaa*," he ordered softly. "Wake and
drink some water to stop the coughing."

But his mother did not rouse herself and sit. He
shook her gently again. Slowly her eyes opened,
and in the moonlight he saw her life force dimming.

"It is my time," she whispered; then another

spasm gripped her. "I will try to go quickly, my son, so that I do not alert the soldiers to our location. I know, as do you, that they wait in the darkness for us."

"Mother . . ." Swift Buck's voice caught. "You must not leave me now. I need you."

A clawlike hand lifted to touch his face. She caressed his cheek. "I knew that I must wait, but until I saw Silent Wind again, I did not know why. She is here now. Her destiny and yours have always been tied to one another. She has come back—now I must go forward. Your father beckons me to join him."

He clasped her hand pressed against his cheek. "Hold on to life," he said. "Soon we will be free. We will be home again. Stay with me."

She shook her head. "I *am* free, my son. Soon I will be free forever. I will soar up into the sky like the mighty eagle. Know that always I will be looking down upon you. Take care of Amoke. Take care of Silent Wind. You must help her to find her place."

"Do not leave me," Swift Buck pleaded, but his mother's hand had already slid from his.

"I must speak to Silent Wind," she said. "Wake her."

"I am awake, *Shimaa*." Silent Wind knelt beside Swift Buck. In the darkness, he saw the sparkle of tears on his captive's cheeks. "You must listen to your son," she said. "He commands you to stay with us."

Laughing Stream turned to Swift Buck. "Leave us for a moment. I must speak to my daughter in private."

Swift Buck wanted to deny his mother's request. He was afraid that if he walked away, even for a moment, she would slip away from him.

"Go," she whispered. "I will still have words for you when I am finished speaking to Silent Wind."

"I will go," he agreed. "But only for a moment. Make your words short. She deserves no better from you."

His mother sighed, a sound that told him what words could not: She was tired of living. Tired of losing. He went, but not far from her side.

A soft sob caught in Silent Wind's throat. He heard her whisper, "You cannot go. I have many things that I must tell you. Words that I could not speak while I grew to be a woman beneath your loving care. I want you to know, to understand—" Her words ended abruptly, and Swift Buck turned to see his mother's fingers pressed against the white woman's lips.

"I know that to love is hard for you, but I also know that you do love me," Laughing Stream said. "You went away because you had to see for yourself where you belong. I knew that one day you would return. Open your heart to The People. Accept your destiny. Accept what others will give you. Because of your father, you do not believe that you deserve these things in life, but you do. Allow yourself to have them. Allow yourself to love, to feel, to hurt. It is part of life. Do not leave this world without feeling all that is meant for you to feel. Forgive him," she whispered, and then Swift Buck saw his mother's hand drop away from Silent Wind's lips.

"Mother?" He heard Silent Wind's choked cry, then louder: "Mother!"

His heart pounding, he rushed to Silent Wind's side and knelt beside her. His mother's eyes stared sightlessly up at the stars, and for the first time in a long while, a serene smile rested upon her lips. Pain and grief rose up inside him, but he could not howl his sorrow to the moon. Instead, he gathered his mother's frail form to him, lifted her, and walked into the night.

As she watched Swift Buck's shadow merge with the darkness, raw and blistering pain rose up inside Rachel. It clutched at her insides and twisted. It wrung a moan from her throat, and if she'd still had the knife Swift Buck had wrestled from her, she would have slashed at her flesh. Tears welled up in her eyes, but this time she could not fight them. She let them fall, let five years of guilt—no, a lifetime of guilt—come pouring from her soul.

Laughing Stream had gone to the spirit world without allowing Rachel to tell her how much she loved her. How much she respected her, how sorry she was that she had left and not returned before now—now that it was too late.

She covered her face with her hands, wanting to cry out for the injustices done to her, past and present. But her grief had to be kept silent, for the night had ears. She balled a fist and stuck it into her mouth as sobs shook her shoulders.

She needed the comfort of another's arms, but there was no other, not now. Laughing Stream had been the only one to hold her when she'd been sad or frightened as a child, and now that comfort was lost to her forever. Amoke stirred, glanced up at her and saw her sorrow . . . and held out her arms.

The response, so uninhibited, so trusting of a stranger, tugged at Rachel's breaking heart. She had never been so innocent herself. Her father had taught her to trust no one at an early age. Always she had guarded her emotions. But here was a child, also mistreated, if not by those who loved her, by her mere circumstances in life—a child who offered Rachel comfort or who wanted comfort herself and was unafraid to ask for it.

Gathering the child into her arms, Rachel hugged her close. The girl snuggled up to her body and rested her small head against Rachel's chest. Slowly Rachel began to rock the child, unsure if the slight motion was meant to soothe herself or the girl. She hummed beneath her breath, an Apache lullaby Laughing Stream had sung to her as a child.

Long after Amoke had settled back to sleep, Rachel held her, rocked her, and hummed the song in her head over and over. Exhaustion overwhelmed her battered emotions, and she settled down on the blanket and closed her eyes, still holding the child in her arms. Just before she drifted off, she remembered Laughing Stream's last words to her. *Forgive him*. Forgive whom? Swift Buck? And had his mother asked her to forgive him for past sins, or sins he had not yet committed?

During their short reunion, Laughing Stream had served as a buffer between Rachel and her son. Now that buffer was gone. What would happen to her now?

CHAPTER NINE

His mother now rested in a shallow grave. Dawn began to streak the sky with vivid colors of pink and purple. There were sunrises as beautiful at the reservation, Swift Buck supposed, but he had not noticed them. There, life had been ugly, and his spirit had only seen the darkness of each new day. The sun topped the distant bluffs and stung his sleep-starved eyes. Swift Buck rubbed them for a moment, then glanced down at the sleeping form of his daughter, wrapped in Silent Wind's arms.

The loss of his mother had obviously weakened him, for he could not find the strength to be outraged by the sight of his daughter resting trustingly in the arms of his enemy. And he would ignore the strange twist of his heart at the sight of them together. Once, he had been foolish enough to envision the children he and Silent Wind would someday have together. He had been a boy then, he realized, a fool in love with a woman who did not know how to love him, or anyone else. He had put those childish dreams behind him. She would not awaken the fool inside him again.

He reached out and shook her. "Rise. We must leave this place."

Her long dark lashes fluttered open, revealing twin pools of deep blue. Her eyes were swollen and red. She had wept. Another stab of conscience struck him. He had left her alone to deal with her grief. She deserved no better, Swift Buck consoled himself. The white woman should suffer. Had his mother not suffered during the past five years, worried over the fate of her adopted daughter?

Had he himself not suffered? Wondering if she would return to him? He had become the brunt of many jokes when all realized that she would not. Had his people not suffered while she and her brother had lived safely in their white world, turning a blind eye to the fate of those who had foolishly given them their hearts?

"Up," he said, his tone harsh with the grief and anger that had become a part of him. "We must go."

Amoke stirred and frowned at him. Her dark brows drew together. Her expression told him that she did not understand why her father would use such an angry tone. Always he had been gentle with his child. He fought hard to keep his temper in her presence. Amoke had enough to fear in the reservation camps; he would not have her fear him as well. Silent Wind, however, was a different matter.

His tone softer, he said, "There is no time to prepare a meal. Find what you can for Amoke. She will eat as we ride."

Releasing his daughter, Silent Wind sat up and looked around. Her gaze touched the blanket she rested upon, and her eyes filled with tears. Her bottom lip, tempting and full, trembled slightly. For a moment, Swift Buck wanted to grab her and pull her into his arms. He wanted to kiss the tears from her eyes and drink from her sweet lips. He wanted to bury himself within her soft flesh and spend his sorrow. But only for a moment.

Amoke rose, rubbing her little eyes. She moved off to find a place to relieve herself. Swift Buck wondered why she did not ask about her grandmother's absence. She would ask, he suspected. When they were packed and ready to leave, she would want to know why her grandmother was not with them. He steeled himself for the task of telling her. She would not understand, being only a small child.

"You should release me now," Silent Wind said. "Let me go back, and you and your daughter will have a better chance of escaping."

Swift Buck ignored her suggestion. He had no

intention of releasing her until he made certain that his daughter was safe with the others who hid in the mountains. He might be able to move more quickly with only Amoke, he admitted. Still, to release Silent Wind was not an option. He wasn't certain he would release her even if it were. She had not suffered nearly enough, in his opinion.

She rose and brushed the wrinkles from her heavy gown. Swift Buck frowned, studying the ugly dress. "Remove it," he ordered softly.

Her blue gaze shot up to meet his. "What?"

"The dress. It is too heavy and slows you down when you ride. Remove it."

"But it's all I have," she argued.

Swift Buck went to her, took her arm, and steered her toward the river. He glanced over his shoulder to see his daughter playing in the sand. Once they reached the water's edge, he leaned against a flimsy tree and crossed his arms over his chest. "You have nothing on beneath this ugly dress?"

Her cheeks flushed. "I certainly have undergarments on, but they are not suitable to wear alone."

"You know that captives are normally stripped naked and made to move around the camp without clothing. It humbles them."

The pink in her cheeks darkened to red. "I am not a captive." She lifted her chin. "I am your adoptive sister."

He smiled at her tactics, although neither his

108

heart nor his loins felt light at the moment. "You used to call to me when the shadows were long and you lay across the fire, sleeping inside my parents' lodge. You would call my name and toss restlessly upon your mats. What did you want?"

Swift Buck saw the motion of her throat trying to swallow. "I did not," she insisted. "I could not speak. You must have dreamed that I called to you."

His brow lifted. "You could speak. You were unaware that words came to you in your sleep. You tortured me with your breathless moans." His gaze moved over her. "I knew what you wanted."

Suddenly she turned her back on him, placing her hands upon her hips. "I don't believe you. I have always thought of you as a brother. If I did in fact call to you, you misunderstood the reason."

Shrugging away from the tree, he approached her. The fragrant smell of her hair flooded his senses. He pushed the thick, tangled mass over one shoulder, watching her body tense.

"You lie. You lie to me and to yourself. You never looked upon me as a brother, just as I never looked upon you as a sister. It shames you to admit this, the same as it has shamed me in the past. But now things are different between us." He ran his finger down the back of her neck, delighted when she shivered. "You are a captive, and I no longer have a conscience to cloud my mind with right or wrong. I can give you what you want—if you are brave enough to take it," he added, taunting her.

She wheeled around. He was not prepared for the slap of her hand against his cheek. The act made a loud smack in the silence. Her eyes burned with blue fire.

"How dare you!" she spat. "How dare you disrespect me and disrespect your mother when her body has not even grown cold! I am ashamed to know you. Ashamed to have ever felt anything but disgust and hatred for you! If I ever called to Swift Buck in my sleep, it was not to the Swift Buck I see before me now. I do not know you. I do not like you. I would never invite your hands upon me. Never!"

Her voice grew loud and shrill. Swift Buck had to silence her before she gave away their location. Placing a hand against her mouth would have sufficed, but instead he placed his lips there. He had not misunderstood her desire for him all those years ago. To admit such would make him look all the more foolish—in his people's eyes, and in his own. She might not want him now, but she had wanted him then, and he would prove it to her.

She did not want this—this moist, heated press of his mouth against hers, the wild beating of her heart, the hot rush of blood to her face and . . . other parts of her body. Yes, she had lied. She had dreamed of him leaning over her while she lay naked upon soft buffalo hides. In her dreams, he had touched her in places forbidden, and he had made her long for things she knew little about. In her dreams, she could allow the weaknesses, the hunger, the desire he stirred within her.

During the past five years, she had tried to put those dreams from her mind. She hadn't lied when she told him that he was no longer the same man. Reminding herself of the truth made her struggle against him now. To her surprise, he pulled back to look at her, his mouth still hovering dangerously close to hers. She expected to see taunting in his dark eyes, hatred, anger—anything but what she did see, if only for a brief flash of time.

Vulnerability. Need. Emotion so dark and deep that she thought she might drown in it for an instant. He blinked, and she could breathe again.

"The dress," he said softly. "Remove it, or I will remove it for you."

She stepped away from him. He was stronger. To resist would be both foolish and a waste of time. She didn't want to go with him, but she wouldn't be the reason he was captured or killed. Challenge shone now in his dark eyes. He liked making her uneasy. She lifted her chin to prove that she would not cower before him.

"Turn your back," she said.

He laughed. "I did not say that you must remove everything. Only the dress."

Rachel raised her fingers to the tiny buttons that ran the length of the garment. Thank goodness it didn't button up the back, or she would have needed assistance. She refused to lower her gaze in shame as she undid the buttons, instead keeping her eyes trained upon his. He did not look at her body as she expected he might, but the fact that he kept staring into her eyes made her more uncomfortable than if he had watched her motions as she undressed.

A hot blush stole over her face and moved down her body. Once the dress was unbuttoned, she pulled it past her shoulders and down her hips and legs. She wore a crisp white camisole beneath, drawers, and a thin petticoat—again, more clothes than she had worn while growing up among the Apaches, but her time in the white world had made her modest.

Rarely was a woman allowed to bare her shoulders and arms among polite white society. Her camisole was low-cut, and her breasts rose proudly above the fabric. She'd done away with wearing her corset due to the insufferable heat.

Swift Buck had kept his eyes on her face, but now he let his gaze drift slowly over her body. She felt as if he touched her with more than his eyes. Her skin tingled, and she had trouble catching a normal breath. Amoke stumbled into the clearing, breaking the tension between them.

"We must go," Swift Buck said, his voice low and husky. Then he swept up the child and headed toward the horses.

* * *

Amoke did not ask about her grandmother. Swift Buck wondered why. Did a child so easily accept that someone was in their lives one moment and gone the next?

No. Silent Wind had not accepted that her father no longer wanted her as a child; she had not accepted that her brother by blood would ignore her when he came to the Mescalero camps, as if he did not know the blond child with a stolen voice. She had hidden from her father. The man was abusive, so Swift Buck understood why she would hide, but always she had looked at her brother with hope when he visited their camp—hope that he might acknowledge her as his kin. Which he eventually had.

Swift Buck's mother had told him that he must help Silent Wind find her place. As they rode, Amoke sleeping in his arms and the reins to Silent Wind's horse tethered around his saddle horn, he was confused about his mother's request. The whites made war on The People. Silent Wind was white. How could she have a place among them? Or had his mother been asking him to return her to her people?

He would, once she had served her purpose for him. Then she could go back to the pale leader, go back to the brother who had treated her unkindly until five years ago, never mind that Swift Buck had never treated her unkindly, even when he considered her a nuisance. Never mind that she had been loved by her adoptive mother, and the child that his mother raised had never once shown her that she loved her in return. Not until it was too late.

Too late, Silent Wind had returned. He glanced across at her. Their horses ran quickly, and she was forced to hold on to the saddle horn to keep from falling off. His eyes strayed to the low neckline of her undergarment. Silent Wind's breasts moved in time with her horse's gait. The heat made her clothes cling to her, and if he looked closely, he could make out the darker circles of her nipples beneath the thin material. He swallowed and glanced away. Even desiring her made him feel as if his emotions betrayed him.

Suddenly something flew past his cheek. Swift Buck jerked his head around to look behind him. Soldiers! He kneed his horse and shot ahead, pulling his captive's horse along with him. Another bullet flew past, and Amoke began to cry.

"Swift Buck!" Silent Wind shouted. "Give me the reins and give me Amoke! They're shooting at you!"

What she asked was impossible. She asked him to trust her with his daughter's life, with the lives of those he had left behind at the reservation. If he gave her control of the horse and his daughter, she might turn and flee. Still, he placed Amoke in danger by holding her. The soldiers were firing at him, not at Silent Wind.

"Swift Buck!" she shouted again. "They won't shoot at me! Give me Amoke! I can keep her safe!"

He had no choice. He must trust Silent Wind, when every part of him told him that he should not. Quickly untying the reins of her horse from his saddle horn, he tossed them to her. She nearly dropped one, and he held his breath. Bending low over her horse's neck, Silent Wind managed to grab the other rein. She straightened, then moved in close to him.

"Place her in front of me," she called. "I'm afraid if I try to take her, I might drop her!"

Another bullet whizzed past them, dangerously close. Swift Buck realized the closer Silent Wind rode to him, the more danger she placed herself in. He tried to pry Amoke from him, but the child clung. Before he could decide what to do about Amoke's determination to hold on to him, Silent Wind slid from her horse onto the back of his.

"What are you doing?" he shouted over his shoulder at her. "You slow us down with three on one horse!"

"I'm saving your life," she shouted at him. "Now they will be forced to stop shooting or risk hitting me in the back!"

Silent Wind was crazy. Killing a woman had never bothered the soldiers before, but then again, the women they killed were not white. The leader would be with them and would not want harm to come to his woman. Maybe her plan would work, but if it didn't . . .

115

CHAPTER TEN

They stood pressed against the wall of a shallow cave, watching the soldiers pass beneath them. The horses took up most of the cave's interior. Swift Buck had one hand clamped over Rachel's mouth and the other pressed against his daughter's. Rachel had been right: The shooting stopped as soon as she'd climbed onto the back of Swift Buck's mount. She refused to consider what might have happened had she not judged the soldier's actions correctly. Below, she saw the rigid form of Franklin Peterson leading his men in the chase.

Swift Buck spotted the captain, too, and his hand tightened over her mouth. Did he really believe she would call out and place him and his daughter in danger? If he did, he didn't know her at all. Amoke squirmed, obviously unused to being restrained by her father. Rachel squirmed, too, disturbed more by the feel of him pressed against her, his scent of horses and earth, than being rendered incapable of speech. She considered biting him.

"Do not," he said in her ear, and she had to wonder if he knew her thoughts. "If you struggle, the white clothes you wear may draw an eye in our direction. I should have made you strip naked."

And she should have let the soldiers shoot him! He had placed his daughter's life in danger, had placed her life in danger as well. She understood his need to escape the reservation, but she could not condone the killing of innocent people to see that his desires were met. There had already been too much bloodshed!

"You were foolish to do what you did," he said, watching the soldiers move away. "You must trust the pale leader more than I thought."

Rachel honestly didn't know what had come over her. She had simply known that she must protect Amoke . . . and perhaps Swift Buck. She had taken a chance—something she rarely did. It had been foolish.

"I did it for Amoke," she told him. "You have dragged her into a war of your own making. If conditions at the reservation were horrid, at least they were peaceful. She was safe there."

"She was starving," he argued. "She was dirty, hungry—and worse, she had become accepting of her surroundings. She knows nothing else. I want to show her the way life should be for an Apache."

Rachel said what she knew to be true, even if it saddened her heart: "The way it *was* is no longer the way it *is* for the Apaches. Why do you want to give her a gift that can so easily be snatched away? It's cruel to give hope where there is none."

He shook his head, his dark eyes now trained on her instead of on the retreating soldiers. "Hope may be all that I can give her. Pride in my daughter's people and what we once were—what we might again be. Life has made you afraid to hope, afraid to reach for what you feel is too difficult to grasp. You want a safe life, a life where you can hide yourself and your feelings away from others. You want no life at all."

Anger rose inside Rachel. He had no right to make such assumptions about her—even if part of her feared that he knew her too well. She *was* prone to run away from danger rather than stand and fight. She had seen the beatings that her father, Hiram Brodie, had inflicted upon her half-brother, had seen the scars crisscrossing his back. When her father had come to the Apache camp, she had hidden from him. She did not have the courage to demand that he acknowledge her as his blood. When she had felt forbidden feelings for Swift Buck five years ago, she had run from him, too.

"You underestimate me," she snapped, and her gaze lowered to the child who now clung to her

118

dirty petticoat. She would save this child, even if it meant stealing her away from her father. Rachel remembered the hope in Laughing Stream's eyes when she'd offered to take Amoke away from the reservation and care for her. She hadn't been able to tell Laughing Stream how much she loved and respected her before she'd passed from one life to another; she would see that her granddaughter lived a better life than what her father could offer.

"We will camp here until we know for certain that the soldiers have moved ahead of us," Swift Buck said. "Prepare something to eat."

He was back to ordering her around. Amoke was hungry, or Rachel would have told him to fix his own meal. He didn't even thank her for probably saving his life today. The Swift Buck she had once known would have—but again, she must remind herself that this bitter, hate-filled man was not the gentle warrior she once knew. And later, she would do something to prove that he didn't know her as well as he thought.

His eyes were heavy. Swift Buck closed them only for a moment, just long enough to soothe the sting. Maybe when they reached the mountains and found better cover, he could sleep. But for now he must stay awake. While he rested his eyes, he thought about the coolness of a mountain river. The scent of pine in the air. The lazy circle of a hawk overhead.

These thoughts comforted him, brought peace to his troubled mind. He did not believe he had slept, but a shuffling noise woke him. In the darkness, Silent Wind's white undergarments, as she called them, stood out starkly. He felt mildly amused that she would try to escape . . . until he saw the small child in her arms.

He rose slowly to his feet. Creeping from the cave, Swift Buck watched while she tried to mount the horse she had taken and hold Amoke in her arms at the same time. He touched her shoulder, and she yipped like a frightened coyote then wheeled to face him.

"You frightened me," she accused, her voice a soft hiss.

His mouth dropped open. She scolded him for startling her, when she planned to run away from him, taking his child with her? He was not amused.

"It does not surprise me that you would try to escape, but why would you take my child from me?"

"I'm only doing what is best for her," she answered. "Amoke will be safe with me in my world. I have money. I can provide for her. She will not starve or be caught up in a war she is too young to understand. Let me take her and return to the reservation. Once I have finished there, I will take Amoke home with me."

It had been a while since he spoke the white language, but Swift Buck had no trouble understanding her words. She wanted to take his daughter from him. She wanted to turn her into a white child.

"Amoke will not fit into your world," he told her. "All that you have will not make her white. Your people will punish her for having dark skin and eyes. She will be unhappy in your world."

"At least she will be alive!" Silent Wind argued.

Swift Buck wrestled his sleeping child from her arms. Amoke mumbled a short protest, but settled her head upon his shoulder and immediately fell back to sleep.

"It is not enough to only breathe in and out," Swift Buck said. "Amoke will know freedom. She will know her own people and our way of life. I am her father. Her path is for me to decide, not you."

Silent Wind's eyes glittered in the darkness. If she said nothing, her anger was evident to him. Swift Buck wondered how she dared to feel anger toward him when she was the one who had wronged him and The People. Today, when she had bravely climbed onto the back of his horse to protect him and Amoke, he thought he might have judged her too harshly, but now she had proven to him that she could not be trusted.

"I will tie you to me at night when we camp to make certain that you do not try to escape again."

In the darkness, he heard her gasp. "I would rather be strapped to a wounded badger!"

Taking her arm, he instructed, "Bring the horse."

Swift Buck trudged wearily back to the cave entrance, holding his daughter with one arm, holding on to Silent Wind with the other. His time spent on the reservation had weakened him. He had no strength to respond to her comment about him. His mood was worse than that of a wounded badger. She should not push him further tonight.

CHAPTER ELEVEN

Long ago she had dared to dream of Swift Buck's arms wrapped around her in the night. She hadn't known that his skin would be smooth and hot, or that his body heat would keep her warm during chilly nights when a fire could not be lit. Rachel lay very still. She hadn't realized that she'd snuggled so close until his arms encircled her and roused her from sleep.

She thought he slept, but she wasn't certain. He might have put his arms around her in an unconscious gesture. For all she knew, he could be dreaming of his lost wife. The thought didn't please her. If he mistook her for his wife, he might take further liberties with her before morning. She lay on her side, his body pressed against her back.

Amoke slept on his other side, no doubt also snuggled close to her father's warmth.

Rachel had been angry when he did in fact tie her ankle to his. What little trust she might have managed to gain from him earlier had been lost when she'd tried to escape with his daughter. She only wanted what was best for Amoke. Why couldn't he see that?

The feel of his warm breath against the back of her neck scattered her thoughts. His hand slid up from her waist and cupped her breast. Rachel's heart lurched.

Was he aware of what he'd just done? His breathing sounded steady and slow, like that of a man deep in sleep. If she stayed still, perhaps he would remove his hand. She waited. The longer she waited, the more aware of him she became. His palm burned on her skin. His thumb suddenly brushed her nipple through her thin chemise. She stifled a gasp.

A moment later, his other hand slid up and mimicked the actions of the first. As before, his thumb brushed her nipple—then both thumbs in unison. The friction against her soft skin sent sensations coursing through her. Her nipples hardened beneath his fingers, and her breasts seemed to swell into the fit of his hands. She knew she should struggle, but instead her body arched involuntarily against him.

His teeth nipped at her neck, her ear. His hands

slid down to her hips, molding her against him. Rachel couldn't contain a small gasp of surprise. How had he managed to hide what he pressed against her beneath a breechclout? She knew the difference between male and female; children often ran naked in the camps . . . but she had no idea that when a boy grew to manhood his . . . Well, what Swift Buck pressed against her backside felt very big, and thick, and hard. She seriously doubted that he was dreaming and unaware of his actions. If he was asleep, she would wake him . . . and not pleasantly.

She jabbed her elbows into his ribs. He grunted in surprise, releasing her in an instant. Rachel turned and brought her knee up between his legs, a defense tactic all Apache women were taught from childhood. Swift Buck sucked in his breath, groaned, and rolled away from her. He sat, his knees drawn up to his chest and his breathing deep and ragged.

Rachel felt a stab of alarm. Had she injured him badly? She'd reacted instinctively. The thought of simply asking him to stop had not occurred to her. She wondered if it would have done her any good.

He raised his head to look at her. Dawn streaked the sky and lit the shallow cave, or she wouldn't have been able to see the tight set of his jaw, or the heat that still glowed in his dark gaze.

"Next time, use your voice to make your displeasure known to me. One day I might wish to have more children."

A hot blush crept up her neck—of embarrassment or anger, she wasn't certain which. "I make my displeasure known now so that there will not be a next time," she said. "Understand that I will protect myself if you try to force yourself on me again."

His response was not one she expected. A small smile lifted the corner of his mouth. "Your lips say one thing to me, but your body speaks a different language. What did you think would happen if you pressed yourself against me in the night? Did you believe I could ignore the feel of you rubbing your backside against me?"

Her face grew hotter. Had she done that before the feel of his arms around her had brought her to wakefulness? "I was asleep," she defended. "Unaware of my actions. I likely wanted your warmth, nothing else."

His smile stretched, flashing white against his bronze face. "I believe your body speaks the truths that your mind will not accept." The smile he wore faded. "I have learned to trust what one does more than what one says. Especially with those who are not of The People. They lie not only to others, but to themselves."

"You'd like to believe that," Rachel huffed, annoyed with him, with her earlier response to him, and with her situation. "I'm sure it would ease your

126

guilt about forcing me if you tell yourself that you are only doing what I wish."

He shrugged. "There will be no need to force you." His dark eyes locked with hers. "Your body is already mine. It has been mine for many years. I will wait until you listen to the stirrings inside you. I will wait until you surrender to me."

His taunting remarks infuriated her. "I will never surrender to you," she assured him. "To do so would mean that you have won my heart, and—"

Given the seriousness of their conversation, his laugh seemed out of place. He shook his head as if she amused him. "You do not understand that the heart does not have to love in order to lust. I have lain with women who did not ask for my heart but only the pleasure I could give them."

His confession shocked Rachel—and also pricked something she would liken to jealousy, were she honest with herself. In her memories of him, not only had Swift Buck been honorable, a noble and kind warrior, but chaste as well. "Promiscuousness is frowned upon by The People," she said. "You would not have disrespected Crooked Nose and Laughing Stream by bringing shame upon them in such a manner."

The mention of his parents hung between them. Too late, she remembered that the Apaches did not speak of the dead. Her heart ached over the loss of her adoptive parents, a loss too recent to have faded. Tears burned her eyes. She glanced away from Swift Buck, but not before she noticed that his expression had also become somber.

"What they did not know did not hurt them," he said. "It is time to move," he added. "Fix something to eat."

Swift Buck untied the rope around his ankle, setting her free. Rachel removed the loop from her own leg, scrambling up and to the packs. Anything to put distance between them. From the corner of her eye, she watched Swift Buck wake Amoke. He touched the child gently, whispered in her ear until she giggled. Amoke stared adoringly up at her father, then threw her arms around his neck. He kissed the top of her head and scooped her up in his arms.

As angry and confused as Rachel felt over what had just transpired between them, something inside her melted at the sight of Swift Buck's gentleness with Amoke. His love for the child shone brightly in his eyes. It occurred to her that maybe she'd been wrong to think of separating them. Maybe she had never understood such love between a father and a child.

Rachel's birth father had never picked her up, or held her, or even noticed her—she remembered that about her father even though she'd been young when her mother died. And Hiram Brodie had proven he had never cared for her by later giving her to the Apaches to raise.

Crooked Nose, Swift Buck's father, had been

kind to her, but always he'd been more interested in his true son and raising him as a warrior. Laughing Stream had embraced her as her own, but Rachel remembered missing her own true mother. She'd been terrified of the strangers she'd been thrust among, and it had taken her time to warm up to her new family.

Maybe Rachel didn't know what was best for Amoke. Maybe she wasn't qualified to make such judgments. It was a matter she would give greater thought. She had to escape Swift Buck in order to save his life—she knew that with certainty.

Franklin would relentlessly pursue them until she had been rescued, but if she escaped and found the captain, she could throw him off Swift Buck's trail. And surely Franklin wouldn't dare harm any of the Apaches left on the reservation in her presence. Would he?

Swift Buck returned to the cave with his daughter. Rachel imagined he had taken the child outside so she could attend to personal matters. Rachel needed to attend to them herself. She feared that her attempted escape last night would take away even her most private moments from her. As she removed supplies from the packs for a cold breakfast, she tested the waters.

"I need to go outside," she said to him. "To attend to personal matters," she added when he narrowed his gaze.

He nodded, and she breathed a sigh of relief. Rachel dropped the supplies on the blanket they had shared, watching Amoke immediately begin to dig inside the pack. She started past Swift Buck only to feel his fingers wrap around her arm.

"I will go with you to make certain you do not become lost."

Rachel cursed silently. It seemed that all her freedom was gone.

As part of a warrior's training, an Apache could go for many days without sleep. The mountains grew nearer, but the days seemed endless to Swift Buck. He had not slept through a night since he had escaped the reservation. Having Silent Wind bound to him when they took time to rest did not help his situation. Swift Buck was aware of her as a woman. Her scent teased him, her body tempted him, and his mistrust of her kept him from being able to fully relax. He knew she planned to escape as soon as an opportunity arose.

He had to make certain no opportunity presented itself to her. True, he might travel more swiftly without her, but he could not lose his hostage until he reached the mountains and found the members of his band who had escaped. If the pale leader and his soldiers found them before they reached their destination, Swift Buck would again use Silent Wind to ensure the safety of his daughter.

Hearing a peal of laughter echo around him, his head turned quickly toward the river where Silent

Wind bathed Amoke. The white woman smiled down at his daughter, then tickled her beneath her chin. Swift Buck hurried toward them.

"Amoke," he scolded, then put a finger to his lips. "You must be quiet."

The laughter dancing in his daughter's eyes faded. Her small mouth trembled. The smile on Silent Wind's lips also faded. She narrowed her sky-colored eyes upon him.

"She's only a child. She should be allowed to laugh."

Annoyed at himself because he had made his daughter's little face sad, Swift Buck glanced around, then ran a hand through his long hair. "Sound carries far when there are not trees or brush to swallow it. You know this, Silent Wind. Do you purposely put us in danger?"

She glanced down at the child, smoothing her hand over Amoke's wet hair. "I would never purposely hurt Amoke. She is the innocent in all of this. I only wanted to see her smile."

Swift Buck allowed his tense stance to relax. His gaze roamed over the two. It was good to see Amoke clean, and even though their rations were few, the girl's face had begun to fill out from her regular meals. His eyes moved to Silent Wind, and fire raced through him. Her long hair hung over her shoulders, but the undergarments she wore—no longer white due to the dust the horses kicked up daily—were wet in places that allowed him to see her skin beneath.

Her rose-colored nipples poked through her hair, teasing him. She had pulled her underskirt up between her long legs and tucked it into her waistband. From the knee down, her legs were bare. Suddenly, water hit him in the face. His eyes shot up to Silent Wind.

"You could use a bath, too," she told him.

Amoke's large eyes widened, her small face turning from one adult to the other. Swift Buck wiped the water from his face. He bent and removed his knee-high moccasins, then walked slowly toward Silent Wind. She backed up a couple of steps, the water rising higher to lap at her clothing. Once he reached Amoke, he lifted her and sat her upon the sandy bank, wrapping a blanket around her small shoulders.

Turning back, he approached Silent Wind. "I could use a bath? No more than yourself. You have dirt on your face."

One of Silent Wind's hands lifted to her face, the other moved to her chest, where it rested as if she could slow the pulse beating at the base of her throat. "Don't!" She held a hand out. "I was only teasing you. I thought you might have forgotten how to smile."

To show her that he had not, he smiled at her now. "I do not remember you being one to tease a man. You should know the trouble that can bring."

She glanced behind him. "Amoke—we should keep an eye on her. She could easily fall into the water—"

Tired of her tactics, Swift Buck lunged forward and grabbed her. She struggled, but he was much stronger and he dunked her under the water. She came up gasping, her long hair covering her face. Swift Buck glanced at the bank to make certain Amoke was where he had left her. His child sat watching them.

Distracted, he wasn't prepared when Silent Wind swept his feet from under him. He tumbled backward into the water, drenching himself. He lay there for a moment, enjoying the feel of the cool water against his skin and the sight of Silent Wind standing with her hands on her hips, her clothes completely transparent. His gaze ran the length of her.

She glanced down and gasped, then hurriedly lowered her body into the water. "That was a trick," she accused. "You did that on purpose just so you could see me, see my, see—"

"I did see," he interrupted. "And I liked what I saw."

Her face, already red from the days they had ridden in the sun, darkened a shade. "You should be ashamed," she said. "Once, you at least had manners."

Swift Buck tried to figure out the word "manners." He kept glancing toward the bank to check on Amoke. His child had lost interest in them and now dug in the sand with a small stick. He turned his attention back to his captive.

"I do not understand manners, but if you are angry because I saw your body through your clothes, I will remove my breechclout and let you see whatever *you* wish to see."

Her mouth dropped open. She quickly closed it. "I have no desire to see anything of yours."

To test her truthfulness, he rose from the water. His breechclout remained in place, although it was wet and clung to him. He watched Silent Wind. Her eyes moved over him; then, as if she realized her actions, her gaze snapped up to his face. He showed her again that he had not forgotten how to smile.

"Arrogant," he heard her mutter.

His smile stretched as he moved toward her. She glanced around, as if looking for a place to hide— a place to run. Suddenly Silent Wind froze, the color draining from her cheeks. Swift Buck followed the direction of her stare. His heart lurched. Amoke still sat on the bank, but she had pulled the knife from a moccasin he had left there, and now she held it in her small hands.

He dared not shout at her for fear she would jump and cut herself. On the reservation, all weapons had been forbidden to the Apaches. Amoke was not familiar with knives, or the damage they could do. Swift Buck moved as quickly as he could toward the bank. He did not want to startle his daughter.

Once he reached the bank, he called her name softly. Amoke glanced up and smiled at him.

"Put it down, Amoke," he said, trying to keep his voice calm. "Put what you are holding down very gently."

His daughter glanced at the knife. Her bottom lip jutted out. *"Dah!"* she said.

Swift Buck tamped down his immediate anger that she would disobey. He drew a deep breath and moved closer. "The stick will bite you," he tried. "It is like a snake."

Amoke had been warned about snakes many times during her two short years of life on the reservation. She frowned, then threw the knife down on the ground. Swift Buck hurried forward and snatched it up before she could reconsider. His knees felt weak, and he collapsed beside Amoke on the bank.

Rachel had been frozen. She breathed a sigh of relief now, then moved toward them. As she approached, she didn't like the words she heard Swift Buck speak to his daughter.

"The snake belongs to me," he explained. "I must show you how the snake will bite so that you will remember never to touch it again. Hold out your hand."

Her petticoat dripping, Rachel hurried from the

water. She didn't think, only reacted. Swift Buck was focused on his daughter, and she easily snatched the knife from his hand. Startled by her action, he glanced up at her.

"You are not going to cut her," she assured him. "I will not allow it."

His jaw muscle tightened. "The lessons we teach our children are not always pleasant, but they are necessary for their survival. Amoke must learn that a knife is dangerous. She must learn that it can cut her, hurt her."

Rachel knew he was right, and that children raised in his world were often less sheltered than children raised in the white world, but she couldn't stand the thought of him hurting Amoke, or anyone hurting a child. She took a deep breath and slashed her palm open with the knife, flinching at the sting. A bubble of blood immediately seeped from the cut. She held her hand toward Amoke.

"Look—the snake that belongs to your father has bitten me. I should not have touched it."

Amoke's dark eyes widened. A small whimper of alarm left her lips. "*Ndiihi*," she whispered.

"Yes, it does hurt," Rachel answered. "That is why we must not touch the snake. It belongs only to your father." Having said as much, Rachel had no recourse but to extend the knife toward Swift Buck. He took it, but he also took the hand she had slashed.

Her gaze met his. Slowly he brought her hand to

his lips, his eyes never leaving hers. When the warmth of his mouth touched her palm and he sucked the blood from the small slash she had made, she couldn't contain the shiver that raced up her back. He smiled slightly at her response, his gaze moving over her. Rachel realized that she stood before him dripping wet. She also knew that her thin undergarments left little to his imagination.

She snatched her hand away and grabbed up Amoke, using the blanket wrapped around the child to block her body from his view. Amoke's ragged clothing had been given a good scrubbing. Rachel moved to a rock where she had left the clothing to dry and gathered up Amoke's things.

"Shouldn't we be moving?" she asked. "We've stayed here longer than we should." She turned and nearly ran into Swift Buck. He took Amoke from her arms.

"Yes, we should be leaving here," he agreed.

Their eyes met and held. For once, she did not see anger glaring back at her, or accusation, only a hint of confusion, and the warmth she'd seen there when he had kissed the blood from her cut.

"To spare a child not of your womb from a hurtful lesson, you would injure yourself? Why?"

She had thought she wanted to see him look at her differently, but now the softness in his eyes flustered her more than hate, or anger, or lust. It made her feel strange—warm and tingly all over.

"I cannot stand to see children hurt," she admitted. "To see a child being abused brings back bad memories for me."

Her gaze moved away from him, but she felt his touch, forcing her face up to his. He said, "I know that the man called Brodie used his fists and his whip upon Cougar. You were not much older than Amoke when you came to us. Did he . . . We saw no scars or bruises on you."

She shook her head, then placed her hand against her heart. "Not on the outside. Only in here."

He stared into her eyes for a moment, and then his hand fell away from her. "We must go."

As she watched him gather the horses, she realized that it bothered him to feel any softening toward her. When hate and anger engulfed a person, there was room for little else. Rachel had learned her own childhood lessons too well.

So much the opposite of her, Amoke stared over her father's shoulder at Rachel. She held out her arms, wriggling her fingers for a white woman, her father's so-called enemy, to come and take her. Rachel couldn't help but smile. She walked to where Swift Buck prepared the horses, balancing his daughter on one hip, and took the child.

When Amoke threw her arms around her neck, Rachel didn't miss the scowl of disapproval on Swift Buck's mouth.

CHAPTER TWELVE

They had reached the base of the mountains. Swift Buck bent, studying the camp the soldiers had left behind. The men had not been careful to hide their tracks; they did not fear a lone Apache, a white woman, and a small child. From what he could tell about the tracks and the campsite, the soldiers were ahead of them by two days. Swift Buck realized they knew that he would try to reach the mountains. They knew the mountains had once been his home. But would they have any suspicion that there were Apaches they had not captured hiding in the mountains?

With a heavy heart, he realized that he had brought trouble on his people, where there had been none. Those who had escaped the massacre would be careful to hide while they prepared any rescue. Still, it had been two years. Maybe they were all dead. Swift Buck could not allow himself to think they might be dead while he had been a prisoner on the reservation. Believing that Gray Wolf and some of the others still lived had been the only thing that kept his spirit alive. That and hate. Hate and his need for revenge.

"How far ahead of us are they?"

He glanced up at Silent Wind. "It is wrong to give such information to the enemy," he told her.

Her lips tightened. "Our supplies are almost gone. I know it is of no concern to you if I starve, but your daughter needs food."

She sounded like an unhappy wife. Swift Buck sighed, then rose, his gaze searching the area. "I cannot stop to hunt now. We must keep moving. Maybe tomorrow."

"That is what you said yesterday," she snapped. "Since the soldiers are ahead of us, I would think it safe to build a fire tonight. A fire would be nicer with a spit of roasting meat upon it."

Her temper was short. So was his. She tried to stay awake during the nights that he tied her to him, and she had gotten little sleep. He had gotten less. Her nearness was the worst kind of torture. He wanted her still, even if she had abandoned him and The People, even though her skin was white and he should only see her as his enemy. Even if her brother was a traitor. None of these things seemed to matter to his body. His weakness for her added to his foul mood.

"Come closer," he instructed her. Swift Buck decided that he would hunt, but he could not use the gun that he had taken from the leader; it would make too much noise. He planned to use an old Apache trick instead.

Silent Wind eyed him warily. "Why?" she asked.

Again his temper flared. "A captive does not ask why she is instructed to do something, but obeys her captor without question."

She lifted a brow, staring down at him with Amoke balanced on her hip. He was beginning to wonder if the two were joined together. He did not approve of the bond that had developed between his captive and his daughter.

"It is my nature to ask questions," she said, tilting her chin in a manner that made her look superior to him. "Now that I can, anyway," she added. "And I refuse to cower to your will as if—"

"As if you had a wise thought in your head," he interrupted. He'd had enough of her sharp tongue this day. Swift Buck rose and marched toward her. She had the good sense to take a step back, but then she planted her feet firmly and waited.

He took Amoke from her arms and set the child upon the ground. "If you wish for me to hunt, then I will hunt," he said to Silent Wind. "But in order to fill your belly with meat, I must first make certain that you will not escape while I am hunting."

Her eyes widened a fraction. "What do you intend to do? Tie me up?"

"That is a good idea," he agreed, and turned toward the horses to retrieve the rope he used to tie her ankle to his each night. She followed him, her hands on her hips.

"What about Amoke? Do you intend to tie her up too? What if she gets into something she shouldn't, or hurts herself? How will I help her if I'm tied up?"

Frowning, he turned to her. "Once, words were dead to you, now you talk too much. Maybe I should put a gag in your mouth to keep you quiet."

Her sky-colored eyes widened again. "You didn't used to be this mean," she said. "We have nothing you could stuff into my mouth that isn't filthy. I ask you to please reconsider."

He almost laughed. His tiredness, he assumed, had made her words humorous to him. Swift Buck realized that she had changed from the quiet girl he knew. This woman was harder to control.

"You will not call out or scream in hopes that the soldiers will hear you?"

As if she were considering, her brow furrowed. "No," she decided. "I would not wish for Amoke to see her father slaughtered before her very eyes. For her sake and not yours, I will be quiet."

"I will not go far," he warned her. "If I hear you call out, I will be back quickly. You will not get to eat fresh meat this night, and I will stuff something

142

foul into your mouth and keep it there until I find the others. Do you understand me?"

She nodded.

He snatched the rope from the packs and motioned her toward a shaded stand of trees. "You have my permission to call out to me if Amoke is in danger," he decided.

Her lips thinned, but she wisely said nothing. Nor did she protest when he made her sit on the ground and tied her hands behind the trunk of the tree. Amoke happily crawled into her lap and seemed content.

Without explaining his actions, he then tore off a piece of dirty material from the hem of the ragged skirt Silent Wind wore. She gasped.

"What are you doing?"

He rose and moved away from her. "Watch and see."

The lace on her ragged petticoat was expensive, she wanted to call to his back, but Rachel knew she'd only anger him further by complaining. She was in a foul mood. Hot, tired, hungry, and homesick . . . although she couldn't say exactly whom or what she felt homesick for. Her gaze strayed to the base of the mountains. Yes, this was what she felt homesick for, she realized. The People's mountain camps. The past.

Rachel watched Swift Buck walk away. Although she had grown up among the Mescaleros, she had seen very few hunts. The women and maidens usually stayed behind unless it was a buffalo hunt; then the most seasoned women skinners would follow the men to take the hides and the meat.

She found herself whispering to Amoke. "Watch your father. He is a great hunter."

Or he had once been. His father, Crooked Nose, was old when Swift Buck was born. From an early age, the duty of providing meat for the family had fallen to Swift Buck. Rachel didn't recall ever being hungry while living with his family.

He walked a short distance from them and did something odd. He tied the strip of lace from her petticoat to a low-hanging branch, then moved a short distance away and hid himself beneath a covering of brush and pine needles. Rachel yawned, wishing she could steal a nap.

She hadn't slept much since Swift Buck had taken to tying her ankle to his at night. She kept remembering what happened the last time she'd cuddled up to him. Afraid she would unconsciously make the same mistake, she'd lain awake for most of the short nights they'd camped. The strain wore upon her nerves, and made her words to him braver than she supposed was wise.

Because he was not the same man she had known five years ago, she knew she should be frightened of him; but she wasn't the same woman, either. She'd been frightened all her life. She had always run away from confrontations—with danger or with her own feelings. She had run away from the Apaches and hidden like a coward five years ago when Tall Blade had tried to kill her.

If she'd have stayed and stood her ground, told The People that he had tried to kill her, and in fact had killed two other women that were a witness to his attack, her brother's life wouldn't have been placed in danger.

Her cowardice had almost cost Clay his life. Rachel was ashamed of that; ashamed of the years she'd hidden from her father and her brother, too afraid to confront either of them about abandoning her. Then she had run away from her feelings for Swift Buck. In truth, she had wanted to find her place in life, to belong somewhere . . . but she really didn't feel as if she'd accomplished that end.

The sight of a deer wandering into her line of vision scattered her thoughts. She whispered to Amoke to remain silent. The deer seemed interested in the strip of lace that hung from the branch. It moved closer, trying to reach up and grasp the strip with its mouth. Swift Buck struck in a heartbeat. He was up and on the deer before it knew what had happened. His knife sliced across the animal's throat, ending the short struggle.

Rachel shuddered in the afternoon heat. She watched Swift Buck quickly gut and skin the deer. The white world had softened her, she realized. Once, such a sight wouldn't have bothered her; now her stomach recoiled at the sight of blood. She glanced down at Amoke. The child seemed unaffected by the display of violence.

"*Dahidaa,*" the girl said, then smiled up at her.

Drawing a shaky breath, Rachel smiled back at her. "Yes, we will eat."

The fire warmed her, and her belly felt pleasantly full. Amoke had already fallen asleep upon the blankets. Rachel's eyes felt heavy, but the grease from the meat still coated her hands and, she suspected, her face as well.

"Could I wash before we sleep?" she asked.

Swift Buck had been staring at the crackling fire. He glanced up at her. "I still wear the stench of blood from the kill," he grumbled. "We will both wash."

That wasn't what she'd had in mind. "I thought we would each take a turn," she said, then glanced down at Amoke. "One of us should stay here and watch over your daughter."

A slow smile crossed his lips. "And you thought I would allow you to wander off without me?" He shook his head. "Amoke will be fine. You know the water is only a short distance away."

She did know that, having filled the canteens earlier. The fire would keep predators away from the sleeping child, and if by chance the soldiers had doubled back, she and Swift Buck could easily hear them. There was no reason to refuse, except of course the obvious one: She didn't want to be alone with Swift Buck. Amoke now served as the buffer between them in Laughing Stream's place.

"Maybe I will wait until morning," she said.

Swift Buck's smile stretched, giving him a devilish appearance in the firelight. "You are afraid. But do you fear me, or do you fear the way your body betrays you? Do you fear you will give in to your woman's desires?"

"Neither," she lied, not sure which she feared more. "I'm tired, is all, and I have decided I'd rather go to sleep now."

He rose and held out his hand to her. "Come. I cannot leave you here alone."

She sighed. "I'm too tired to try to escape. What if I promise to sit here until you return?"

A frown twisted his mouth. Knowing it was useless to argue, she reached for his hand and allowed him to pull her up. A current ran from his fingers to hers and all the way up her arm. She quickly ended the contact. Again a slight smile turned up the corners of his mouth. He walked toward the water. She followed.

While she bent by the water's edge and washed her face and hands, she heard him shuffling beside her. A moment later, he stepped into the water. She glanced up and felt her mouth drop open. He had removed all his clothing. She supposed she made some sound—a gasp, or, more embarrassing, some type of strangled croak. He turned his head, glancing over his shoulder at her.

147

"I am covered in dirt and blood," he explained. "Stay where I can see you until I have finished."

He walked into the water, and her gaze roamed across his broad back, his muscled buttocks and his long legs. Night had fallen, but the moon was full and bright overhead, allowing her to drink her fill of the sight of him. Embarrassed that she had stared rather than quickly glance away, she lowered her gaze. Yet not before his male perfection had been etched in her mind.

She watched the water ripple in the moonlight, saw her own blurry image staring back at her. The darkness distorted her features. The woman who stared back looked half wild. Rachel quickly glanced away from the disturbing reflection. She resembled the girl of her past—wild, silent, and pathetic. She no longer was that girl, the one who had been cowed by an abusive father, her heart broken by her family's abandonment of her!

Sounds of Swift Buck bathing reached her ears. Curious, Rachel glanced up and watched him. The water on his skin caught the moonlight and silhouetted his body against a dark night. He was magnificent—all male, and perfectly at home in his rugged surroundings. Something deep within her stirred as she watched him: a hunger long suppressed; a desire to belong to him, to belong to someone; an endless, aching need to find her place.

But then she remembered that she was here with him not because of her own desires, but because he had taken her as his hostage. She remembered that he no longer thought of her as he once had, and that now his heart was full of hate and a bitter hunger for revenge against her race. Her feelings for him were remnants of a past lost to both of them. The future looked bleak for the Apaches; the present was uncertain and dangerous. And in the midst of it all, she sat watching him in the moonlight, lost in so simple a pleasure.

He moved toward her, the water receding around him as he drew nearer. She understood that she should look away from him. White society would demand she be shocked, enraged really, that a man would bare himself to a young woman's eyes. But Rachel hadn't been raised in a white society. She'd been raised among people who wore as little clothing as weather permitted. The Apaches were comfortable in their skins.

Swift Buck had nothing to be ashamed of—his body was lean and muscled, smooth and strong. Her gaze swept over him, settled between his legs, and she felt her brow knit.

"The water is cold."

Her gaze shot up to his face, and her cheeks exploded with heat. "Yes," she agreed, fighting to keep her gaze riveted upon his face.

"Something confuses you?"

The light of mischief danced in his eyes. Something did for a fact confuse her, but it wasn't something she could comment about. The night Rachel had cuddled up to him and he had pressed against her, what he hid beneath his breechclout had felt much larger than what her eyes had just seen.

"No," she answered. "I thought we should hurry back to check on Amoke."

He nodded, turned, and bent to retrieve his breechclout and moccasins. Rachel's gaze immediately dropped to the muscled contours of his backside. The night chill had started to set in, but she felt as if her face were on fire. Swift Buck apparently did not possess a modest bone in his body.

"It is not big all the time."

Her gaze snapped up to his face again. He had turned and stood adjusting his breechclout.

"What are you talking about?"

"The thing that confuses you."

The heat flushing her face intensified. "I told you, I am not confused."

"I will explain."

"Explain what?" she demanded.

Suddenly he reached out and took her shoulders in his hands, raising her to her feet. He stared down at her; his eyes still alight with mischief.

"You are still a maiden," he said softly.

Of course she was still a maiden. Both white society and the Apache culture frowned upon intimacy between men and women who were not joined to one another. And Rachel had never felt either desire or curiosity concerning the matter.

Well . . . she hadn't felt either for the past five years.

"I don't see where that is any of your business," she snapped. "Or why we are speaking of it," she added, trying to move from his hold. Swift Buck's hands tightened upon her shoulders.

"That is why you do not know that a man is not the same at all times."

She sighed. "I am aware that no one is the same at all times. At some times you are worse than others. Like right now, when you know I wish to go back to the camp and you will not allow me to do so."

He threw back his head and laughed. The sight might have intrigued her had she not strongly suspected that he was, for some reason, laughing at her.

"What do you find so humorous?" she asked.

"Your innocence," he explained. "I am speaking of the part of me that makes me a man. The part between my legs that you were staring at when I left the water."

The night chill had started to seep into her bones, but his words immediately brought another rush of heat to her cheeks. "I-I was not," she lied.

His hand moved up from her shoulder, his finger brushing her bottom lip. "When a man desires a woman, he grows hard and long with his need for her. He changes so that his body can join with hers. But for a man, this is torture if he cannot complete the act of giving a woman pleasure, of finding his own pleasure with her."

She feared that her eyes were like twin full moons in the sky. Rachel didn't know a lot about intimacy. Since Laughing Stream was younger than her husband had been, not much had taken place beneath their blankets. Because it was her duty, Laughing Stream had tried to explain such matters to Rachel, but she had never paid a great deal of attention. She had never pictured herself as a wife, a mother—maybe because the only man she could envision herself joining with had been forbidden to her.

"I change for you now," Swift Buck pointed out, his dark gaze still staring down at her. "I change because you stand close to me. I change because the feel of your skin beneath my hands excites me. I change because you smell like the flowers that bloom in the meadows of the Sacred Mountains. I change because your eyes tell me that when I touch you, you feel the same desire flowing through you as I feel."

She did feel something. Something that made her hot and cold at the same time. Something that made her ache inside and lower, where her legs joined together. Even the sound of his voice, deep and husky, added to the ache, made it spread up her body until her nipples hardened and her breasts swelled. Clay, her brother, had once warned her about seduction. About how a man could use words to bend a woman to his will. Words, he had told her, that were not always true.

"How you can you desire what you also despise?" she whispered. "When a heart is full of hate, how can there be room for anything else?"

His hand fell away from her face. "What happens between my legs has nothing to do with my heart."

She supposed she would have been appalled were she not tired and confused. Her weariness lowered her defenses. "It is not the same for me," she said. "I don't understand what it means 'to walk into the flame,' but your mother tried to explain. I think it means to walk into it with more than desire, with all your heart. That is one thing neither of us can give each other. I am going back to camp to check on Amoke."

He didn't try to stop her, which Rachel felt grateful for since her emotions were so confused. He was right—her lips said one thing and her body another, because she still burned for him. But there was one thing Rachel wanted more than pleasure, more than anything: love unconditional. She wanted to be loved by someone who didn't *have* to love her. She wanted to be loved by someone who knew everything about her and loved her anyway.

"The life we have been given is difficult," Swift Buck called to her back. "Sometimes it is better to take what you can get and forget about what you want."

CHAPTER THIRTEEN

Swift Buck closed his eyes and breathed deeply. The scent of pine was stronger now. Although his people did not stay long in one place, he liked their summer camps in the mountains the most. He felt a sense of coming home, his joy bittersweet because his mother was not with him to see this place she also loved.

He glanced at his daughter, riding before Silent Wind, her dark eyes so much like his own, wide with wonder. His heart swelled with pride. Amoke would walk in the ways of her people.

With a will of their own, his eyes strayed to Silent Wind. To his surprise, her eyes were closed and a smile curved her full lips. Was she remembering too? She had also once claimed these mountains as her home. There were bad memories, he knew—those of her white mother dying, and the animal, Hiram Brodie, giving her away like a possession he no longer wanted. But by her smile, he knew she carried good memories with her as well.

"We must take the back trails," he told her, watching her eyes quickly open. "The soldiers are soft and will follow those trails that are easiest."

"The soldiers may be soft, but their leader is not," she told him. "I don't think Franklin Peterson is a man easily discouraged."

Her words delivered a short stab of jealousy. To his ears, her words sounded like praise for the pale leader.

Silent Wind had cleverly taken to having Amoke sleep between them now. Her words from the night he had bathed in front of her still haunted him. She had said that to walk into the flame, one must walk into it with one's whole heart. He did not believe his heart was still whole, but in the moment she had whispered those words to him, he had admitted that he wanted that from her: her heart. But why?

For revenge because she had once hurt him? Because she was his enemy and only a total surrender would appease his thirst for revenge against her and her people? Or had she awakened the boy in him with her words?

"I wish Amoke could see the waterfall," she said suddenly. "I suppose the truth is, *I* would like to see it again."

The place she spoke of was one of great beauty, one that humbled a man and brought peace to the soul. It was not a place easily reached by either horse or foot, however, and Swift Buck was not certain that it would be wise to take the time. Still, the excitement dancing in Silent Wind's eyes made saying no difficult, when he should have no trouble refusing her.

Of course, it was possibly a place where his brothers would hide. Few outside of The People knew of its existence. Maybe there would be no harm in showing the waterfall to his daughter. Maybe he would find what few remained of his band there. He nodded consent, and Silent Wind cast him a rare smile—as if in her excitement she had not realized the gift that she had given to him. She turned the smile upon his daughter.

"We are going to a beautiful place," she told Amoke. "The water falls from the top of the mountain a long way to a clear pool of water below. When the sun in the sky hits the water at a certain time, a rainbow of many colors shines through the water."

Swift Buck allowed the sound of her voice to wash over him. Her tone was soft and as beautiful as a wooden flute. Silent Wind, the child who did not speak, was silent no more. Nor was she truly Silent Wind any longer. The white world had changed her. He was surprised to admit that the changes in her were not all bad ones. Her inner strength was greater. She fought her childhood instincts to withdraw inside herself and avoid conflict. She stood up to him now, when once he did not believe she would have had the courage.

She was still his enemy, he told himself. He must not soften his heart toward her. Once, his feelings for her had made him weak, and he could not be weak now—not when he had won his freedom and his daughter's. Not when the lives of others depended upon him.

Silent Wind must mean nothing to him. His body could desire hers, but he could not walk into the flame with her. Not with his whole heart. Not even with a piece of it, that small corner from the past.

"Look!" Silent Wind pointed to the sky.

Swift Buck glanced up, and he knew he still had a heart because he felt it breaking. A pair of eagles circled high above their heads. He remembered what his mother had said to him before she left for the spirit world. She had said that soon she would be free forever. She would fly high in the sky like the eagle and look down upon him.

He watched the birds circle together, swooping low, then soaring higher. His spirits lifted. He imagined the eagles as his father, Crooked Nose, whom he had lost the year that Silent Wind had left them, and his mother. He wanted to believe that his parents were free at last—that they were now free *forever*.

"Aren't they beautiful?" Silent Wind whispered

beside him. Her face was flushed, her eyes bright.

"Yes. Very beautiful," he agreed.

"You are thinking of them, aren't you?"

Such insight into his thoughts disturbed him. He knew of whom she spoke. "You know our ways. We do not speak of those who are gone."

A frown settled across her mouth. "It is different in the white world. The whites believe that speaking of those who are gone keeps their memories alive. They speak often of those departed. And . . . I think to do so brings them comfort."

"The pain is still raw," he said, because he felt that she wanted to speak of his parents and he did not. Amoke, he noticed, did not seem interested in their talk. His daughter had still said nothing about the missing one among them.

"Why does Amoke not ask about the one we cannot speak of?" he wondered, and realized that he had spoken the thought aloud.

Silent Wind shrugged. "I don't know. I wonder the same thing. They were very close—I could tell that even in the short time that I saw them together. Why don't you ask her?"

Because of his people's customs, asking his daughter would not be easy for him. Curiosity would not leave him alone, however, and he glanced at his daughter and asked softly, "Amoke, where is your *shiwoye*?"

The child looked around as if she were searching.

Then she looked up at the sky and pointed at the eagles that circled overhead.

A lump formed in Rachel's throat. Did Amoke mean she thought her grandmother was in heaven, or her grandmother was now a bird? Either way, Amoke's answer clearly affected Swift Buck. His dark eyes misted for a moment, and then he quickly glanced away. Maybe he was right, and the pain was still too raw to speak of those lost.

They rode on in silence, but as always, Swift Buck glanced around, looking for possible trouble. In the mountains, danger took many forms. As serene as the landscape appeared, and as much as it soothed her, the mountains were filled with wild animals and possible enemy tribes, and of course somewhere, Franklin and his men still hunted them.

She wanted to be rescued by Franklin, she supposed. The life Swift Buck had stolen her from was the one she had chosen five years ago. Because of Swift Buck's hatred of the whites—herself among them—there seemed to be no place for her in the Apache world. And Rachel wasn't certain that she would want one . . . not the way things were now.

She knew she couldn't deal with the hardships, the danger, and the warring. If her life with her brother and his wife had not been all that fulfilling, at least it had been safe.

At the same time, Rachel didn't want to see Swift

Buck or Amoke hurt in order for her to be rescued, which was why she still needed to escape from him. She wasn't sure what to do about Amoke. She wanted the child to be safe and well taken care of, yet Swift Buck so obviously doted upon his daughter, and Amoke was so clearly taken with him, that Rachel felt confused about the issue. Was emotional happiness more important than safety and security?

The questions continued to plague her as they rode. Her train of thought weakened as the mountains drew them deeper into their welcoming embrace. She had once taken the beauty surrounding her for granted, but now the sights and scents took her breath away.

Swift Buck reached over and plucked Amoke from Rachel's saddle, pointing out different landmarks to his daughter. Rachel couldn't deny that watching them together, seeing Swift Buck's love for his only child, made her feel soft and warm inside. She had never envisioned him in the role of father, but it clearly suited him.

As the sun bore down on her, she thought of the cool, clear water that pooled beneath the waterfall. She saw herself bathing in the pool, washing the dust and sweat from her body. Then a vision of Swift Buck, tall, naked, and proud, flashed through her mind. Maybe it hadn't been such a good idea to suggest showing Amoke the waterfall. She hadn't been able to get the enticing picture of him in the moonlight out of her thoughts. Nor could she banish the sound of his deep, husky voice, or the feel of his hands burning into her skin.

The afternoon heat suddenly felt stifling. A trail of sweat trickled into the valley between her breasts. She knew that the higher they moved up into the mountains, the cooler the air would become. Trying to bear that thought in mind, and dismiss the other disturbing memories, she urged her horse onward up the rocky trails.

A day and a half later, they had to leave the horses behind. Rachel hadn't taken that necessity into consideration when she'd made her request to see the falls; the lack of a horse would greatly deter any chances of escape for her. Once, she had run wild in these mountains, but now she was older, wiser, and she knew that Swift Buck held an advantage were she to try to escape on foot.

He built a makeshift corral using fallen timber. A small stream ran through the area, so the horses would not be without water during their absence. He stripped the animals of bridles and saddles, carefully concealing the tack beneath brush he had gathered. Rachel watched him intently, making note of where the tack was hidden in case an opportunity arose for escape, admitting that she felt pride over his adeptness. Apaches were wonderful with horses, whether it was caring for them, training them, or stealing them from their enemies.

He carried a small pack of supplies with him and a couple of blankets. Rachel wasn't surprised when he threw the items upon the ground before her and told her to carry them. It wasn't only the duty of a slave to carry her master's belongings, but Apache women often carried the family's household belongings when moving from one camp to another.

She had often helped Laughing Stream do so, and never questioned why the women often walked and carried heavy items while the men rode. The men were the protectors. They needed to have their hands free and the height of a horse beneath them to help them spot danger.

"Come," he said. "We will go."

Rachel tied the supply pack around her waist, stuffed the blankets beneath one arm, and reached for Amoke's hand.

"No, Amoke will ride on my back," Swift Buck said. "She cannot keep up with our strides."

He motioned his daughter to him, bent, and allowed her to crawl up on his back and place her arms around his neck. Amoke giggled, and Rachel couldn't help smiling, regardless of the burdens she carried. They were a lot lighter than carrying a child on her back, even if Amoke was small.

The trio set off up a rocky incline that would have proven impossible for the horses to maneuver. Only halfway up, Rachel caught herself huffing for breath, her underclothes clinging to her with sweat. She had grown soft during the past five years.

Once, she could have scrambled along the trail as easily as Swift Buck. He paused, waiting for her to catch up, and she thought he would berate her for slowing him down, but he said nothing when she reached him, just set off again.

Once they reached the top of the incline, the view below made the journey worthwhile. A valley of tall grass spread out like a blanket beneath them and she heard the soft roaring of the falls, could in fact see it spilling from the next peak, falling gracefully down the mountainside into the clear blue pool below. She sucked in her breath. Swift Buck allowed Amoke to slide down his back. The child hurried to stand beside him, her eyes round. Rachel felt Amoke clasp her hand, and she smiled.

Only after they had stood staring for a short time did Rachel notice that Amoke held on to her with one hand and held her father's hand with the other. The three were joined, like a family. She quickly shied away from the thought. They were *not* a family. They would *never be* a family. Rachel was not about to spend her life with a man who couldn't love her. She knew the sting of rejection in that area all too well.

No; Swift Buck's heart belonged only to his daughter now, and what part Amoke did not own was filled with hate. It was said that time healed all wounds, but Rachel didn't believe that was true. Some wounds lasted a lifetime.

The journey down the other side of the hill was

faster than the journey up. At times, the path became so steep that Rachel slid rather than walked. More dust coated her filthy undergarments, and the prospect of a bath became even more appealing.

Their walk across the meadow was easy in comparison, but they hadn't traveled high enough into the mountains to escape the heat. The waterfall created a gentle roaring noise. Rachel ran to the pool beneath and bent, scooping the clear, cool water into her palms to drink. The refreshing liquid moved down her throat, quenching her thirst and cleansing the dust from her mouth.

"Not too much water," Swift Buck warned. "Too much will make you sick."

Rachel knew that, but she'd forgotten how wonderful the mountain streams tasted. She sat back on her haunches and wiped a hand across her mouth. Amoke ventured near the water's edge and peered down into the shallow, clear pool.

"Would you like to go in the water?" Rachel asked the child.

Amoke nodded her head enthusiastically.

"I must scout the area," Swift Buck announced. "If you wish to bathe yourself, do so now, and hurry, so that you are finished when I return." His dark gaze had been roaming the area; now it lowered to her. "Unless you wish for me to find you naked."

If this was an attempt at teasing her, Rachel was not amused. "I will hurry," she assured him. "And my clothes are so filthy I don't intend to take them off."

He shrugged, a smile tugging at his mouth. "When you get them wet, you might as well be naked."

Her bulky gown was stuffed in the supply pack. Rachel thought it might be a good time to don it again. She suspected Swift Buck wouldn't like the idea, so she kept her intentions to herself.

Deciding that Amoke's clothes needed to be washed as well, she didn't bother to undress the child as they walked into the cool water. She waded to a spot deep enough for her to sit, but not over Amoke's head. She wished she had a bar of soap, but the sandy bottom of the pool would have to do for scrubbing. Swift Buck watched them for a moment, then moved away. Tall pines surrounded the pool, and soon she lost sight of him.

Amoke splashed and played in the water while Rachel saw to the more serious subject of washing the child and herself. The sand left a gritty feel on her skin. She glanced at the waterfall and remembered a time in her past when she'd stood beneath the outer edges where the water only trickled. It would be a wonderful way to wash the sand from her skin and clothes.

She rose and took Amoke's hand, leading her around the shallow rim of the pool to where the water cascaded down the mountain. Amoke blinked in surprise when Rachel led her beneath the spray. Rachel smiled to assure Amoke that the water trickling down upon them wouldn't cause her any harm. She still saw no sign of Swift Buck when she glanced around the area.

Once she felt that she and Amoke were thoroughly rinsed, they returned to where they had left their belongings. Rachel took a blanket and dried Amoke the best she could. When she suddenly felt the prickly sensation of eyes on her back, she stiffened and slowly turned her head, hoping to find Swift Buck standing there.

It was not Swift Buck she saw, but Franklin Peterson.

CHAPTER FOURTEEN

The captain quickly brought a finger to his lips, his eyes darting around the area. He waved a hand, and several soldiers crept from the trees. Rachel's heart did not lurch with sudden joy, but instead with sudden worry over Swift Buck. If he returned, he would walk into a trap. Amoke looked past her, saw Franklin, and let out a loud wail.

"For heaven's sake, shut her up!" Franklin hissed. He stormed forward and snatched the child, covering her mouth with his hand.

Rachel rose, and instincts she didn't know she possessed took over. "Give her to me this instant," she snapped at the officer. "You're frightening her!"

A moment later he yelped in surprise. "Damn

child bit me," he swore. "Here," he shoved her at Rachel. "If you don't keep her quiet, she will alert the Apache that we are in the area. Where is he?"

"I-I don't know," she stammered. "He went off somewhere." Her hand slipped off Amoke's mouth, and the child let out another wail, louder this time.

Franklin's face turned dark red. "Please," he insisted. "Keep her quiet."

Rachel hugged Amoke to her, praying that her cries wouldn't bring Swift Buck running blindly back to her rescue . . . but no, she knew him better than that. He wouldn't rush in but would find a vantage point from where he could see what was happening without being seen himself.

"Men," Franklin called. "A few of you stay and give me and the lady protection, the rest of you spread out and search. If you see the savage, shoot to kill." He holstered his weapon as five soldiers surrounded them, all with weapons drawn, their gazes scanning the area.

"Thank God you are alive," Franklin said, his eyes roaming her body.

Rachel realized that she still wore her undergarments, knew they were wet and clinging to her. "My gown," she said softly. "Please allow me to dress."

"Do so quickly," he agreed. "I want to get you out of here and to safety."

He joined the circle of men surrounding her, all with their backs turned. Rachel grabbed the packs and dug out her drab gown. She quickly shuffled into the dress, thinking how heavy it felt, and how restrictive. She wrapped a blanket around Amoke and picked her up.

"All right, I am decent now," she said.

Franklin turned and frowned at the sight of her holding Amoke. "We could move faster without the girl," he said.

Rachel bristled and held Amoke tighter. "We're not leaving her here to fend for herself," she assured him.

He waved a hand through the air. "No, of course not. Besides, if my men don't find the savage, he might come after her and give us another chance to capture or kill him."

Would Swift Buck come after Amoke? She felt certain that he would, if there was an opportunity to do so without it being suicidal. But Rachel didn't see how the circumstances could be anything but dire for him. Franklin had brought along a good number of men. Of course, Swift Buck had always told her that one Apache warrior defending his home or family was more dangerous than twenty armed white soldiers.

"Can you ride?"

The captain's question seemed rather silly to Rachel. She wasn't injured in any way. "Of course I can ride," she told him. "How do you think I've managed to get this far?"

He flinched slightly over her sharp words. Rachel's worry about Swift Buck made her temper short. She regretted snapping at Peterson and realized that she wasn't acting like a rescued hostage. She supposed a true hostage would have thrown herself at his feet and wept with relief.

Franklin pressed his lips together. "Forgive me for showing concern," he said. "I've been worried sick about you, you know."

Further shame rose to the surface. "No, forgive me," she whispered. "I-I'm not myself. I am grateful to you."

His eyes suddenly had trouble meeting hers. "I know you have been through a horrible ordeal, but you are safe now. Come—we'll have to walk a short distance to the horses."

The soldiers fell into step around them, their weapons raised in readiness for any danger that might arise. Rachel followed the captain, her heart breaking as she watched little Amoke's head swivel around, obviously in search of her father. Amoke was only a baby, but she obviously understood what the soldiers' uniforms meant, and Rachel felt the girl's small body trembling. A child her age shouldn't have to be afraid, and Rachel wondered again if a safe life in her world wouldn't be better for the girl.

Their horses were not very far away, and Rachel soon found herself mounted with Amoke settled before her in the saddle. Two men rode double in order for her to ride with Amoke. Rachel felt warring emotions. Franklin's rescue had saved her the trouble of escaping from Swift Buck, but this wasn't what she had planned.

She had wanted more time to decide what to do about Amoke, and admitted that if she had escaped on her own, she would probably have left the child with her father. Now the choice had been taken from her. If Franklin had captured only her—what was she thinking? Captured? No, rescued. If Franklin had *rescued* only her and not Amoke too, Swift Buck would have no reason to risk his life to get her back. He would have taken Amoke and moved on to find the Mescaleros who had not been captured or killed, if any in fact remained.

Her stomach knotted, mostly due to her worry over Swift Buck being captured or killed, and partly due to the way the soldiers would glance at her, then quickly glance away. Even Franklin seemed to have difficulty looking steadily at her.

Thankfully, the camp the soldiers had set up wasn't far. Rachel wasn't surprised to see that Franklin had erected a tent. The man did like his comforts. A few soldiers milling around the camp stopped to gawk at her as she rode past. Amoke issued a small whimper of alarm, and Rachel hugged her tighter.

"When we dismount, hurry into my tent," Franklin said beside her. "Away from curious eyes."

She had to wonder what was so interesting about her. The men surely knew their mission was to rescue her, along with, she felt certain, killing the

Apache who had dared to escape the reservation. She supposed they had assumed she'd be dead by now. Maybe they had been searching for a body and not a living, breathing woman.

They stopped before Franklin's tent, and he quickly dismounted, coming around to help her down. Amoke threw her arms around Rachel's neck, obviously afraid of the white man holding up his arms to receive her. Rachel was forced to awkwardly dismount with the child clinging to her.

"Go inside," the captain said. "I must give my men orders. I will join you shortly."

With Amoke still holding tightly on to her, Rachel hurried inside the tent. It was cooler, and curiosity about the tent immediately overwhelmed the child. Amoke ceased her whimpering to look around.

"You will be all right," Rachel whispered in Apache to the girl. "I will not let anyone hurt you."

"Father," Amoke said, her lip trembling.

"He is hunting," Rachel assured her. "You must be brave for him while he is gone."

Rachel sat Amoke upon the dirt floor and swiped a hand through her own hair. Her fingers couldn't pull through the curling, tangled mass. She straightened her dress, only then realizing she wore no shoes. Her underclothes were still damp beneath the heavy dress. Amoke's clothes were damp as well. Rachel made sure the child had a blanket wrapped around her. Amoke cuddled the blanket to her and lay down. She shoved a thumb into her mouth and closed her eyes.

Rachel envied Amoke the ability to act upon her body's demands. If Amoke was tired, she simply went to sleep. Rachel started to pace, keeping one ear trained for the possible sound of gunshots. *Please,* she prayed silently, *protect Swift Buck from the soldiers.*

Franklin entered a moment later. He frowned at the sleeping Amoke, then moved to pick up a couple of packs stored in one corner. "Mrs. Stark was kind enough to gather a few of your things in case we found you alive."

Bless Nelda Stark, Rachel thought as she accepted the small packs from Franklin. Inside were her riding clothes, an extra pair of boots, and, thank heavens, a brush.

"Are you hungry? Thirsty?"

"No," Rachel answered. "But thank you for asking," she added, remembering her manners. A tense silence fell between them. Franklin took up the pacing that Rachel had abandoned.

"Miss Morgan . . . Rachel, first, I want to assure you that this savage will pay for what he's done. I want nothing more than to kill him myself, and envy my men who are hunting him. But first, I must assure myself that you are coping with what has happened to you. You might feel certain understandable inclinations. But although taking your life might seem the only honorable—"

"Taking my life?" Rachel interrupted. Franklin wasn't making a bit of sense. "Why on earth would I do that?"

He glanced at her, then quickly glanced away. "I'm assuming that the savage . . . well, I know what these savages do to white women given the chance. You have been his captive now for several days and nights. I can only assume . . ."

Rachel knew exactly what he assumed. It was the same thing her brother had warned her about. "You would assume incorrectly," she bit out. "He did *not* force himself upon me."

Franklin's head snapped toward her. "Do you really expect me, or anyone, to believe that?"

She was tired, scared, and simply didn't give a damn what Franklin wanted to believe. Rachel shrugged. "You may believe whatever you wish, but I'm telling the truth."

He resumed his pacing as if he hadn't heard her. "I suppose once you return to Washington, there will be no need to tell anyone about your unfortunate encounter with an Apache in New Mexico. When a woman has wealth, which you have indicated to me is your situation, a man has a tendency to overlook anything undesirable he might later discover about her."

Suddenly suspicious, she asked, "Are you that type of man?"

He misunderstood her question. "Would you like for me to be?"

She was so naïve at times. Rachel realized that it had never been her that Franklin Peterson was interested in, but the wealth she had claimed when she first met him.

"You hate this life," she suddenly saw. "You believe that having a commission as an officer in the Army is beneath you and an embarrassment to the person you once were before the war took everything from your family."

Franklin brushed a speck of dirt from his uniform. "War is a dirty business. I would be lying if I said I didn't hate this stinking country, or that stinking fort I'm in charge of, or these stinking Indians I am forced to deal with on a daily basis. I was meant to have the finer things in life, and I resent that, instead, I am forced to labor like a common man. But have no fear; the savage will pay for his arrogance—for what he has done to you, and for making me look like an incompetent fool in front of my men. That is one part of my position that I do enjoy. Punishment."

She shuddered at the thought of Franklin with a whip in his hands, punishing a former slave for some slight transgression. "He did nothing to me except use me to help him get his daughter and his mother away from the horrid conditions at the reservation," Rachel said. "There is certainly no need to kill him on my account."

As if suddenly recalling something that had slipped his mind, Franklin asked, "What happened to the old woman? I realize now that she wasn't with you."

An aching sense of loss squeezed Rachel's heart over the reminder. "She died," she said softly. And Rachel understood in that moment that Franklin was in part to blame for Laughing Stream's death. If conditions had been better at the reservation, if the Indians were given proper rations of food and medicines to treat their illnesses, her adoptive mother might still be alive.

"Well, she was of no importance anyway," Franklin said coldly. "I never considered her a threat."

No importance? Rachel suddenly felt the urge to fly at him with her nails and claw his eyes out. But of course she could not. Instead, she was forced to say nothing. It would do Swift Buck no good for her to lose what little standing she had with Franklin.

"You have rescued me. Why don't you just let him go? I'd like to return to the fort where I know I am safe. And of course, once I've finished my work at the reservation, I'll be anxious to return to my home."

"I cannot let him go," Franklin argued. "He must serve as an example to the Indians he's left behind. If I don't bring him back slung face-down over a saddle, he will become some kind of hero to them and inspire more rebellion."

Now was the time to appeal to Franklin's softer

side, if he did indeed have one. Rachel drew a deep breath. "If conditions at the reservation improved, they would have no reason to want to escape."

He ceased his pacing and glanced at her. "Rachel, you do not know these people. They will always have a reason to rebel against authority. If it isn't the lack of food, the foul-tasting water, or the cramped living conditions, it will be something else. They will not be satisfied until they have things the way they used to be."

Her courage mustered, she said, "Then perhaps you should consider that."

His mouth dropped open. He closed it with a snap. "Consider just setting them free? Then what? We're back to warring with them because they slaughter innocent settlers over land issues. When will you understand that it is either them or us?"

Never, she supposed, but she wouldn't say so. She knew that there was no middle ground left for her. She would have to choose, but how could she? Her skin was white—her past was Apache. The two halves of her tugged and she was pulled first one way and then another.

"I do not know the answer," she said softly, rubbing her forehead where a headache had begun to throb. "I am tired, and I ask you to leave me so that I can change and rest for a while."

Franklin sighed. "Of course. I should have been more thoughtful to your needs." His posture as straight as ever, he marched to the opening of the tent, then paused. "I do have one question. The day we almost caught up with you and the savage, why did you slide upon the back of his horse, forcing me to call a halt to the shooting lest you were hit by mistake?"

She could have lied and said the Apache ordered her to do so, but she was too tired to lie. "I was afraid the child would be hurt. She is innocent of any wrongdoing."

"She is an Indian, Rachel. We cannot see her as innocent. As I've told you before, little savages grow into big savages."

Her patience lost, she turned on him. "She is not a savage," she bit out. "She is a little girl, hardly more than a baby."

"She is a child with no future," he said flatly.

Rachel lifted her chin. "Not if I have my way in the matter. I intend to take her back to Washington with me and raise her in a place where she will be safe."

Franklin sighed again; then his eyes softened. "Rachel, there is nowhere on earth safe for that child. And all the money in the world will not change her skin from red to white. To believe so is to set yourself up for heartache and ridicule. I'm telling you this for your own good, and for hers. If you strap yourself with that child, no decent man will have you for a wife, I don't care how wealthy you are. The child will always be an outsider in the world you think to give her. She will be persecuted and spat upon. She will hate you for the life you've given her."

Rachel was struck dumb by his words. He didn't wait for a response but exited the tent. Was what he said true? Were there no compassionate people left in the world? If she took Amoke away and raised her as her own, would the child hate her for it one day? Would Amoke end up like Rachel—torn between two cultures, feeling as if she didn't belong to either?

Rachel went to the child and bent down beside her. She smoothed the dark hair from her sweet, round face. They were alike in many ways, she and Amoke. Both had lost their mothers at a young age. Both had been uprooted from one home and sent to another, but unlike Rachel, Amoke had a father who loved her. All Rachel had been thinking about were her own concerns. Swift Buck loved his child. He was right. Amoke's path was his decision to make, not Rachel's. She only hoped that Swift Buck lived to see the morning, much less to see his daughter grow to womanhood.

Swift Buck lay on his belly, watching the activity of the camp below. The soldiers hunted him, but they were no match for an Apache who knew the land. He could blend in with his surroundings, and, more than once, a soldier had passed right by and not noticed him among the brush and trees.

His first instinct when he had heard his daughter

cry out was to rush to her side, to make certain that Amoke and Silent Wind were not hurt, but he had forced himself to go slowly. Swift Buck was glad that he had, or he would have been dead or captured by the pale leader and his men by now. He had watched helplessly as the soldiers took Amoke and Silent Wind away.

The soldiers outnumbered him, and an Apache warrior knew when to fight and when to run, but he could not leave Amoke behind. He had lost his mother already. He would not lose his daughter as well. But how would he get to her? The camp was well guarded. He knew that Silent Wind and Amoke stayed inside the leader's white tent. The path to that tent was littered with soldiers.

Rage boiled inside him when he saw the leader come and go from the tent as he pleased. Was Silent Wind happy to be free? Was she happy to be with the leader now? And did she still think to take his daughter from him and raise her in the white world? She would do so only over his dead body. His daughter belonged with her people.

A bullet splintered the tree he stood behind. Shouts went up among the soldiers. They had spotted him spying on their camp. Swift Buck had no choice but to run, but he would be back.

CHAPTER FIFTEEN

Rachel's heart pounded in her chest. Not long ago, she had heard gunshots. She tried to concentrate on brushing Amoke's hair, but her gaze kept straying to the tent opening as she expected Franklin to enter at any moment and tell her they had killed Swift Buck. She didn't want the child to sense her distress, and Amoke had enjoyed watching Rachel tug the tangles from her own hair, so she had taken her brush to Amoke's hair in a ploy to distract the child.

It wasn't working. Rachel had not been surprised to hear Franklin report that sightings had been made of the Apache they hunted. Swift Buck would not run away and leave Amoke behind—even if it meant risking his life. Since Franklin was smart enough to realize Swift Buck would not leave without his daughter, he had doubled the guards inside the encampment. He'd told Rachel they would not leave without the body of the Apache to take back as an example to others.

Franklin coughed discreetly outside and asked permission to enter. Rachel could hardly get the words of permission past her paralyzed throat. He entered, his face red with anger.

"Gone," he bit out. "Like a wisp of smoke. There one minute and gone the next. This savage is sorely testing my patience."

A sigh of relief escaped Rachel's lips. She gave Amoke her brush to play with and rose, her knees none too steady.

Hoping to sway Franklin into leaving the camp, she said, "I would like to return to the fort. I'm certain that the Starks are worried about me, and I'd like to put them at ease that I am all right."

Franklin stared into her eyes. "Are you? I still find it difficult to believe that the savage didn't touch you. His kind has no honor, no conscience, no—"

"And what about your men?" Rachel interrupted. "What about their honor? I understand that they often force themselves upon the young Indian women you hold as prisoners at the reservation."

He straightened—if that were possible, since he always held himself perfectly erect. "Who told you this? One of the women? She's lying."

"The bruises on her face told me," she answered. "Bruises don't lie. How could you allow such things to go on?"

To his credit, a deep blush stained his cheeks. "Rachel, I do not condone such behavior, but you must understand, my men rarely have an opportunity to mix with women of their own race. They become unmanageable if I do not allow them an occasional outlet for their frustrations. I don't approve, but if it keeps them from deserting, I must at times turn a blind eye to their transgressions."

"And you call yourself a gentleman," she sneered. "You sicken me."

His gaze lowered, as if he couldn't meet her accusing stare. "I'm sorry to hear that. I've made no secret that I feel quite the opposite about you. You can't imagine how relieved I was to find you alive. I would have never stopped looking for you."

She hated the slight softening she felt toward him. He did appear genuine in his concern on her behalf. "And if I told you that the Apache did molest me, would you still feel the same way about me?"

His gaze shot up to her. "Of course I would. You can hardly be held accountable for something beyond your control. Even if others would judge you, I know how cruel this land can be. I hate it, and hate what it has made me become—but to survive, I suppose one must become as harsh as one's surroundings."

Although she could never condone Franklin's turning a blind eye while his men abused the Indians, men and women alike, she did realize that Franklin was a product of his past, just as she was. He'd been raised to believe his white skin made him superior to all other men. She supposed that if anyone was to blame for the kind of man he'd become, it was his parents, just as hers had affected the way she viewed others and life itself.

Still, just because her father was an abusive man did not mean that Rachel shared Hiram Brodie's cruel nature. He had broken her heart with his dismissal of her, but he had not made her behave in the same manner he did. Franklin should see the wrong in his own thinking, especially where men of a different color were concerned . . . yet he chose not to.

But was Swift Buck any different with his hatred of whites? Yes, she had to admit. Swift Buck had reason to hate them. He didn't judge solely by skin color, but by actions. The Apaches had been shown through the years time and time again that a white man's word could not be trusted.

Hoping Franklin would leave, Rachel turned her back on him. She saw Amoke trying to stick the brush she played with into her mouth.

"*Dah*," she scolded the child, then bent beside her, gently taking the brush from her small hand.

"You spoke to her in Apache," Franklin said at her back. "How do you know the language?"

Her heart gave a sudden lurch. "I think the word I said means 'no.' I heard her father say it on more than one occasion when she was doing something she shouldn't."

He said nothing for a moment, which made her even more uneasy.

"Maybe we should pretend we are torturing the child to force her father out of hiding."

His suggestion made Rachel's blood run cold. Swift Buck would never allow anyone to hurt Amoke. She scooped Amoke up protectively into her arms.

"I will not allow you to misuse the child. He is only one man, Franklin. I would think an army could capture or kill him without resorting to torturing small children."

She meant to goad his manly ego, and her tactic seemed to work. He gave her a curt nod, his eyes chilling when he smiled at her.

"You're right; he is only one man. I will give it another day, then I may have to revive my plan to use the child as bait."

Unconsciously Rachel hugged Amoke tighter to her. The captain left, and she realized that she had only one choice if he intended to use Amoke to lure Swift Buck out of hiding. She would simply have to escape Franklin and his men and return Amoke to her father. How she would slip past the soldiers, and how she would explain her actions once she returned, she didn't know. All she knew for certain was that she had to act quickly.

He could wait no longer. Swift Buck knew that each day that passed, his chances of being captured or killed increased. He needed to see that Amoke was safe and well. He needed to continue the search for his lost brothers. He did not trust the white leader to show honor where his daughter was concerned . . . and maybe the man would not show honor where Silent Wind was concerned, either.

Swift Buck had not seen much of Silent Wind outside the leader's tent. Was she all right? It should not matter to him, Swift Buck told himself. He should care nothing about what became of Silent Wind. She had chosen her path; let her walk it, even if the path was strewn with stickers. But he might have use of her, he reasoned. He still needed a hostage in case the soldiers caught up with him. He could use Silent Wind to trade for his freedom, and his daughter's. If the leader still considered her a worthy trade.

The man might believe she had been ruined. Swift Buck knew that white men often judged a woman over circumstances she could not control. The pale man might believe that Swift Buck had taken her to his bed. He smiled at the thought. It would make the leader crazy to think that a savage had touched her soft skin, had held her close, had buried himself inside her warm, tight . . . He shook his head.

His mind must remain focused upon what he must do. Tonight he would sneak into the camp and rescue his daughter. He had been watching, knew where the guards were stationed. And maybe he would steal Silent Wind back again, too.

Tonight was the night. Rachel tried to stop her shaking hands and present a poised picture for the guards who escorted her and Amoke to perform their private duties each evening. Franklin had wanted to see to the task himself, but he soon tired of the many trips a young child had to make out into the forest. He had assigned five men to the duty, and all were seasoned soldiers, armed to the teeth.

She had no idea how she would escape the men, or how she would find Swift Buck once she had, but Rachel knew she must act. She now realized that no matter how young Amoke was—how innocent and beautiful, Franklin and his men only saw her as a savage, an enemy. They would use her to draw Swift Buck out and kill him, without a care for the trauma they would cause the child, or concern that she might get hurt or killed in the process. Rachel wasn't about to let such a thing happen.

They were escorted into the woods not far from the camp. Night had almost fallen, and she was still unsure just how she intended to escape the guards and how far she could run before an alarm was shouted. She also wasn't sure what she would tell Franklin when she returned, if she did manage to find Swift Buck and give Amoke to him. The truth maybe. Not all of it, but the truth that she was worried about the child's safety and thought she was better off with her father.

He would be furious that he had lost what he considered his bait to trap Swift Buck, but what could he do to her? Rachel shivered in the night air, not wanting to contemplate the question further. Doing so wouldn't help steady her nerves. They had reached a secluded area and the guards stopped; then they began to spread out, surrounding her and Amoke.

"Please," she said, "could you move out farther to give me greater privacy?"

"The captain said we're to stay close," one man responded.

"Well, the captain is not a woman and sorely embarrassed to have an audience every time he must take care of personal matters," she snapped. "I find I cannot attend to my business with all of you breathing down my neck. If you'd rather stay out here half the night, it's fine with me."

"We can move out a bit farther," the guard agreed, then motioned the others to spread out. "But you'd best hurry. We'd all like to get back to our gambling."

Rachel didn't see that she'd really accomplished

much. The problem was, there were too many guards to elude. She could possibly handle one guard, but five? Amoke tugged on her skirt. She suspected the child did in fact need to relieve herself. Rachel tried to come up with some type of plan while she helped Amoke. She had nothing to bribe the men with. She had nothing to use as a weapon—not that she would shoot them, or knife them. She hated violence.

There must be some way, something she could use to sway at least one of them into looking the other way. But even if she did manage to soften one man's heart to the plight of the child, how would she deal with the others?

"Hurry it up," one of the guards called. "I'm getting tired of standing around out here."

The men were getting antsy. Rachel bent and whispered to Amoke to stay still. Silently she approached the man closest to her.

"Could I have a word with you?" she whispered.

He turned, his eyes widening for a moment as if her request surprised him. "A word about what?"

She moistened her suddenly dry lips. "It's about the child."

His nose wrinkled. "She sick or something?"

"No," she answered. "I was wondering . . . well, I was wondering if you have children of your own."

He frowned. "Not that I know of. 'Course, if you look real close, some of them squaws at the reservation have some real light-skinned papooses." He winked at her. "But since they'd spread their legs for any man, who's to know which of us fathered their stinkin' little savages?"

She'd obviously picked the wrong guard to appeal to. The man made her ill. "Never mind," she said, then turned to go back to Amoke.

The man grabbed her arm. "Now, hold up a minute. What did you want to talk about?"

"Nothing," she answered, trying to tug her arm free.

He held tight. "I was hoping maybe you'd come sneaking up on me because you are lonely and need some special attention."

"Lonely?" she repeated, confused.

His grin resembled a leer. "We all know that Apache gave it to you every night he had you, probably during the daytime too. The captain gave us orders to treat you with respect, but maybe respect ain't what you want. I figure the captain's too obsessed over killing that buck to give you what you got a hankering for now. Am I right?"

Her first instinct was to slap his ugly face. Bile rose in her throat over his indecent suggestion, but she fought down both the sickness and the urge to strike him. Her voice shook when she said, "I wouldn't do anything with the other men present."

His eyes narrowed, and he glanced around. "I could get rid of them, but we'd have to hurry or someone might come looking for us. The captain would have my hide if he caught me between your legs. He still likes to think of himself as a gentleman, and you a lady." He snorted his opposite opinion.

Stomach churning, heart pounding, she nodded. "Get rid of them, then." Rachel had no intention of letting the man touch her; she would look for a rock to knock him unconscious. She hadn't wanted to resort to violence, but in this case, it looked as if she had no choice.

"Hey, what the hell is taking so long?" one of the guards shouted.

"The little Injun has the runs!" he shouted back, then winked again at Rachel. "The rest of you boys go on back and finish our poker round. I'll wait for the brat to finish!"

She heard the crunch of boots against pine needles. All four of the other men approached.

"You sure about that, Truitt?" one of them asked. "The captain said—"

" 'The captain said,' " the man called Truitt mimicked. "Hell, ain't nothing going on out here. That Apache wouldn't have the guts to come this close to the camp. Go on back and watch my hand. You know them boys from Texas cheat given any opportunity."

A grumble of agreement followed. "All right," one said. "But hurry it up. If something happens to the woman and the brat, the captain will have us court-martialed and hanged."

Rachel's heart pounded louder as she watched

191

the other men move back toward camp. They'd barely gotten out of sight when the man called Truitt fumbled with his belt buckle.

"Let's get to it," he said. "Hike up them skirts."

CHAPTER SIXTEEN

Rachel took a step back. The man dropped his gun belt and started to unhitch his pants. While he was distracted, she bent and searched for a rock. Suddenly she found herself pushed down to the ground. The smell of sweat assaulted her. The man shoved his hands beneath her skirt and groped. Rachel tried to bring her knee up as she'd done with Swift Buck, but the guard had her legs pinned down.

His foul scent gagged her, and was made worse when he pressed his plump lips against hers. Rachel's first instinct was to scream. She opened her mouth, recalled that she must be silent, then felt the man's tongue snake into her mouth.

Her fingers tightened around the rock in her

hand. She bashed it against the man's skull. He grunted in surprise, then rolled off her. She was up in an instant and ran and grabbed Amoke. The man's groans and curses as he sat holding his head in his hands told her that she hadn't hit him hard enough. He wouldn't stay down for long. She took off through the forest, her progress slowed by having to carry Amoke.

She glanced over her shoulder, terrified that the guard would rouse himself and shout an alarm. She ran into a tree. No, not a tree, she realized a second later. Trees didn't have arms. Fear clawing at her belly, she glanced up, expecting to see one of the soldiers. Instead, she saw the handsome face of an Apache warrior.

"Thank heavens," she breathed, then shoved Amoke into Swift Buck's arms. "Take her and go quickly. I managed to escape the guard, but I think he's chasing us."

Amoke squealed in delight upon seeing her father and threw her little arms around his neck. He smiled softly at her before his expression hardened and he glanced back at Rachel.

"You give me my daughter?"

There wasn't time for lengthy explanations. Rachel glanced over her shoulder again. "She belongs with you in your world. Go. Hurry, before the guard—" But her fears materialized before she could finish the sentence. The guard came crashing through the brush, winded but also armed. He skidded to a halt at the sight of Swift Buck standing with her and Amoke. His gaze flew to Rachel.

"You Injun-lovin' bitch," he cursed. "You tricked me!"

He lifted his gun, aiming—at which of them, Rachel wasn't certain. A knife sailed past her, landing with a soft thud in the man's chest. Horrified, Rachel watched the guard stagger, then fall to the ground.

Her head slowly swung back toward Swift Buck. "You killed him," she whispered.

"I had no choice. He would have shot me, and even if he missed, his gun would have alerted the others."

She knew that he had only been defending them, but Rachel felt responsible for the man's death. The violence sickened her. At least she could make up a story to tell Franklin, and there was no one to dispute her.

"Go quickly," she said again to Swift Buck. "Other soldiers will come to check on the guard and me. Take Amoke and get as far as you can from the soldiers."

"You will stay?"

For a brief moment, as their eyes touched, she felt torn. She had to remind herself that she had chosen her path five years ago, and she must stick to her decision. "Yes, I will stay," she answered.

His jaw tightened, but he turned away from her without a word—not even a thank-you for aiding him in getting his daughter back. Amoke stared over his shoulder, then let out a loud wail, holding her arms out to Rachel. The child's voice carried in the still night.

"No, Amoke," she heard Swift Buck warn, but his daughter paid him no heed. She let out a sharper cry.

Rachel's heart broke as she watched the child struggle against her father's hold, stretching her small hands out to her in appeal. Amoke's dark eyes glittered with tears in the coming dark. Rachel had become very attached to the child in their short time together. Another loud cry sounded, and Rachel knew she had no choice. Amoke would alert the soldiers. She wasn't old enough to understand the danger she placed them in, or why people kept coming and going in her life.

"I'll go with you until you and Amoke are safely away," Rachel said to Swift Buck, then gathered up her skirts and ran past him. He caught up with her quickly and took the lead. Darkness fell, and Rachel stumbled many times over rocks or tree branches in their path. In the distance, she heard a shout. Swift Buck heard it also and he increased his speed. She didn't know how he could run so fast carrying Amoke, but she was thankful for his Apache upbringing.

And, she supposed, her own. Even though she had grown soft in the white world, the past few days spent with Swift Buck had toughened her up.

A few days ago, she'd be huffing and puffing from her efforts. Her eyes adjusted to the darkness, and she felt as if she and Swift Buck were two wolves racing through the night.

They ran over slopes, across moonlit valleys, their hearts pounding in tune with the sound of their footfalls. Animals scurried from hiding places, startled, as they passed. There was no time to think about what creatures roamed in the darkness; a greater danger followed fast upon their heels.

They reached the horses before Rachel could make out their dark shapes. To her surprise, the animals were saddled and ready to go, as if Swift Buck had known he would need to make a fast escape this night. Rachel stopped and placed a hand against the stitch in her side.

"Go," she panted. "I'll tell them I escaped from you."

"No," he said simply, throwing Amoke up onto his saddle, where the child knew to clutch the saddle horn. "You will go with us. I have decided it will be so."

She snorted at his arrogance. "*I've* decided otherwise," she informed him. "I helped you to get Amoke back; you owe me my freedom."

He reached out, grabbed the front of her blouse, and tugged her close to him. "I owe you nothing. Many years ago my parents took you into their lodge. They fed you, they clothed you, and they loved you when no shared blood said that they must. You repaid their gifts to you by running away—deserting them as if they were nothing to you. One brave act does not make up for all that you have done. I may need you to bargain with if the soldiers catch up with me. Now move."

Swift Buck shoved her toward her mounted horse. Rachel knew that to stand and argue with him would only allow the soldiers more time to catch up. She'd make him think she would go with him, then turn her horse and race toward the soldiers' camp. She mounted, waiting for him to throw her the reins, but he did not. Instead he took them and wrapped them around his saddle horn; then he quickly jumped up behind Amoke in the saddle. He smiled at her, his teeth flashing in the darkness.

"Hold on tight," he warned.

To race through the night with the wind blowing in his hair while his horse, surefooted beneath him, jumped over logs and slid along rocky paths his eyes could barely see, was a joy that Swift Buck had once feared would be lost to him forever. The only thing that dampened his excitement now was worry over Amoke and Silent Wind.

If he'd had only himself to worry about, he would say to himself *It is a good day to die* and rush headlong into whatever the night brought. But he did not have only himself to think of. He slowed his mount as they made their way up a steep slope, holding tight to Amoke and hoping Silent Wind would not fall off . . . or jump off in defiance of his decision to keep her as his captive.

She was angry with him. He felt her hostility even if he had no time to see it in her eyes. She had done a brave thing tonight. She had risked herself for his child. It was not a thing that she might have done five years ago. She would have been too frightened of being punished. Or maybe he had not known everything that went on in her mind as he had once believed. Maybe there had been more to her than he could see, because the outside of her was so pleasant to look upon that he had not looked deeper.

The old feelings stirred inside him, and he fought their return. One brave act did not erase years of hurt. She had chosen another life five years ago; she had made the same choice tonight. Nothing had changed between them. He must remember this when past desires rose up and tempted him to make a fool of himself over her again.

She did not wish to be at his side, but back with the soldiers. The pale leader. He could force her to accept him upon her mat, but he could not force her to give him her heart. She had no heart, he reminded himself. Maybe the other should be enough.

Lost in his thoughts, he was not prepared when a dark shape appeared from nowhere and knocked Silent Wind from her horse. A hatchet caught the moonlight's glow. Swift Buck grabbed his daughter, sprang from his horse, and pulled the gun he'd taken from the pale leader on the day he'd escaped the reservation.

He did not have time to raise the gun before a body slammed into him. He stumbled and fell, turning so he would land upon his back so that Amoke would not take the brunt of the fall. A dark face immediately loomed over him, a knife raised, but he recognized the man.

"Would you kill one of you own?" Swift Buck asked, his heart slamming against his chest.

The knife hesitated. "Swift Buck?"

"It is good to see that you still live, Gray Wolf."

The leader of the Mescalero band quickly called an order to his companion. A figure appeared above the crouching form of Gray Wolf.

"Is it you, Swift Buck, or your ghost come to haunt these familiar lands?"

"It is me, Blue Feather, and my daughter, Amoke."

His child was suddenly lifted from his arms and held up into the night. "She has grown," Gray Wolf commented, then handed her to Blue Feather and held out his hand to help Swift Buck to his feet.

"What about the woman?" Blue Feather asked. "Even in the dark, I can see that her skin is white. My hatchet wanted her silver hair for my scalp belt."

"She is my captive." Swift Buck allowed Gray Wolf to help him up.

"I am not his captive," Silent Wind said, and all turned to look at her. She now stood, brushing dirt from her white-woman's clothes. "I am Silent Wind," she continued, using Apache, even though Swift Buck knew she remembered that Gray Wolf also understood the white words her brother had taught them as boys.

"I took Silent—the white woman and used her to escape from the soldiers at the reservation." He glanced around. "They might be following."

Gray Wolf tensed. "You brought soldiers here?"

Swift Buck once again felt the weight of guilt. "I want my daughter to be free, to walk in the ways of her people. I did not know if there were any of you left, but I knew I must make certain before I gave up hope."

"Your wishes should not come before the safety of your people."

"He did not lead the soldiers here." Silent Wind came to stand nearby. She took Amoke from Blue Feather's arms. "The soldiers came here because they assumed this was where Swift Buck would hide from them."

"Does your woman speak for you?" Gray Wolf asked.

"I am not his woman," Silent Wind snapped.

"No," Swift Buck agreed. "She is my captive, and

though once she did not speak, now she is never quiet."

"We must go from this place," Gray Wolf said. "Our camp is two-days' ride. We must be careful to leave no tracks for the soldiers to follow."

Swift Buck understood the seriousness of the situation, but also, inside, his heart soared to see two men he never expected to see again. He had hoped Gray Wolf still lived. The man had been one of his best childhood friends. Cougar, Silent Wind's brother, had been another. The three of them had been always together during the summer months, when the Mescaleros camped in the great mountains. Swift Buck's memories were a mixture of joy and sorrow.

He retrieved Silent Wind's horse and took Amoke from her arms. "Climb onto your horse," he ordered, then once again wrapped her reins around his saddle horn. Gray Wolf and Blue Feather left, returning with branches they had cut from trees. They disappeared again, this time bringing back their horses, each with a deer tied across its back.

"We will ride behind and drag the branches to cover our tracks," the Mescalero leader told Swift Buck. "If Silent Wind is now a captive, we cannot trust her to do this. You have your hands full with the child. Follow the North Star and ride hard."

Swift Buck nodded and kicked his horse out, pulling Silent Wind's horse along behind him. To put distance between them and the soldiers, they would only stop for short rests and there would be little conversation. Once they reached the Mescalero camp, there would be time for words and reunions.

Excitement churned his blood at the thought of seeing some of his people again. How many were there? Would it be enough to attack the fort and rescue the others? And what was Silent Wind thinking now? Did her heart beat with joy to see people she had not seen in many years? Or did she dread facing those she had abandoned five years ago?

CHAPTER SEVENTEEN

Rachel was terrified of reaching the Mescalero camp, unsure of what to expect from people she hadn't seen in five long years. Would they feel about her the way Swift Buck felt? Would they see her now as only an enemy, and not as one who had been raised among them?

For the past two days, Swift Buck had set a grueling pace, and she hadn't had much time to worry over what type of reception she would receive at the Mescalero camp. Nor had there been much conversation between Swift Buck, Gray Wolf, and Blue Feather.

She had to admit that Apache resolve was a force to be reckoned with. Swift Buck must have been bursting with questions, as was she, but he kept his attention focused on putting distance between them and the soldier's camp. He had acted as if he hardly noticed her. It irritated her more than a little that he would force her to come with him, then ignore her as if she didn't exist.

Gray Wolf and Blue Feather followed his lead, ignoring her as well, but she had seen more than one curious glance pass between the two Apaches.

"How much longer?" she asked, her legs aching from many hours in the saddle.

"A captive does not ask questions but only follows orders," Swift Buck said. "My order for is you to be quiet."

She glanced behind her and again saw a look pass between Gray Wolf and Blue Feather. They shared a small smile on her account, she suspected.

"I am certain that Amoke is also tired," she persisted. "The journey has been difficult for her."

Swift Buck slowed his mount so her trailing horse could catch up. "Do you hear Amoke complaining?" he asked, a dark brow raised.

Amoke was nestled against her father, fast asleep. Rachel envied the child—because she could sleep, not because she was nestled against Swift Buck's warm, smooth chest. A woman who complained was considered a curse to an Apache man. Rachel didn't plan on making Swift Buck's life pleasant.

"We have had little to eat in two days," she went

on. "My legs ache, my back hurts, and the sun is blistering my face!"

He rolled his eyes heavenward as if appealing to a greater being, but slowed to a stop. Gray Wolf and Blue Feather stopped beside them.

"How much farther?" Swift Buck asked Gray Wolf.

"Not long," the leader answered.

"Will you take Amoke while I see to my captive?"

Gray Wolf glanced at Rachel, smiled again, and nodded. "Do you need my knife to cut off her tongue so that she does not speak again? Or maybe you will cut off her ears, since she does not listen with them anyway."

Swift Buck seemed to consider Gray Wolf's offer. Rachel wasn't frightened. She didn't believe Swift Buck would harm her. But then, men often behaved differently in the company of other men. Swift Buck had been lording her captivity over her even more than usual during the past two days.

Warily, she watched Swift Buck lift Amoke and hand her over to Gray Wolf. Swift Buck dismounted and took the canteen that hung from his saddle horn. Rachel thought he meant to bring her a drink, but instead he poured the water on the ground, making a small puddle.

She would have thought he was crazy except another full canteen had been given to Gray Wolf and Blue Feather, and water was not far away. In the distance, she heard the sound of a rushing stream.

He walked to her horse. "Join me."

Rachel wondered what he would do if she refused. A glance at Gray Wolf and Blue Feather told her they were wondering the same thing. And maybe they were hoping to find out. With as much dignity as she could muster, Rachel dismounted.

Swift Buck bent, grabbed a handful of mud, and slapped it onto her cheek. Rachel gasped, her hand flying to her face.

"That was not funny," she cried.

"It was not meant to be," he countered. "I did this once for Cougar's woman. Her skin was pale the same as yours, and I used mud to keep the sun from burning her face and neck."

Rachel had been absent during the short time that her sister-in-law had been a captive among the Mescaleros. Melissa had been given to her brother to make up for Rachel's death. Only Rachel hadn't been dead, as the Apaches believed; she had been hiding high in the mountains from the murdering Tall Blade.

"Why were you tending to my brother's wife?" she wanted to know. "I thought she belonged to Cougar during her captivity."

Swift Buck scooped up another handful of mud. "I was in charge of her until we brought her to our camp and gave her to your brother. I had her tied to me for days. The journey was long."

A tiny spark of jealousy ignited in Rachel's belly. Whenever Swift Buck had been mentioned during the past five years, Melissa would always smile as if she had a secret. What secrets did her brother's wife and Swift Buck share? She started to ask, but another handful of mud landed on her face, close to her open mouth.

"Smear the mud over your face and neck," Swift Buck instructed. "Unless you would like me to do it for you."

Annoyed by her sudden jealousy, she lifted her chin. "Since you have had practice with my brother's wife, perhaps you should do it. You can tend to me just as you tended to her."

A corner of his mouth curved up. "If you wish."

"I do," she assured him.

The moment his hands touched her skin, she knew she'd made a mistake. How could so simple an act cause her heart to flutter and steal her breath away? She stood very still, trying to ignore the gentle way he touched her. While he rubbed the mud over her face, he bent his head close to hers, staring down at her.

She lost herself in his dark eyes. Time seemed to stand still, and everything else faded into the background. He had a tiny scar above his left eyebrow. He'd had it for as long as she could remember, but she didn't know where he gotten it. She reached up and touched the scar.

"What happened here?"

"Your brother gave me the scar the first time the man named Brodie brought him to visit our camp."

"Cougar did this?"

"We were both very young boys. I told him that to be one of us, he must prove he could fight. He pushed me down, and I fell on a rock and cut my skin open."

"What happened?"

He smiled. "He became one of us."

She smiled back, but then as if he remembered that Cougar was no longer one of them in his opinion, Swift Buck's smile faded.

Strange, but she hadn't noticed that the grooves on either side of his mouth had deepened. They made him look older than his years. He was the same age as her brother, ten years older than Rachel, but at times he looked twice that.

The past five years had taken a toll on him, and, safe if not fulfilled in her new life, she hadn't known of his suffering, or the suffering of all the Mescaleros. Her brother, she realized, had kept much of what he knew or suspected from her. He might have even been trying to spare her any worry over events she could do nothing about. Rachel resented him for it now.

Swift Buck's hands lowered to her neck. She wondered if he felt tempted to put them around her throat and squeeze, but again his touch was gentle. Gone were the teasing lights in his eyes, however, and now a different light shone there. He spread the mud down her neck, his fingers pushing aside the collar of her shirt to afford him better access.

His eyes still held hers when his hands traveled down her throat to her collarbone, then lower. Her gaze shot past him, wondering what Gray Wolf and Blue Feather would think of his boldness.

"They cannot see," he said softly. "My body blocks you from their view."

Blushing, she realized that she should have been more concerned about Swift Buck's boldness than about who might see him with his hands halfway down her blouse. She stepped back from him.

"We're holding up the others," she reminded him.

Another smile twisted his mouth. "And you are very anxious to see the people you abandoned five years ago. Yes, you are right; we should be moving."

Yes, somewhere deep inside, Rachel longed to see the Mescaleros again. But she was also afraid of how they would think of her now. Her two closest friends among the Mescaleros had been murdered by Tall Blade when they had tried to help her get away from him.

As she turned from Swift Buck and mounted her horse, emotions swarmed over her like bees that had been disturbed in their hives.

The sight filled Swift Buck with great happiness and greater pain: Below them, nestled in a valley beside a rushing stream, were tepees, horses grazing, and children running through the camp. Swift

Buck's eyes stung. He was home, but he wished his mother sat beside him and saw for one last time the land that she loved, the life that she knew. A shadow crossed overhead, and he glanced up. An eagle soared there.

Silent Wind made a soft noise and drew his attention. The shimmer of tears filled her eyes as she stared down into the valley.

Gray Wolf and Blue Feather raced ahead of them, sounding a cry to alert those below of their return. Heads turned upward, and The People rushed to greet them.

It was in this moment that Swift Buck saw how few there were—no more than a two dozen, and most of them women and children. His heart sank.

"Where are the rest of them?" Silent Wind strained in his saddle, searching below.

"Dead or captured," Swift Buck assumed.

The excitement that danced in her eyes dimmed. She sat back in her saddle, her eyes round in her mud-caked face. "So many . . . I thought . . . that is, I had hoped what we heard was not true."

What could he say to her? The truth was hard to accept, but not accepting it would change nothing. His heart hardened against her. Her people had done this to his, reduced their numbers and forced them to either waste away on reservations or hide like ghosts.

"Look below you, Silent Wind, and tell me you are proud of your people. Tell me that, at this moment, you are happy to wear your white skin."

When her gaze lowered and she did not answer, he thought he had shamed her into silence. But then she lifted her head and stared at him.

"As proud as you were when you learned that one among you had killed two of my friends, and that he had blamed it on a caravan of whites. As proud as you must have been to realize that you had slaughtered innocent people for the crimes of an Apache warrior."

Silent Wind had forgotten an important truth in her story; Swift Buck now reminded her. "He was not all Apache. He was your father's son. It was his white blood that made him do those horrible things."

Silent Wind flinched, and Swift Buck wished he could take back the words spurred by hate and resentment. Silent Wind had not known that Tall Blade was her half-brother. No one had known until the brave had tried to kill Cougar, and then, during their battle, he had told him the reason that he hated him, hated Silent Wind, hated everyone with white blood. Tall Blade's mother had shamed her Apache husband with the trapper called Brodie. She had lain with the white man for trinkets, and she had borne the man a son. Tall Blade was that son.

When Tall Blade's mother's husband learned the truth, he had killed himself, which was a serious crime among The People. It had brought shame upon the family. Only Tall Blade had known why he'd done it, and later, he had killed his own mother so that no one else would learn of her affair and his shame.

"I know the sins of my blood family too well," she said. "Do you believe, when I see these mountains and my heart is filled with good memories of your mother and father, that the other ghosts do not appear to remind me of the shame in my life, as well?"

Now Swift Buck felt his own shame. His hateful words had brought this haunted look to her eyes— this look she had worn like a favorite cape in her youthful years. Before either of them said more to slash at wounds that would never heal, he nudged his horse forward, gently shaking his sleeping child.

"Wake, Amoke, and see your people. Now you will walk in the ways of your grandmother and grandfather and of theirs before them. You will walk in the ways of your father and mother." Again sorrow was mixed with his joy. So many gone. So many taken from The People too soon.

CHAPTER EIGHTEEN

As nervous as she had felt about her reunion with
the Mescaleros, Rachel couldn't help the joy that
rose up inside her. When The People recognized
Swift Buck, their excitement was like that of a
mother welcoming home a long-lost child. She
watched the exchanges from her horse. Many
hugged Swift Buck, and a few women wept with
joy to see him. Amoke's eyes were round as she was
passed from one Apache to another, all of whom
exclaimed over her beauty and how much she had
grown since last they saw her.

Rachel recognized many present. Most had aged
more than might be expected in five years, but she
understood why. Worry and strain not only weakened a person on the inside, but made their mark

visible on the outside as well. Younger children gathered around, watching the reunion with curiosity. Rachel had not seen them before, and wondered which parents they belonged to.

There were two boys, twins and exact replicas of one another, who she immediately recognized must belong to Gray Wolf and his wife, Jageitci. Gray Wolf's wife was half Spanish, and she had what some called the "sight." Early into her pregnancy, Jageitci had told the tribe that she would produce twin boys. Rachel had always respected and admired the former captive who had stolen the leader's heart.

She found the woman in the small group. Jageitci was still beautiful. As if Rachel's curious regard had been felt by all present, they began to turn and stare at her.

"Who is the white woman with her face smeared with mud?" Mesa asked. The girl had been thirteen when Rachel had left the Mescaleros. Mesa had grown into a lovely young woman.

Rachel's eyes moved to Swift Buck. He stared at her for a long moment, then lowered his gaze.

"She is a captive. I took her as a hostage from the fort to help me and my daughter escape the reservation."

A captive? A hostage? Why didn't he tell them she was Silent Wind, one who once walked among them? She glanced at Gray Wolf and Blue Feather, hoping one of them would reveal her true identity, but neither spoke. Then it occurred to Rachel that she no longer needed someone to speak on her behalf. She could speak for herself.

She'd barely gotten her mouth open when the women rushed toward her, all whooping so loudly that she didn't suppose they could hear her anyway. Arms pulled her from the horse's back. Hands tore at her clothing. Rachel tried to slap the women's hands away, but someone ripped the shirt clean off her back. Fingers dug into the waistband of her skirt; the material gave a second later. She was down to her underclothes, and she'd be damned if she'd let them strip her of those.

"Stop!" she shouted. "Listen to me!"

Someone punched her in the stomach. She doubled over and fell to the ground. Fingernails scratched her face and fingers grabbed at her long hair, tugging. The pain brought tears to her eyes. A figure loomed over her. Mesa, whom she had just a moment ago thought so lovely, held a large, thick tree branch aimed at Rachel's head. Mesa drew back to strike, but suddenly a large hand clamped over her arm. Through the tears swimming in Rachel's eyes, she saw Swift Buck.

"Enough!" he barked. "You will kill her."

"White whore," Mesa growled, then spat on her. "She does not deserve to live."

Mesa's words stirred the women up again, and Rachel feared that Swift Buck could not stop them. She scrambled back on her hands and gained her unsteady feet. Glancing down, she noticed that her petticoat was shredded and a large tear in her chemise was gaping open. She glanced up and saw the women crowding toward her again.

A small figure darted through them. Amoke was suddenly at Rachel's side, clutching her torn petticoat, with big tears in her eyes. Rachel reached down and plucked the child up. The women all gaped at her.

"I am not a captive," Rachel said in Apache. She realized that earlier, in her panic, she had spoken in English. "I am not a white whore, either," she called. "I am Silent Wind. I was once a sister to you—the adopted daughter of two whose names we can no longer speak. A sister in truth to the mighty Cougar, who you once called brother and who fought for many years by the Apaches' side."

Jageitci stepped forward. "Silent Wind?" she whispered. "Is it really you?"

"No," Swift Buck answered before Rachel could. He stormed forward and took Amoke from her arms. "She is no longer Silent Wind. She goes by her white name and chose her path five years ago when she and her brother abandoned The People. Cougar once fought by our side, but where is he now? Where has he been while the whites slaughtered our women and children? When they killed or captured our warriors? When they forced us to live on their filthy reservations and treated us no better than camp dogs?"

All eyes swung toward Rachel for an answer. She swallowed the lump in her throat and straightened her shoulders. "Cougar has kept his promise to The People. He fights for you in Washington with words. When I learned of what has been happening to The People, I went to the reservation with supplies and medicines to help those who are confined there. I have embraced the white ways, but in my heart I have not forgotten you, and neither has my brother."

"Then where is he now?" Gray Wolf demanded, and she knew that, like Swift Buck, the leader also felt hurt and confused.

"He is in a white man's jail," she confessed. "When he finally heard the truth of what had happened to the Mescaleros, he attacked the man who ordered the massacre and nearly killed him with his bare hands. My brother has much of the white man's money, but he has few friends in the white world willing to help him in his fight for Indian rights. The lawmakers and politicians kept the truth from him, and in turn, Cougar has kept the truth from me. We did not know of this ruthless campaign against the Indians, Apache and Navaho alike, until recently."

"And now that you do know, where does your loyalty lie?" Gray Wolf asked. "Are you white, or are you Apache?"

She was neither, but Rachel didn't know how to

explain that to The People. Most things were cut-and-dried with them.

"Would you kill a white man?" Swift Buck asked, and she cast him a dark look.

"You know I would not," she answered. "But neither would I would kill an Apache. I hope a peaceful solution can be found so that no more have to die."

"You hope for the impossible," Swift Buck said.

"Your adoptive brother is right," Gray Wolf agreed. "I saw these dark days years ago in my visions. There will be more killing. Whites and Apaches will die. I will tell you what I once told Cougar: You are either with us or you are against us. If you are against us, you are our enemy."

Where war was concerned, she was with neither the whites nor the Apaches, but that answer would not suffice in the circumstances. Rachel supposed she could lie and say otherwise, but she wouldn't.

"The ones who raised me among you taught me that to lie is wrong. I made a choice five years ago. I chose because I hoped to find my place, but now I realize there is no place for me. Not in this war of one people against another. Bloodshed is never a good answer."

"We are women the same as you," Mesa said, her voice still full of hate. "And women do not like war, but when war is demanded, we pick up what weapons we can find and fight to defend our own and our way of life. To fight, you must love what you are fighting for. Maybe this is the reason Silent Wind cannot fight. Her heart died long ago. She loves no one."

Rachel supposed The People had the right to think that of her. She had never been good at expressing her feelings, even if she'd had a voice to do so. The trauma of being abandoned by her birth mother, and then her birth father and her birth brother, had made her afraid to care. With love came pain. She suffered her shame and hurt in silence, hoping that one day the painful memories would fade and she would not remember that bad time in her life . . . but the memories had never faded.

"Hear me now," Swift Buck said. "I do not claim this woman as my adopted sister. I do not claim her as any family to me. She is my captive and will remain so until I decide that she is no longer useful to us."

Rachel seethed with anger toward him. Had she not shown him that she only wanted to help his people? Had she not shown him that she cared for Amoke? Cared enough to risk her life so that Amoke and Swift Buck could be together? Why could he not soften toward her? At times she felt as if the distance between them was closing; then he would reopen the wounds and force the distance to return.

"So, you will have her as you have always wanted," Mesa spat, her dark eyes flashing. "Once, you could not win her; now you force her to be with you. I say this is wrong and that Silent Wind should be given to another as a slave."

Swift Buck's face darkened with either anger or embarrassment at Mesa's barbs. Rachel had almost forgotten that White Dove, Swift Buck's wife, had been Mesa's older sister.

"I captured her. She belongs to me," Swift Buck insisted, but his gaze softened upon the young woman. "Mesa, we have both lost those we hold dear. I understand your need to lash out at the living, but my heart does grieve for those who you also miss in our world."

Mesa's stormy eyes filled with sudden tears. "You never loved my sister," she accused. The young woman nodded toward Rachel. "It was always *her* on your mind and in your heart. Go ahead, make a fool of yourself again." Mesa turned and shoved away through the crowd. A moment later, Rachel saw her running through the meadow toward the stream.

There was an awkward silence. Swift Buck stood tall, his stance proud and somewhat threatening, she thought. He dared anyone to dispute his claim on Rachel, and she resented being treated like a possession. Mesa's declarations also unsettled her. Secretly, she might have once known that Swift Buck had feelings for her that were not brotherly, but she hadn't known that anyone else knew.

"It will be as you say, brother," Gray Wolf finally

announced. "Now come inside my tepee and meet my sons. Allow Jageitci to fix us something to eat. Blue Feather will . . ." His voice trailed off, and everyone followed his gaze to see Blue Feather traveling across the meadow in the direction that Mesa had gone. "Someone will take the horses and care for them," he amended. Gray Wolf then looked at Rachel. "What do you wish to be done with your captive?"

Visions of being staked outside the tepee and struck or spat upon by everyone going past came to Rachel's mind. But this band had not taken many captives, so she could not know how she would be treated by them—and the only two captives she knew of had ended up married to men of the tribe. Well, Cougar had considered himself a member at that time anyway.

"She will try to escape and return to the soldiers if given an opportunity," Swift Buck answered. "I wish her to come with me inside your tepee so I may keep an eye on her."

Gray Wolf nodded and turned away. "Come, then, and bring her."

The tension seemed to drain from The People. Not so for Rachel. She admitted that Swift Buck was right: If given a chance, she supposed she would escape and return to the soldiers, if for no other reason than hoping her return would appease them and they would give up searching for Swift Buck.

When Swift Buck turned and followed Gray Wolf, she knew it was understood that she would follow him. Rachel didn't balk over her duty. Better to be inside Jageitci's tepee and away from curious eyes until she adjusted to her situation—if it were possible to adjust to being a captive among her own people.

Again Rachel caught herself. Neither by right nor by blood could she claim the Mescaleros as her people. Now her only link left to the Mescaleros, Swift Buck, had disowned her as family. She wondered if he had more than one reason for doing so. Maybe if he broke that tie in the Mescaleros' minds, they would not think it wrong for him to desire her in his bed. And now that they had reached their destination, she wondered how long it would be before Swift Buck would demand her presence in his bed.

It was his right as her captor, but nothing would make it right in her eyes.

CHAPTER NINETEEN

It was good to be home. Although Gray Wolf and Jageitci's lodge was not as fine as it once had been, Swift Buck thought it was comfortable and served its purpose. Gray Wolf's wife had fixed them a filling meal. Silent Wind sat alone, while Swift Buck and Amoke sat with Gray Wolf and Jageitci and their twin sons, Tokota and Nanton. The boys tried to make Amoke laugh by making funny faces, and Swift Buck smiled over their antics. He heard Silent Wind's stomach grumble from where he sat and felt guilty that her status did not allow her to eat with them.

"The stew will turn bad before morning," Jageitci said, her eyes downcast while she stitched a shirt for her husband. "I will either have to throw it outside or someone will have to finish it."

"I will—" Nanton began, only to grow quiet beneath his mother's stern look.

Gray Wolf glanced at his wife, then scratched his chin. "We do not throw food away. Not when so many are starving. You know this, wife."

"I was thinking we could give the remainder to the captive. Then we do not have to go against the ways of our people, or attract animals to our camp by throwing it out."

Swift Buck watched the exchange with quiet amusement. He remembered that Jageitci usually got what she wanted from her husband, and Gray Wolf made a game of his surrender to his wife's wishes.

"Nanton indicated that he would finish the stew. He is growing. He needs to eat," Gray Wolf said.

Without glancing up, Jageitci said, "He is growing *out*, not up." She sighed. "I think he gets this from my side. My people were short and plump."

Gray Wolf smiled. "I thought you did not know your people."

"Only on my mother's side," she reminded him, never missing a stitch. "But my father was not a tall man, and he was round. As I remember, he would always have more to eat than his belly needed."

The leader's gaze strayed to his sons. Neither paid attention to the conversation, but instead continued to entertain Amoke. She giggled at their silliness.

"Maybe you are right, wife," Gray Wolf admitted. "If it is permitted by Swift Buck, the captive may have what is left of the stew."

Swift Buck turned to Silent Wind. "Are you hungry, woman?" he asked.

She shrugged. "Since I am your captive, I suppose that is up to you. Am I hungry?"

Her show of spirit irritated him. He knew she was starving; the grumbling of her belly had told him so countless times while the family ate and she was forced to sit and watch without a bowl of her own.

"A woman who does not eat cannot work. And it is a slave's place to work," he said.

"What work would you have me do?" she asked. "You have no lodge of your own that I can—"

"You will care for Amoke." He cut her off, then reached forward and filled his bowl with stew.

"Amoke is not work," she told him. "Amoke is a pleasure."

He rose and took her the stew. She reached for the bowl, but he would not release it, forcing her to look up at him. "Then I will find something for you to do that you will not consider a pleasure . . . or maybe you will."

He let the implication rest between them. She stared at him blankly for a moment; then her eyes widened. She tugged the bowl from his hand and began shoving the stew into her mouth with her fingers.

"You must accept the hospitality of our lodge tonight," Gray Wolf said. "Tomorrow the women will make a new lodge for our returned brother and his family."

Swift Buck's family was small now. He wished that his mother and father would have provided him with brothers and sisters; he and Amoke would have stayed with them since he had no wife. While he had been married to White Dove, he had stayed with her family, as was the tradition.

"I thank you," he said, and both Gray Wolf and Jageitci nodded acceptance.

"I will make a bed for Amoke among my children," Jageitci said. "Will you and your captive require one sleeping mat or two?"

"One." He smiled when Silent Wind choked on her stew. "I must keep her tied to me during the night, or she will try to escape," he explained.

Jageitci lifted a brow, but she did not glance up from her sewing. "Swift Buck and my husband might enjoy time alone outside to smoke from my husband's fine pipe and talk while I prepare our sleeping mats."

Swift Buck had many things he wanted to discuss with Gray Wolf. He wanted to know the leader's plans for a rescue of those left at the reservation. He wanted to know if Gray Wolf had found other bands to join with them . . . or if there were even others left to fight.

"Yes, we will smoke and talk for a while," Gray

Wolf agreed, and he rose to get his pipe.

Swift Buck glanced at Silent Wind, who sat licking stew from her fingers while she watched them. He knew she did not feel uncomfortable around Jageitci and he felt no qualms about leaving her alone with the woman. Amoke still played with Gray Wolf's sons, although he could see by the drooping of her eyes that soon she must be put to bed. He rose and followed Gray Wolf from the tepee.

Rachel wished she had a water basin, a washcloth, and a towel. She'd been so hungry when Swift Buck handed her the stew that she hadn't wanted to ask for an eating utensil.

Jageitci seemed to read her mind. "I have cloths for washing and a pan of water heating over the fire. I make my sons wash every night before they climb into their sleeping mats. My husband too," she added with a smile. "You are welcome to use what I have."

"Thank you. It is good to see you again," Rachel said, and she meant it. "Also, thank you for seeing to it that I had something to eat tonight."

"I could tell that your grumbling belly bothered Swift Buck. He would not want to see you go without food, even if he has declared to all that you are his captive."

"I refuse to be his captive," Rachel told her. "It is silly for him to call me 'woman' when he has known my name since we were both children."

"Swift Buck was almost a man when you came among the Mescaleros," Jageitci reminded her. "I was not here in those days. Your mother? Why is she not with you?"

For a moment, Rachel thought Jageitci meant her white mother, and felt confused because the woman knew her story and that her mother had died when she was a small child. Then she realized that Jageitci asked about Laughing Stream.

"She is gone," Rachel answered. And that was all she needed to say, because the Apaches did not like to speak of death, or even to say the word.

Jageitci bowed her head. "I am sorry. I liked her very much. The same as her son, she had a gentle spirit."

"Her son no longer has a gentle spirit," Rachel fumed; then she moved to the fire to accept Jageitci's offer to wash. The mud caked on her face would probably dirty the whole pot.

"These horrible things that have happened to The People have changed many." Jageitci handed over a strip of clean cloth. "It is strange for me to hear your voice," she added. "For so long you did not speak."

Rachel dipped a generous strip of cloth into the warm water. "It took me two years in the white world to say a sentence without using an Apache word," she confessed. "My sister-in-law worked very hard to teach me what my mind had forgotten."

"How is Huera?" Jageitci asked. "Is she well? Does she have children?"

The Apaches had called Melissa Huera because the word meant light hair. "She is very well. She has two children. Her son, Daniel, is three, and her daughter, Anna, is only a year old. They are both beautiful children, and I miss them."

"And do you miss the world that you chose?" Jageitci asked. "Did you find what you went searching for?"

Rachel didn't want to admit that she hadn't found what she'd been searching for; she was no longer certain exactly what it was she had hoped to find. "I miss some things about my world." A nice big tub full of steaming water and scented soap. "But I am not sure that I found what it was I went searching for," she admitted. "I am still looking."

Gray Wolf's wife gave a sad smile. "Some look for what is right under their noses. You came back. Maybe your heart knows what it searches for more than your mind."

"I did not come back for *him*," Rachel snapped, and realized how defensive she sounded. She took a calming breath and began to wash the mud from her face. "I came back to help The People."

Rachel didn't know if Jageitci would have disputed her claim, because before the woman could comment, a guest entered the tepee. It was Mesa, and although she greeted Jageitci with respect, her eyes shot insults at Rachel.

"I have come to see my niece, Amoke," the young woman explained. "Today was difficult for me. Amoke is all that I have left of my family. Seeing her reminded me of those we cannot speak of, and it saddened my heart."

"I understand," Gray Wolf's wife said gently. "Go and see her. Hold her and play with her. She should know her family."

Rachel continued to scrub her face while watching Swift Buck's sister-in-law. Mesa bent beside the children. She spoke softly to Amoke and took her in her arms. Amoke, so open with her love, smiled up at Mesa, and the young woman visibly melted.

"She has the look of your family," Rachel commented. "And that of her father's."

Mesa's smile faded. "You look like none of us," she sneered. "You should have left the mud on your face. To see your white skin reminds us of your people's treachery. Do not believe that just because you once walked among us and we accepted you, it will be so again. Much has changed since you and your brother turned your backs upon us."

Lowering the cloth to her neck, Rachel wasn't certain how to respond. She should have expected this treatment—had in fact suspected that most of The People's attitudes toward her would be the same as Swift Buck's. Still, she had hoped in a small corner of her heart that she would be welcomed as warmly as Swift Buck had been welcomed home. That had been a foolish dream.

"Do not forget, Mesa, that Huera fought beside you to keep you from being captured by Comanches," Jageitci said softly. "Or that when you were indeed captured, it was Cougar who went and brought you home, and Cougar alone. The People despise the Spanish who have tricked, deceived, and enslaved them over the years, and yet, half of the blood that runs through my veins is Spanish. You cannot judge everyone by the actions of some."

Mesa blushed over the put-down, but her expression did not soften. "While it is true that Huera became a friend to me in her time among us, and that Cougar was once a great and respected warrior to The People, neither of them are here now. They were not here to help us fight the soldiers who attacked our tribe. Silent Wind was not here either, but living among those who do not even count us as human. Had they all stayed and fought and died with us, I would feel different."

Rachel could try to explain her and her brother's absence once again, but she felt it would matter little to Mesa. As Swift Buck often said, actions spoke louder than words. Mesa touched Amoke's small cheek, set the child aside, and left the tepee.

Jageitci sighed. "You will have to win them back to you. It will take time . . . and courage."

"I am hoping that Swift Buck will release me now," she said. "He has made it safely back to his people and has no reason to continue to hold me captive."

For a moment, Jageitci did not respond; then she said, "Understand that if you go again, you can never come back. Think on this before you beg too much to be released. Now, you will help me fix our sleeping mats."

Rachel's pulse leapt. Tonight she would be forced to sleep beside Swift Buck, and Amoke would not be there as a wedge between them!

CHAPTER TWENTY

The dream had returned. Rachel knew it was a dream because she had had it before. Many times. Swift Buck bent over her, staring down into her eyes. She lay naked upon a thick buffalo hide. He ran his fingers across her skin, causing her to arch against his touch. Bravely she reached up and grasped the back of his neck, pulling his lips down to hers. They were firm but warm, and they melted into her. Then his body pressed against hers and his naked heat engulfed her.

"Walk into the flame with me," he whispered, his voice a husky caress against her ear. "Do not fight a battle you cannot win. You are mine. You have always been mine."

She came awake with a jolt. Rachel opened her

eyes and found herself looking at a bare, smooth male chest. She quickly glanced up. Swift Buck stared into her eyes just as he had in her dream. She was pressed snugly against him, and she felt the hard proof of his arousal against her. She swallowed, hating the loud gulp she made.

It brought a smile to his lips. The buffalo robes were soft beneath her, and she had slept like the dead, regardless of her worry that Swift Buck would demand his rights as his captor. She knew it was now morning by the weak light that filtered in from the open tepee flap.

"You still talk in your sleep," he said.

She recalled what she'd been dreaming about and felt her face flush. What had she said? What had she done? What should she do now? Deciding that she needed distance between them in order to think straight, Rachel tried to move. Swift Buck's arms were around her, and she couldn't budge.

"The others—" she whispered.

"Are gone," he informed her.

"But Amoke—" she tried.

"Jageitci will look after her."

"Breakfast—"

"Is prepared and waiting for us whenever we choose to rise." He pressed a heated kiss against her neck. "I would rather nibble on you."

She'd always had trouble waking with a clear head, instantly aware of her surroundings and ready to face the day; now it took her a moment to remember how he'd turned the people against her. How he had declared her to be a captive, and an enemy in their eyes. She recalled the reason why she should not be lying in his arms, or enjoying the contact of his skin with hers.

"I suppose I have no choice but to submit to your lustful intentions," she said. "You said you would not force me, but you are not the man I once knew. The one whose word I could trust."

Swift Buck sighed, then lifted his head to look at her. "You do that well."

"Do what?"

"Try to make me do the opposite of what I wish. You are a woman. I am a man. We are here together upon these soft robes, and no one will disturb us. Why can you not enjoy the pleasure I give to you?"

She answered honestly. "I do not feel pleasure."

He smiled. "That is because I have not yet given it to you. If you do not enjoy what I do, I will leave you alone."

"I am not a child," she scoffed. "I will not fall for your tricks."

His dark gaze pinned her. "No, you are not a child. It is time for you to become a woman."

"I *am* a woman! Nothing you can do will make me either more or less of one."

"We will see," he said. Then he lowered his mouth to hers.

She tried to resist, clamping her lips together. He

teased her bottom lip with his teeth, then ran his tongue along the contours of her mouth. He continued to nibble and tease until she felt her blood turn hot in her veins. His gentleness would always be her downfall. If he used brute force she could resist him, but a tender onslaught weakened her will. She opened to him, her arms straying from her sides to curl around his neck.

He deepened the kiss, exploring the cavern of her mouth, his tongue teasing hers until she joined him in the dance. He pressed her more firmly against him, and the torn, gaping chemise she wore allowed skin against skin. A fire leapt to life between them. His flesh was muscled, hot, and smooth against hers. Her breasts were pushed together and rubbed against his broad chest. The slight friction teased her nipples until they hardened.

His mouth, warm and moist against hers, traveled down her neck, nipping and sucking a path of fire across her sensitive skin. He gently rolled her onto her back; then his head dipped lower. He pushed aside the torn edges of her chemise, exposing her breasts. She felt a moment of modesty and tried to bring her hands up to cover her nudity, but his arms pinned hers at her sides.

"You have no reason to feel shame," he said, his voice very low and husky. "You are beautiful to me. I worship all that makes you a woman."

And he did worship her. His head lowered, and he traced the aureole of her nipple with his tongue;

then he took the hardened bud into the warm, moist recesses of his mouth and sucked gently. She gasped, her body involuntarily arching against his.

Babes suckled at their mother's breasts. She had never imagined a man doing so, and had never suspected that a man doing so would cause such strange yet pleasurable sensations to course through her. He paid homage to the other breast, going back and forth between them until she squirmed beneath him.

Her fingers twisted into his long, dark hair. How could what he did to her upper body affect her lower body as well? She felt heat flood the private place between her legs. The harder he sucked, the more discomfort in that area she felt. She began to throb, to ache, to rub against him with some need that she did not understand. He groaned and pressed his shaft against her leg. He was long and hard, and suddenly she understood what her body craved. The joining. His body and hers.

"No," she moaned. This was not right. And yet it was. Somewhere deep inside she wanted this with him—had wanted it since she first saw him as a man through a woman's eyes. But that was long ago, before she had run away from him, before war between his people and hers had made him into someone else, had made her into someone else in his eyes as well.

"Stop," she said firmly. "You said you would not force me."

He lifted his head and slid up her body. "Do I not bring you pleasure? Do I not make you burn with the same need that I have for you?"

To answer no would be to lie. His face was so handsome staring down at her that she felt another moment of weakness. But she could not be weak. He had waged this war between them. He didn't want her, only her surrender—which in his mind would be a form of revenge against both her and the whites he despised.

"Your needs and mine are not the same," she said. "I cannot give myself to a man who claims to be my enemy. I cannot give myself to a man whose heart is full of hate."

"You cannot give yourself to any man," he answered. "Because to give, you must let go of something, and you cannot let go. You are afraid," he accused softly. "You have always been afraid." He rolled off her and sat up. "Run away now. It is what you do best."

His words pricked worse than his easy dismissal of her. Yes, once she had been a coward. But her refusal to couple with Swift Buck as if they were animals had nothing to do with fear. Did it? No, she assured herself. To give her body, she must be willing to give her heart . . . and she could not let go of that, because she was afraid. Afraid to love, afraid to live, afraid to feel.

She hated Swift Buck for knowing her too well.

* * *

Swift Buck battled himself to let her rise and move away from him. His need for her ached between his legs. She fired his blood like no other woman. He supposed it would always be that way, regardless of the changes in their world, and in themselves. He hated the whites, and she was white, but he could not truthfully say that he hated Silent Wind. He resented her for the pain she had brought him, and for abandoning his mother and The People, but he did not hate her.

His gaze slid to her as she fixed them each a bowl of leftover breakfast—cold corn cakes and raw berries, from what he could see. She had trouble working and holding her gaping undergarments together. If it were just him and her, he would not mind the flashes of smooth, rounded flesh she kept affording his eyes, but he did not like the thought of other men seeing what he wanted to be meant only for him.

"I will ask Jageitci to find you something to wear," he said. "You cannot work in those torn clothes."

She lifted a brow. "I thought captives were to roam naked through the camp. To humble them."

Her wise mouth always surprised him. She had been a quiet and obedient child in his mother's lodge. Some things about her had changed much; other things had not changed at all.

"You may go naked if you wish," he offered.

Her answer was a dark look before she indicated his bowl. "Do you wish to eat? Because I do, and I know my place is to wait for you to finish."

He rose and moved to the cooking fire that had no flame but still gave warmth. As he settled, he asked, "Why did Mesa come last night?"

"Besides to insult me with hateful words, she came to see Amoke."

Thoughtful, Swift Buck studied his bowl of cold corn cakes and berries. "Mesa has lost all of her family," he explained. "Her parents, her grandparents, her brothers—all were killed by the whites. It is a hard thing for one so young to deal with."

"Yes," Silent Wind agreed softly. "Amoke will be good for her. She does not know yet how to hate."

His gaze lifted to her, his pale captive. "No. Amoke gives her small heart easily—too easily, I fear. She does not know color."

"I wish we all could be as innocent again."

Swift Buck ate. There was no point in responding. They could not go back. They could only move forward.

"The one we used to call White Dove," Silent Wind began, then paused as if hesitant to continue. "Did you love her?"

Pain squeezed his chest for a moment. "I tried to."

Rachel did not say anything else, and he was glad. He nodded toward her waiting bowl. "You may eat."

She took up her bowl, maybe glad like him that

if they ate, they'd have no reason to speak to one another.

"What did you learn from Gray Wolf?" she asked.

That was another subject he would not discuss with her. He was saddened by what he had learned. Since the Mescaleros' numbers were so small, they had sent out one man every six months to search for others, hoping to gather enough warriors to attack the fort and rescue their people from the reservation. None of the men sent out had returned. Gray Wolf feared there were no others, and that the men had been either captured or killed by soldiers.

"Did you hear me?"

"I will not discuss such things with a captive."

"Then we will discuss another matter," she persisted. "Now that you and your daughter are safely among your people, you should release me."

Jealousy nearly overcame him. "Do you really wish to return to the pale leader of the fort? Does he still want you even after you have been my captive?"

"He does not hold against me what is beyond my control," she said, her tone cold. "And it is the fort I wish to return to, and of course my continued care for those at the reservation."

"I cannot let you go," he said. "Gray Wolf agrees that we may have further use of you as a hostage.

Also, if the white leader had you back, he might kill his prisoners on the reservation."

"I would never allow that to happen," Silent Wind insisted.

He smiled at her naiveté. "One woman will not stop the pale leader. You do not see this man for what he is. Killing the Indians at the reservation would be no different to him than killing a pack of coyotes."

"Or a herd of wild mustangs," she said, then quickly closed her mouth as if she had not meant to speak. "So, I am to stay," she finished with a sigh.

"For now," he agreed.

Amoke came running into the tepee. The girl smiled and ran straight into Silent Wind's arms.

"Where have you been? I missed you," Silent Wind teased, then pulled her tighter into a hug.

Although his feelings were hurt that Amoke had not come to him, Swift Buck made a startling realization in that moment, watching the two of them together. Silent Wind had a soft, serene expression on her face, one he had not seen her display with anyone else. She *could* love, because she clearly loved his daughter. And, not as surprisingly, Amoke loved Silent Wind in return.

CHAPTER TWENTY-ONE

It took two days to complete Swift Buck's tepee. Rachel was allowed to help, but only in a slave's capacity. While the other women worked, laughing and talking amongst themselves, Rachel had to stand a ways apart and bring things when they demanded them.

The older children were in charge of watching the young ones while their mothers worked. Rachel had been so distracted with making certain Amoke was being taken proper care of that once she was cuffed on the side of the head for not paying attention.

A few of the men, and there were very few, had gone out to hunt, Swift Buck among them. Rachel was happy for him—to see him mounted on a horse with other Apaches, going off to find food for his family. Seeing him that way had brought back memories for her—memories of how she would watch him when he wasn't looking, thinking how strong and handsome he was, how proud a woman would be to have him as her own.

"The dress does not fit you too badly," Jageitci commented. "It is a little short, but the tall moccasins help."

Rachel had been preoccupied again and didn't realize that Jageitci had approached her. The woman's arms were laden with furs to cover the tepee floor, and Rachel helped her by taking an armful.

"No, the dress is fine," she said, following behind Jageitci, as was now her place. "Thank you for finding me something to wear."

"Swift Buck is possessive of you. He did not want other men looking at your exposed skin. You should be thankful for that; otherwise you may have had to run through the camp naked."

The tepee was fully stretched upon the poles, although some women still worked outside. Jageitci entered, and Rachel followed her inside. The lighting was dim due to the thick hide walls and only the small opening above.

"All have donated items to give Swift Buck comforts for his lodge."

Rachel smiled to herself. Jageitic had forgotten that she had lived among them and knew that this was customary. No one in the tribe owned more than another. They shared everything, even food. It was not that way in the white world, where some liked having more than others and showing off that fact to everyone.

A cooking pit had been dug in the center of the tepee, and Rachel and Jageitci began spreading robes on the ground around the pit.

"If these robes could talk," Jageitci said, then grinned at her.

Rachel burst out laughing, then quickly covered her mouth. The women outside would frown over her enjoying herself, even a little.

"It is so strange to be here and yet feel as if I do not belong," she told Gray Wolf's wife.

Jageitci raised a brow. "I thought the reason that you left was because you did not feel as if you belonged here."

Spreading a thick buffalo pelt on the ground, Rachel said, "I did not feel as if I belonged, but now I realize how it *truly* feels to be an outcast. At least back in the days when I lived among you Mescaleros, I did not feel as if anyone questioned my right to be there."

"You were accepted," Jageitci agreed. "You took that for granted, and now you see that you had more of a gift than you knew."

The woman was right. Curious, Rachel asked, "Do you still have visions? Can you still see the future?"

Jageitci shook her head sadly. "No. The gift left me when my sons were born. Maybe it is better that it did. I would not want to see something horrible happen to them. Women's lives are bad enough as it is. We shouldn't have to worry and imagine the worst for our children."

"I do worry for Amoke," Rachel confessed. "I had thought that maybe she would be better off in my world where she would be safe and I could provide many nice things for her, but now I realize she would not be happy there."

"No," Jageitci agreed. "I am thinking maybe *you* were not as happy there as you thought you would be, either."

"I was not unhappy," Rachel said.

"But neither were you happy," Jageitci guessed. "I once lived in a different world, also," she reminded Rachel. "I could not go back there now. And if my sons would be safer there, they would not be happy either. This life, as hard as it is at times, is the best life. An Apache cannot be happy any other way. And now I am Apache."

Rachel realized she would have been better off if she'd accepted that she was one way or the other, instead of allowing herself to be trapped in the middle between both worlds. Maybe her brother hadn't done her such a favor by insisting that she be given a choice. Sometimes having a choice only confused a person.

Mesa entered the tepee with a few items to donate. She held a doll made of cornhusks in her arms. "I want Amoke to have this doll," she said. "It once belonged to someone who would have wanted Amoke to have it, even though it is one of the few possessions I have left from my family that soldiers did not destroy."

"I will tell her to treat it gently," Rachel said, thinking it was a very touching gesture by Mesa to part with the doll since she had nothing left from her family.

Mesa glared at her. "I will tell her that myself. You are not her mother. It is not your place to instruct her in any matter. Swift Buck should send you back to your people. He should not let his daughter, who is too young to know you are her enemy, become attached to you."

The young woman had gone too far. Rachel rose and faced her. "I am not Amoke's enemy! I would never hurt her. I . . ."

"She loves the child," Jageitci finished for Rachel. "Why do you not say what is really bothering you, Mesa? Why do you not tell Silent Wind that you want your sister's husband for yourself? That you have wanted him always? Why do you not tell her that even though Blue Feather has asked you to join with him, you refuse, hoping Swift Buck would return and you could take your sister's place in his empty bed?"

The young woman's face turned bright red, even

in the dim lighting. Rachel waited for Mesa to confirm what Jageitci had said.

"Witch," the young woman muttered instead, then swept out of the tepee.

"Who does she call a witch?" Rachel asked after a short silence.

"Me," Jageitci answered. "You are the woman standing in her way to Swift Buck as a husband. I am only a witch."

Although Jageitci tried to make light of the incident, Rachel didn't feel amused. "It would be right," she said. "An Apache brave often takes his widowed sister-in-law for a wife so that he can provide for her. No one would frown upon a joining between Mesa and Swift Buck. Although Mesa is young, she would be a good wife for Swift Buck. She would be a good mother to her niece."

Raising a brow, Gray Wolf's wife said, "You should tell Swift Buck these things that you have decided for him."

Still not in the mood for teasing, Rachel began tidying the tepee. "There is no reason that he should not remarry and provide Amoke with a mother."

"There is one," Jageitci said softly. "You. A man should give his wife his whole heart. How can Swift Buck do that when his has already been taken? White Dove was very brave to accept him as a husband. He treated her kindly, he did things to please her, but everyone knew, even she, that he could not give her a heart that belonged to someone else."

Sudden tears pricked Rachel's eyes. "His heart is free now," she assured Jageitci. "He does not see me as he once did, and now his heart is full of hate. I pity the woman who wins it."

"Do you?" Jageitci asked. "Or do you envy the woman who teaches him to love again? He is a prize, Silent Wind. Why do all of our women see that but you, when you should be the one who sees it above all others?"

Rachel didn't answer. She knew the answer; deep down, she had always known the answer, but she could not speak it.

Heaving a frustrated sigh, Jageitci finished her chores and headed toward the tepee's exit. "You do not deserve him." Suddenly she stopped. Slowly, she turned and narrowed her gaze upon Rachel. "But that is the answer. You do not feel as if you deserve him, or any man's love."

A tear made a slow descent down Rachel's cheek. She did not speak, wished she still could not so that no one would expect answers from her. Ashamed of her tears, she turned her back and began going through the items donated to Swift Buck's lodge.

"I hurt for you," Jageitci said softly. "To allow one man, so many years ago, to instill this belief in you and make it grow until it has wrapped around your heart and choked all else, saddens me greatly. Only you can chop the vine down, Silent Wind.

Though others have tried to do it for you, only you can rid yourself of the weed that keeps you alone, keeps you from finding your place."

Jageitci left Rachel to her tears, and left her with something to think about. Could she win Swift Buck's heart back? Along with the hearts of the Mescaleros? Did she have the courage to even try? Life with the Apaches would be difficult, dangerous, in all probability, deadly. Her brother would not like her to stay with them under current circumstances. Yet Clay had made his choice. Shouldn't Rachel now be able to make her own?

So many things to think about. So many things to consider. If she loved Amoke . . . if she cared for Swift Buck . . . wouldn't the best thing for both of them be to have a woman in their lives that fit totally into their world? A woman like Mesa, who was bitter because of what the war on the Mescaleros had taken from her, but who . . . maybe could mend Swift Buck's heart. Rachel didn't know.

The only thing she knew for certain was that when Swift Buck rode into camp a few hours later, a big deer slung over the rump of his horse, she felt her insides flutter and nearly melted beneath the dark, heated onslaught of his eyes.

Swift Buck was pleased with his new lodge. He was pleased that his daughter had thrown herself into his arms upon his return and greeted him with a quick, slobbery kiss on the lips that shocked all who witnessed it. He was also pleased to find Silent Wind in his lodge, wearing deerskin, her hair in long braids as he once remembered her. She had made his new lodge comfortable, and a part of him remembered imagining this in his dreams. Him. Her. Together. Beneath one tepee. Alone.

Only they were not alone.

"The People are talking," he said.

Silent Wind glanced up from stirring the stew she had made with a portion of the deer meat he had brought back. "And what are they saying?"

He reached down and played with the fringe of his moccasins. "They are saying that maybe it would be better if Amoke stayed with another family until a decision is reached about you. They believe she is becoming too attached and that this is not good for her."

When Silent Wind said nothing, he glanced up. She was not looking at him but at the stew. Her brows were drawn together, and a frown shaped her mouth.

"Maybe she should stay with Mesa."

"Mesa?" He was surprised she thought so, since Mesa had been hateful to her.

Rachel rose and went to where Amoke sat playing and ran her hand over her hair. "Mesa is her aunt. Amoke should know her family."

"Mesa is young and—"

"And she would make a good wife for you."

Swift Buck blinked. "A wife?"

"Amoke needs a mother. You need a wife. Mesa is family. It makes sense."

He was shocked. "When did you make these plans for me?"

"Today," she answered, then returned to her place by the fire to stir.

Swift Buck felt insulted. "And you would not mind if I take Mesa as my new wife?"

She shrugged. "I suggested it. Why would I do so if I minded?"

Now he felt more than insulted. He rose and sat beside her. Grabbing her braids, he pulled her face close to his. "If I want a wife, I will choose one myself. Do you understand?"

Her deep blue eyes stared into his. Slowly she nodded. "I was only trying to be a helpful slave to you."

He could not resist the closeness of her lips. The other morning when she had kissed him back, when she had wanted him even if she would not allow herself to surrender, he had thought that her feelings for him were changing. He had hoped that he could penetrate more than her body, but the shield that she used to guard her heart was too thick. Was it only for revenge or for his male pride that he sought from her what she would not give?

The brush of his lips against hers made her shiver, and he released her braids and pulled her closer. He liked the way she felt against him, her soft, womanly curves pressed against the hard planes of his body.

She opened her mouth beneath his, not to allow him inside, but to say, "Amoke . . ."

Swift Buck pulled back and glanced at his daughter, who was watching them curiously. He sighed and released Silent Wind. There was still the matter of Amoke to settle.

"I think Amoke should stay with Gray Wolf's family for a while," he said.

Silent Wind also glanced at the child, and he saw tears fill her eyes. "Before, I did not speak what is in my heart concerning Amoke. I can see where you want to send her away from me, but do not send her away from her father. She may not understand. She may think you do not want her."

As Silent Wind's father had not wanted her. Again he knew that somewhere inside him his heart still lived, because he felt a tug, a twinge. "It would cut me like a knife if Amoke ever thought such a thing," he admitted. "And maybe you are right. She has lost too many people in her young life. It would not be good for her spirit to think she has lost me as well."

"Then you will not send her away?"

At the sight of his daughter's big dark eyes staring at him, he shook his head. "No. I cannot send her away. My heart needs her close to me."

He felt the soft touch of Silent Wind's hand upon his arm. When he looked at her, he saw deep gratitude shining in her eyes in place of her earlier tears.

"Thank you. For Amoke's sake," she added. "You are a good father to her."

And it bothered him to think so, but Silent Wind would be a good mother for his daughter. She might not make a good wife for him, and in the Mescaleros' current circumstances, he could not even consider taking a wife, but Amoke had managed to draw love from the woman when Swift Buck had not. Maybe he had been wrong about Silent Wind. Maybe she had changed during the past five years.

Before he could give the matter too much thought, a visitor arrived. Swift Buck glanced accusingly at Silent Wind when Mesa asked permission to enter. Silent Wind smiled back at him.

CHAPTER TWENTY-TWO

Rachel found Swift Buck's obvious unease around Mesa amusing. He would barely look the young woman in the eye and he spoke little to her. It made for an awkward situation, since Rachel knew that Mesa did not care for her. Still, she tried to be cordial.

"Would you care for something to eat?" Rachel asked the silent young woman.

Mesa shrugged. "If you have not poisoned the food, I might have a bowl."

Rachel filled a bowl with stew and placed it before Mesa. She waited until the young woman took a bite before she said, "If I had poisoned the food, I would not tell you."

Mesa's chewing ceased, and Swift Buck's mouth turned up at the corners.

"She is insolent for a captive," Mesa said to Swift Buck. "You should beat her."

"She should be punished," he agreed; then his gaze pinned Rachel and heat flared in his dark eyes. "I will think of something."

A small shiver raced up Rachel's back. Was it fear or anticipation?

Rachel rose and retrieved the doll Mesa had brought earlier. She had wrapped the gift in some old cloth so Amoke would not see it. She handed the bundle to Mesa. "I know you would want to give Amoke the doll."

Mesa blinked at her in surprise, then took the bundle from her. Rachel reclaimed her seat, waiting for Swift Buck and Mesa to finish so she herself could eat.

"Eat," Swift Buck allowed, then turned to Mesa. "What have you brought for Amoke?"

Unwrapping the bundle, the young woman showed him the doll. "It belonged to Amoke's mother. I thought Amoke should have it.".

Swift Buck took the doll and held it gently, staring down at the child's toy. "It must be hard for you to part with it."

Mesa straightened, thrusting out her breasts. "I am not a child."

He glanced up and smiled at her. "I did not mean

for you to think I thought so. I only meant that I know you have little left from those of your family who are gone."

"Oh." Mesa tossed her braids. "That is true. But now you and Amoke are my family."

Curious as to what Swift Buck would say to the girl's bold move, Rachel barely touched her food.

"That is true," Swift Buck agreed. "You are Amoke's only aunt, and you are like a little sister to me."

Mesa frowned. Then she smiled, rather slyly. "The same as Silent Wind was once like a little sister to you?"

Rachel's eyes darted between the two of them.

"No," he stated simply. "Silent Wind is not of my blood."

"Neither am I," Mesa challenged.

"Silent Wind is . . ." Swift Buck stopped, obviously having trouble coming up with a suitable term for her.

"Your whore," Mesa provided unkindly.

Gripping her bowl, Rachel felt tempted to throw the contents in the girl's face. She was no longer amused by the exchange.

"No," Swift Buck said softly. He handed the doll back to Mesa. "Silent Wind is my woman. You are still a little girl in my eyes. I will always see you that way. To let you believe otherwise would be wrong."

Suddenly Mesa clutched the doll to her chest as if she were indeed a child. Rachel knew that a blush had exploded in her own cheeks because she felt the heat in her face. Swift Buck had, in a way, managed to insult both of them.

Mesa shoved the doll back at him. "You give Amoke my gift. I must go."

He refused to take the doll. "Mesa, you should give her the doll. It is yours to give," he insisted.

Rachel could see that the girl was now clearly uncomfortable in their company. Despite her anger at Mesa, she said, "I need to go outside for privacy. I know you do not trust me and would wish to make certain that I do not stray too far." She looked at Swift Buck meaningfully.

"I will get Amoke," he sighed.

"No," she insisted. "Mesa can stay here with Amoke. It will be a chance for her to give Amoke her gift."

His dark brows shot up in sudden understanding "Would you stay with Amoke?" he asked Mesa.

She nodded. Rachel was surprised when the girl grudgingly cast her a grateful glance.

Rachel and Swift Buck left the tepee and walked toward the stream that ran alongside the camp. The night chill made her shiver, but it was nice to be out in the moonlight, to smell the strong scent of pine and see the dark sky dotted with thousands of stars overhead.

"It was considerate," he said. "What you did for Mesa, even though—"

"She called me a whore?" Rachel provided. "It was only a little more insulting than when you corrected her and told her I was not your whore but your woman."

He suddenly stopped and pulled her around to face him. "You *are* my woman."

"I am your captive," she argued.

He smiled.

Rachel wanted to bite her tongue. He had gotten her to refer to herself as his captive even though she had refused to do so ever since her capture.

"Very clever," she muttered; then she tried to move around him. He blocked her path.

"I thank you for the work that you did to make my lodge comfortable."

Flustered that he'd thanked her, she didn't know what to say. His thoughtfulness was more in line with the old Swift Buck she had known and not the changed one.

"I wanted to be certain that Amoke has a good place to live." Now, why had she said that? She had also wanted Swift Buck to be proud of his new home.

"You do much for her," he said. "Maybe more than you should."

"But you said that it is my duty to care for her," Rachel reminded him.

"It is not your duty to feel too deeply for her," he countered. "It will make leaving her harder for you."

Her heart lurched—partly due to the thought of leaving Amoke, partly to the possibility of being released. "Will I be leaving?" she asked. "And when?"

He shook his head. "I do not know. Gray Wolf and two others scouted yesterday. The soldiers have not left. They still hunt for us."

She was surprised that he divulged as much to her, but not surprised by the information itself. "I told you that as long as you hold me prisoner, Franklin will not stop looking. Now you've made him more determined by killing one of his men."

"I had no choice," he said. "The man would have shot me, or you; maybe Amoke would have been the victim of his bullets. Survival is not easy, nor are the choices we are forced to make to maintain it."

Rachel hadn't forgotten that she had been the cause of a man's death. The guard was crude and disgusting, but he was a man all the same, and it was not her place to decide if he lived or died. That was the place of the Great Spirit. The night chill crept into her bones, and she turned from Swift Buck, rubbing her arms to restore warmth.

"I hate war," she said. "I hate the violence of it, and the innocents who are trapped in the middle. Why doesn't Gray Wolf order the Mescaleros to flee these mountains? It's not safe here now for The People."

His hands suddenly replaced hers, rubbing her arms and sparking far more heat than her own had done. "There comes a time when a man must stand

and fight for his beliefs, for his way of life. The People are tired of running. They are tired of hiding. Like the reservation, it is no life at all. There is more honor in fighting, in dying, than in becoming a slave to the white man's ways."

She couldn't bear the thought of more Mescaleros being slaughtered at the hands of the soldiers, and at the same time, she knew that the Apaches would be just as merciless when dealing with the soldiers. She had come to New Mexico to help The People, never imagining that she would be caught in the middle of a war. Or that she might be the spark that ignited the killing all over again. She suddenly felt very alone, trapped between two worlds.

"Do you find this man, this pale leader of the fort who searches for you, more honorable than you find me?"

In the moonlight, she turned to look at him. She studied his handsome features, searching for the proud yet gentle warrior she once knew. But he was no longer gentle. These were not gentle times. Swift Buck fought for his people, for his way of life.

Franklin's motivations were much less noble. The captain fought simply to control. He fought because it was his job. He fought because these people were only wild mustangs to him—animals he must destroy because in his mind they were bothersome and served no purpose.

"No," she whispered.

His head bent, and his lips moved closer to hers. "If you were forced to choose between us, would you choose him?"

The intensity of his eyes staring into hers demanded an honest answer. "No."

If he had smiled as if he'd won a victory, or if he had looked smug about the answers he'd managed to win from her, she would have protested when his mouth brushed hers lightly, like the soft touch of a feather dropping from the sky. She closed her eyes, desperately needing gentleness in the harsh reality she'd been forced to live in.

She did not protest when he pulled her closer. She needed his warmth against the cold that penetrated not only her body but also her heart. He kissed her eyes, her cheeks, but when his mouth returned to hers, he kissed her with less tenderness. He kissed her like a man kissed a woman. She opened to his insistent probing, her body warming when his tongue caressed hers, teasing her until she answered the challenge.

Her arms encircled his neck. Something uncurled inside her. Something that had been sleeping. Again and again their mouths parted and found each other again. Their warm breaths steamed on the cold mountain air. He teased her relentlessly, nipping at her bottom lip, then sucking it gently into his mouth. She clasped the sides of his face to keep him still, and again their mouths joined. His hands slid down her back, he pressed her hips against his, and she felt his blatant desire for her. She pressed back. He groaned and the next moment she had a sturdy tree at her back, the rough bark scratching her skin. She did not care.

His mouth was everywhere—on her lips, on her neck. He cupped her breasts through her sturdy doeskin dress, squeezing her gently. She wanted to feel his hands holding her without the dress between them. His head bent, and then his teeth nipped at her nipples through the soft material, making them harden with anticipation.

He moved back up, capturing her mouth again, and then he slid his hand down and lifted her leg, wedging himself into a position that allowed the part of him so totally male against the place that made her a woman. He did not relinquish her lips, and the slow, steady stroke of his tongue inside her mouth matched the movement of his hips against hers. Warm, moist heat flooded her lower regions. She ached and burned for more than the teasing friction he caused, muted by the cruel covering of their clothing.

She moaned her frustration and pressed harder against him. His breath exploded in a muffled Apache curse; then he pulled away. He took her hand and nearly dragged her toward his lodge. But he didn't have to drag her; Rachel found herself hurrying behind him, her mind focused only upon one thing. More. She wanted more.

Both of them were breathing hard by the time

they reached the newly constructed tepee, and Swift Buck pulled her inside. The cooking fire had banked and spread only a soft glow around the tepee's small interior. He pulled her to the soft hides spread on the floor. It was natural for both of them to first search for Amoke.

They made out her small form, sleeping peacefully, her new doll clutched in her arms. Rachel breathed a small sigh of relief along with Swift Buck. Then her eyes snagged a less appealing sight. Amoke was not alone. Mesa slept peacefully beside her.

Swift Buck muttered another Apache curse.

CHAPTER TWENTY-THREE

Rachel did not have to like Mesa, but she did feel grateful for her unwanted intrusion into Swift Buck's life. What had Rachel been thinking the other night? How had she come so close to surrendering to Swift Buck? She might have, but would never know, because Mesa's presence had brought her to her senses before Swift Buck could tempt her further into the flame.

He was not happy about his new living arrangements. Mesa had informed them the next morning that she would live with Swift Buck and Amoke. They were her only family left, and it was his duty as her brother-in-law to care for her.

Only one person besides Swift Buck seemed less pleased about Mesa's decision. Blue Feather. Rachel felt sorry for the young man. He clearly loved Mesa, but she could not see beyond her own childish obsession to have what had clearly been denied to her: her dead sister's husband.

Swift Buck could not refuse to do his duty to Mesa or he would insult not only her but also the ways of his people. Rachel supposed it was just as well that Mesa had come to live with them. Her presence had put a damper on the dangerous feelings that had sprung suddenly to life inside Rachel. But then, she supposed those feelings were not so sudden. She had acknowledged them long ago; she had just never acted upon them.

"Gather more wood," Mesa demanded, nodding toward the small bundle in Rachel's arms. "That is not enough. I like a nice fire each night to keep me warm."

Fighting the urge to growl at the young woman, Rachel walked about picking up more firewood. Mesa, it seemed, counted Rachel as her slave as well. Worse, Mesa had taken over Rachel's duty of caring for Amoke and tried to keep them apart as much as possible. Rachel could stand the cold treatment she received from all the women of the band except Jageitci, who was still nice to her, but she cold not stand being kept away from Amoke. She had fallen in love with the little girl.

Swift Buck was in another meeting with the Mescalero men, no doubt plotting what they would do about the soldiers and about the Apaches still trapped on the reservation. He didn't know that Mesa bossed Rachel around and had taken over the task of watching Amoke. Rachel glanced longingly now at Swift Buck's child, playing next to the water as Mesa sat beside her.

"Gather more," Mesa ordered, her voice harsh, and the women working around Rachel snickered. "I do not have a man's arms to keep me warm at night. But then, I am no man's whore," she added, bringing more snickers from the women.

"But you would like to be," Rachel muttered beneath her breath. Unfortunately, the women heard her remark and they laughed out loud. Mesa was on her feet in an instant.

"What did you say?" she demanded.

Rachel continued her work. "Maybe you should turn your eyes elsewhere for a husband," she suggested. "Blue Feather would not mind keeping you warm at night."

"Blue Feather is a boy," Mesa scoffed. "When I go to my joining mat, I want a man, and one who knows what he is doing."

The women erupted into wild calls over her daring remark. Rachel thought they were all quite enjoying themselves. Since she was not chastised for her bad behavior, Mesa grew bolder. She marched to where Rachel stood.

"You know that when Swift Buck joined with the one we used to call White Dove, he came to live in my family's lodge as is the custom. He may not have given the one we called White Dove his heart, but he gave her plenty to moan about and cry out about late in the night beneath their robes."

Mesa wanted to make her jealous, and since she could not do so by bragging that Swift Buck had an interest in her as a woman, she resorted to low tactics. Even the other woman frowned their disapproval over Mesa's bad manners.

"It is a shame your family is gone," Rachel said. "You are a spoiled child who could still use their discipline."

Acting very much like what she'd been accused of being, Mesa struck her. Rachel stumbled back from the blow, dropping her bundle of firewood. She tasted blood in the corner of her mouth.

"You will not speak to me that way! You are nothing here! Just like all of your kind, you think you are better than us!"

The enraged girl lifted her hand as if to strike again, but Rachel wasn't going to stand still for it. She started to warn Mesa that she would fight back, but her gaze strayed past Mesa and what she saw made her heart lurch in sudden panic. She did not see Amoke.

Mesa charged her. Rachel sidestepped the girl and raced to the water's edge. "Amoke!" she called, glancing around frantically. "Amoke!" she called louder.

The other women rushed to her side. All started calling for the child.

"There!" Mesa screamed.

Rachel stared where the other woman pointed and saw a tiny dark head bobbing in the water as the current carried her away. Rachel jumped into the water. Its icy fingers took her breath away, but she simply gasped for air and swam to where she would also be pulled into the current.

Rachel used the fast-moving water to swim with all her strength. She was terrified, terrified for Amoke. The icy water was dangerous enough, but Amoke was too young to know how to swim. From the side of the stream she heard women screaming, women urging her on as they raced beside the water.

Closer now, she saw the tiny dark head bob, even heard Amoke crying and coughing. Rachel felt a burst of strength and pushed onward, her arms starting to shake with the strain. She finally reached Amoke and grabbed her close. The child threw her arms around her neck. That was when Rachel realized that the current was too strong for her to escape it—not with Amoke clinging to her. She glanced around, searching for a rock, a tree, anything ahead in their path she could grab hold of.

She saw nothing. Nothing but a thick tree that had fallen and might serve as a bridge to cross the rushing stream. But the branch was too high for her to grab. A figure suddenly appeared ahead on top of the tree bridge. She almost cried with relief. It was Swift Buck. He had a rope that he quickly tied around his waist, then secured to the thick branch he stood upon.

When Rachel and Amoke passed by him beneath the bridge, she thought for an instant that he had decided not to risk his life to save her and Amoke, but she should have known him better. He waited until they passed beneath, then jumped. He almost landed on top of them. His strong arms encircled them both. The rope was not long, and soon they came to a jarring halt.

She looked behind them and saw Blue Feather and Gray Wolf atop the branch. They held the rope and were pulling them back. Arms reached out, and Rachel handed Amoke up. Jageitci had climbed onto the branch and took the child from her husband, wrapping a blanket around her. Swift Buck lifted Rachel next, and Blue Feather's strong hands clasped her arms and hauled her up. Her legs were so weak that she had to crawl along the branch to reach the bank, but she did, spurred by the sight of Jageitci hurrying back toward camp with her precious bundle.

Wanting to be sure that Swift Buck had made it from the water, Rachel glanced over her shoulder. He rushed toward her. He stopped, dripping wet. "Are you all right?"

At her nod, he continued on, racing after Jageitci. It seemed everyone raced away while Rachel struggled to pull air into her lungs and to rise on still shaking legs. Someone reached and helped her up.

She was surprised to see Mesa, tears coursing down her cheeks. She put Rachel's arm around her neck, and together they ran after the others.

"Here, here!" she heard Stone Woman shout. "I have already started my cooking fire. My lodge will be warm."

Swift Buck had caught up with Jageitci, and now he carried Amoke. He followed the woman into her tepee. Others were gathered around but hung back. Rachel had caught her breath and let go of Mesa. Both of them raced ahead, and neither asked for permission to enter Stone Woman's lodge.

Swift Buck had placed Amoke next to the fire. His daughter's little lips were blue and trembling. He hurriedly peeled off her wet clothing and began to briskly rub her arms and legs. Rachel knelt beside him and helped. Mesa started crying again, soon joined by Amoke, who Rachel knew cried because the circulation had returned to her little limbs and they tingled painfully.

As they worked, someone draped a blanket over Swift Buck's broad shoulders. Rachel had trouble keeping her teeth from chattering uncontrollably. To her surprise, a blanket was also draped around her. She didn't have time to glance up and see who had thought her worthy enough to receive such consideration.

Soon Amoke's lips returned to a healthy color and her protests grew louder. Her skin was now pink and warm. Rachel considered that a good sign.

She worked extra long on the girl's little feet, having seen too often the ugly results of frostbite.

Swift Buck wrapped Amoke in a dry blanket and picked her up. He left the tepee with her. Rachel followed, as did Mesa, she noted. Once inside Swift Buck's lodge, Rachel was relieved to see that someone had come in and started a fire. It was warm now and she longed to get out of her wet clothes.

Jageitci entered with a pot. "I have warm soup," she said, placing the pot over the fire. "You should get some down her," she instructed Swift Buck; then she glanced at Rachel. "And you should have some, too. Get out of those wet things now before you catch something bad."

Teeth still chattering, Rachel nodded. She'd been careful to be modest beneath Swift Buck's roof. Even though he made her sleep next to him each night, she always kept her dress on. She knew he was too concerned right now over Amoke to care whether she stripped in his presence or not. She did so as quickly as she could, then grabbed a blanket and wrapped it around her before joining him next to the fire.

Gently he spooned warm soup into Amoke's little mouth. She ate, but her eyes grew heavy and soon she refused the food, drifting off to sleep. Swift Buck continued to hold her, staring down as if looking for any sign that all was not normal. When he seemed satisfied, he laid his child next to him. He sighed and then looked up at Rachel. She had never seen him look so angry.

"How could you let this happen?" he demanded, but he kept his tone soft. "Your duty was to watch over her! A duty you said would be a pleasure! A duty I trusted you with because I thought you had grown to love her!"

Startled by his accusations, she didn't know what to say. She felt crushed that he would believe for one moment that she didn't love Amoke, that she wouldn't risk her own life for his daughter.

"Do not blame her," Mesa spoke up softly. Rachel had forgotten her presence.

Both she and Swift Buck glanced at the girl, who still had streaks of tears coating her cheeks.

"It was my fault," the girl continued. "I took the duty away from Silent Wind because I knew it would hurt her not to be near Amoke. The hate inside of me has caused this horrible thing to happen. My own bitterness and jealousy has led to almost killing my niece." Her voice caught, and for a moment she could not continue. Then she gathered herself and glanced back up at Swift Buck.

"I hit Silent Wind today. I struck out in anger over what her people have done to ours, and I was so wrapped up in my hate that I was not watching Amoke near the water. But then when Silent Wind jumped into the water to save Amoke, when she risked her own life, I knew I was wrong about her. She is not the same as those who killed all of my family. And you are right, Swift Buck. I am still a child. Only a child would behave the way I have done, and I am deeply ashamed."

"You should be," he said, and his voice was neither kind nor gentle. "Leave us," he ordered. "Now I must beg Silent Wind to forgive my own hateful words."

The girl quickly rose and, with a sob, left the tepee.

Swift Buck glanced after her, then sighed, as if he was sorry for his harsh dismissal of her. It took a moment for his dark eyes to meet Rachel's.

"Tell me what to say. Tell me how to erase my hurtful words. You . . ." He paused, catching a breath. He bowed his head and closed his eyes tight for a moment, then glanced back up at her. "You saved my daughter's life. What can I give you that will ever be equal to the gift of one who is like the sun to me in this dark world?"

Her eyes misted with tears at the depth of his emotion. She had thought he couldn't love, but she was wrong. She knew what she should ask for— her freedom. But she could not make herself say the words. In her heart, she wasn't certain she wanted to be free of him.

"Mesa," she answered. "What I ask is that you go and ask her to return. You and Amoke are the only family she has left. No one knows better than I what it is like to have no one want you."

* * *

No one want her? He had wanted her forever, it seemed. Swift Buck felt a deep shame that he had treated this woman the way he had since she had come back to his people. In his heart, he now wondered if all of his resentment toward her had been because she had not felt about him the way he had felt about her. Her skin was white, but today, she had proven that her heart was the same color as his. She *could* love; she *did* love. She loved Amoke. Should he feel bitterness toward her simply because she could not love him?

He reached out and gently touched the split corner of her mouth. Tomorrow he would tell Gray Wolf about a decision he had reached. He must let Silent Wind go. This was not her war, and he had dragged her into it. She should not suffer for the sins of her brother. She had made a decision five years ago, and just because it was a choice Swift Buck did not like, that did not mean her choice had been wrong.

"I will go and get Mesa," he said. He rose and turned away from Silent Wind. His pride had cost him much throughout his life. He turned back. She was staring after him, and the look in her eyes was soft.

"Forgive me," he said.

CHAPTER TWENTY-FOUR

He had come back to her, her gentle warrior. Rachel had seen that last night when he had asked for her forgiveness. She had seen it when he displayed the depth of his love for his daughter. This man was the one she remembered. The one she had dreamed of—the one she had fled from five years ago because of her confused feelings. He was also the man she had thought was forever forbidden to her. She had believed herself unworthy of him— and maybe she was, but she was still happy to see him again after all this time.

Rachel hummed to herself as she and Mesa worked on a new dress for Amoke. A short distance away, she saw Swift Buck talking to Gray Wolf. She wondered what word they had of the soldiers. She knew scouts went out weekly to spy on Franklin's men.

"Do you think Blue Feather is handsome?" Mesa asked, distracting her.

Rachel smiled. "I think he is very handsome."

Mesa pursed her lips. "I will probably join with him. Someday," she added. "When I feel that I am a woman."

"He will be lucky to have you."

Mesa nodded. "Yes, he will be."

They both burst out laughing. Their laughter turned heads in their direction, but no one frowned at them. Instead, The People smiled and went about their duties. Rachel's actions the day before had raised her status considerably among the Mescaleros.

And something had also changed between Rachel and Swift Buck. When Swift Buck had left to bring Mesa back, Rachel had lifted Amoke and carried her to her own bed. She had held the girl's little body close, sharing her heat with Amoke until she drifted to sleep. This morning, Rachel had awoken with Swift Buck curled around the both of them. It had felt right this time—the three of them together.

The sound of raised voices turned her head once again toward Swift Buck and Gray Wolf. They were clearly arguing. Curious, Rachel asked Mesa to look after Amoke, who sat playing with her doll. Rachel rose and made a pretense of gathering wood, moving ever closer to the men in hopes of overhearing their conversation.

"We cannot set her free," she heard Gray Wolf say. "The soldiers are not far from our camp, and we may have need of Silent Wind as a hostage. You told me that the leader does not know she was once one of us."

"We do not need a woman to hide behind," Swift Buck said. "Silent Wind does not belong here. She wants to go back to her world. I owe her this for saving my daughter."

"You would risk the lives of all for her," Gray Wolf accused. "What if she tells them how to find our camp? What if she leads them to us?"

"She would not do that," Swift Buck defended. "She does not want to see war continue between her people and ours. She has said this to me many times."

"She may not want war, but maybe she would like to see us all confined to the reservation so that there is no more war. And you said yourself 'her' people. How can we trust her to go against the whites by keeping silent about us?"

Swift Buck drew a deep breath and shook his head. "It is not right to keep her here. She would not betray us. I know this about her. She could have betrayed me many times while we hid from the soldiers, but she did not. She went against them to bring Amoke back to me when the soldiers took Silent Wind and my daughter to their camp. We will wage war upon the soldiers anyway. What difference does it make if we let Silent Wind leave?"

"Because we need to surprise them," Gray Wolf answered. "So many of them, so few of us. You know our plan—to surprise them and attack when they are still only looking for one Apache, a white woman, and a child. A surprise ambush will be our only hope of defeating them. Of killing all of them so they bother us no more. Then, with half of their men gone, we will next wage war upon the reservation. We will kill all of the soldiers there, and our people will be free."

Rachel had heard enough. Her stomach churned at the thought of a handful of Apaches going up against a regiment of soldiers. They would be slaughtered. All the talk of war and killing made her feel physically ill. She hurried back to where Mesa and Amoke sat in the tepee.

"What is wrong?" Mesa asked. "Your face is whiter than normal."

"Nothing," Rachel lied, but her hands were trembling and she saw that Mesa noticed.

"You look as if you will be sick," Mesa said, wrinkling her nose. Her eyes suddenly widened, and she glanced around. "Are you with child?" the girl whispered.

"No," Rachel assured her. "Swift Buck and I, we have not . . ." She let her voice trail off.

Again Mesa's eyes widened. "You have not? Why? He loves you. And I can tell that you love him. Why do you deny yourself the pleasure of becoming his? Of making him yours?"

"It is complicated," Rachel explained. "We are from two different worlds now. And we are both trapped within a war. This is no time for love."

"It is the best time," Mesa argued. "He could die tomorrow. We could all die. This time may be all the time that you are given. I know too well that in the blink of an eye everyone you love can disappear. Consider what I have said."

Rachel was already considering all that Mesa said. She had waited for so long to gain the courage to take something she wanted. She wanted Swift Buck, and if she could not have him forever, was it wrong to want him for at least one night?

"There is also the problem of privacy," Rachel said dryly.

Mesa's dark eyes sparkled, and she grinned mischievously. "All you have to do is give me a sign when you are ready, and I will make certain Amoke and I sleep elsewhere that night. But if you plan to stay, you will have to get used to making do inside a crowded tepee."

The prospect of staying had been dancing in her mind, but now Rachel knew she couldn't stay. She must come up with some plan to stop the Mescalero men from being slaughtered by the soldiers. If she found her way back to Franklin, could she convince him to leave well enough alone and return to the reservation?

And, if she escaped, maybe Swift Buck and the Mescaleros would assume she had gone to warn the soldiers of a surprise attack, and then the Apaches would abandon their plans. Of course, she would have to let Swift Buck know she had overheard his conversation with Gray Wolf—either that, or she would have to make him reveal their plans to her.

"What sort of sign will you give?"

Lost in her thoughts, Rachel was brought back to the present by Mesa's question. "I do not know," she answered. "I do not even know if I have the courage to do such a thing."

"What sort of thing?"

They both jumped; then Rachel breathed a sigh of relief to see Jageitci.

"Silent Wind wants to walk into the flame with Swift Buck."

Rachel felt her face flush, and Jageitci lifted a brow. "Swift Buck has much patience. I assumed that had already taken place between them."

"Silent Wind wants privacy," Mesa continued. "We are thinking of a sign she can give when she is ready, and I will take Amoke and go sleep elsewhere."

"You must come to my lodge," Jageitci said. "That way, Silent Wind does not have to worry where you are. A woman should have nothing on her mind but what she is doing and what is being done to her when she—

"Ssshhh," Rachel whispered, her face blazing as

she glanced around them. "This is a private matter, not to be discussed with all who happen to pass by. Besides, as I said, I am not certain if I want . . . if he will even want—"

"He will," Jageitci assured her. "All men want to do that with a woman."

"Spotted Dog did not," Mesa argued. "Remember, he was banished by our people because he liked men more than he liked women."

Rachel tried to refrain from rolling her eyes. The conversation had become ridiculous. She had reservations, but now she dared not share them with Mesa or Jageitci. They already knew far more than they should about her and Swift Buck's private relationship. There was another problem besides privacy and finding her courage: Swift Buck had never said the words that might unlock her heart and give her the courage to believe she was worthy of him.

"Silent Wind."

She jumped again. This time the voice was low and husky. She glanced up and saw Swift Buck standing over her.

"Tonight I must speak with you in private."

Considering what she and the other women had been discussing, Rachel knew her face was red again.

"I would like for Mesa and Amoke to stay with me tonight," Jageitci said, smiling broadly. "My sons enjoy playing with Amoke, and I told Mesa that I would help her sew Amoke new clothes. We can work on them tonight."

Panic suddenly engulfed Rachel.

"I thank you for your hospitality to my family," Swift Buck said. He glanced at Rachel, but she couldn't seem to find the words to respond.

"Tonight," he said to her. Then he walked away.

"Tonight," both Mesa and Jageitci whispered, grinning at her.

Tonight? Rachel feared she would be ill again.

Silent Wind looked beautiful tonight. She wore her hair loose around her shoulders. Swift Buck had not seen the dress she wore, but suspected it was one Jageitci had given to her. Her eyes were bright. Her cheeks were pink. But he sensed that she was nervous.

He was nervous as well. Swift Buck did not know how to tell her that he could not release her. He could never repay her for saving his daughter's life, but he at least thought he could give her what she most desired—her freedom. A chance to return to her own people.

"Today I asked Gray Wolf to allow you to leave," he told her. She said nothing, which surprised him. He had thought he would have to interrupt her excitement to tell her the rest. "He feels that you still may be useful as a hostage."

"I understand," she said softly. "And I thank you for asking him on my behalf."

What he would say next was difficult. "But although I cannot allow you to leave The People at this time, I can give you your freedom from me. I no longer think of you as my captive. You are free to stay elsewhere if you desire."

Rather than make her happy, his words seemed to have had the opposite effect. Her face fell. "You wish for me to stay elsewhere?"

"What I wish is of no importance, since I no longer claim you as a captive. You may now do as you wish."

Her eyes suddenly narrowed upon him. "I could always do as I wished. I never accepted the role of captive."

This was not going as he had planned. He meant to make peace with her tonight, but she seemed determined to wage war with him instead.

"Then I am only saying that I now agree with you. You are not a captive."

"And you wish for me to leave you?"

He chose his words carefully this time. "I would understand if you choose to do so. And if you would like to stay because you have grown close to Amoke and Mesa, I would understand that as well. I will not demand that you sleep next to me. You may have your own sleeping mat."

Her tempting mouth formed a frown. She lifted her chin in the manner that annoyed him. "You do not want to sleep with me?"

For a moment, he thought she was asking one

thing and he was speaking of another. He must have mistaken the look of challenge in her eyes. "I find it difficult to sleep with you," he said. "I have . . . desires."

"And you believe that I do not?"

What was this game she played? His heart began to pound loudly. The tepee seemed suddenly too warm.

She did not allow him to answer. "No, you do not. Now I remember what you said to me the day that you took me from the reservation. You said that a man wants a woman beneath his robes whose touch does not freeze him like a winter wind."

She reached out and ran her fingers down his arm. He shivered, but not because her touch felt cold.

"Does my touch disgust you?"

"No," he assured her. "I said things then, when I first saw you again, that I did not mean."

"You meant them," she argued.

He hung his head. "Yes, I did. My heart was full of hate. My pride had suffered because of you. I wanted to punish you. It was not right. I know now that I cannot make you . . . that you felt differently than I did those many years ago—that you always have. My eyes only saw what they chose to see. My ears only heard what they chose to hear. That does not make what I saw and heard true."

She lowered her gaze. "And what about what has happened between us these past weeks? What about the night by the stream, when we were both hungry for one another? Do you believe you imagined my response to you?"

That night was burned into his memory. Every night since, he had wondered what would have happened if Mesa had not been present in his tepee.

"You were not thinking clearly."

"That is not true," she said, glancing up at him again. "I only surrendered to feelings I have been fighting for many years. When I lived among The People and I became a woman, your ears did not hear a lie when I called to you in my sleep. You saw the truth in my eyes. You were not mistaken."

He was confused by her words. Always she had denied him; now suddenly she said all the words that he had waited too long to hear.

"Then why?" he demanded. "Why did you leave? Why did you not come back? Was it because my skin was not white? Was it because you did not think that I could provide for you? Why?"

She shook her head, and beneath her lowered lashes he saw a tear trace a path down her cheek. "You look for faults within yourself that kept me from you, but the fault was inside of *me*. I did not believe I was worthy of you." She glanced back up at him, her eyes swimming with tears. "I did not think I was worthy of any man. I was afraid to give my heart when it had been broken too often. Every time my brother came to our camps, I thought it would be the time that he reclaimed me, but it took so long. Every time, my heart would break again. Soon I learned to shield it. I learned to ignore the pain . . . to deny all that I felt inside."

Swift Buck had known that she had suffered over her father's abandonment, her brother's coldness toward her, but he had not known the depth of her suffering.

"You were loved among The People," he said gently. "The one who was my mother and is gone loved you like a child of her womb. How could her love not heal the pain you had suffered because of your father and your brother?"

"She was a woman, Swift Buck. I knew my own mother loved me. My pain did not stem from not being loved by my mothers, birth or adoptive. My pain stemmed from not being loved by a man. My father and my brother—they planted the idea in my head that I could not be loved by a man, that I did not deserve to be loved. If they, my own family, could not love me, how could anyone else?"

Her pain became his pain. He ached for her. "You know about your brother Cougar? You know why he acted as he did toward you?"

Silent Wind wiped the tears from her cheeks. "Yes, now I know, but for many years I did not, just as he did not know the reason that he was treated as he was by our mother. But my father . . . there is no excuse."

Before he said anything, Swift Buck also searched for answers—answers besides the obvious one, that there was no good in Hiram Brodie. The trapper had been a crude, selfish brute. But Silent Wind knew that about him, and still she blamed herself for his faults.

"There may be one," Swift Buck said. She glanced up at him, a spark of hope in her eyes that nearly broke his heart. "Maybe because he did love you so much, he gave you to people he knew would care for you better than he could. He was a trapper, Silent Wind. A man who lived more in the wilderness than he did in his home. He was always gone, setting his traps and trading his furs. That would be no life for a young daughter."

"The life Amoke has been handed is also difficult for you, and for her," she argued. "But you have not abandoned her."

He scooted closer to her. "But remember the other night? I said to you that I might send her away for a while, and in my heart it was because I thought that would be best for her. Just as you thought taking Amoke to live in your world would be best. I thought she would be too young to remember that we were apart for a while, but you have proven to me that is not so, and now I am thankful that you did not let me send her away. Not even for a short time."

Silent Wind ran a hand through her hair. "Do you really believe that my father only gave me away because he thought it was best—because he hoped that I might have a better life than what he could give me?"

Swift Buck did not know. Brodie had not been an honorable man; still, he had been Silent Wind's father. She needed to find something good about the man, so that she could take pride in herself. He bent close to her.

"Your brother has said to me many times throughout the years that, when your father gave you to The People, it was the kindest thing he could have done for you."

She stared into his eyes for a moment. "That is true. It *was* the kindest thing he ever did for me. The People accepted me when my own would not. I might not have come to know you if I had stayed up on the mountain with my father and my brother. He gave me a gift, even if he did not know it."

Swift Buck cupped her face in his hands. "You must let it go, Silent Wind. The hurt. The hate. The shame. It is time for you to put those bad memories in your past where they belong. You cannot move forward until you do. I know that what I ask of you is difficult, but I believe that to do this, you must do the most difficult thing you may face. You must forgive your father."

Suddenly she sucked in a deep breath. Her eyes widened. "Before the one we called Laughing Stream left this world, she said to me, 'Forgive him.' I thought she meant you, but now I understand that she did not. She meant him, my father.

She knew that unless I could forgive him, the anger that binds my heart would never allow me to give it wholly to anyone."

He had resented her for being the last to speak to his mother, but now he understood that Silent Wind had needed her last words more than he had.

"Can you?" he asked. "Can you forgive him?"

CHAPTER TWENTY-FIVE

Rachel thought hard about his question. Her father had had a sickness—an obsession with a woman who could not love him. She had read the story of her mother and Hiram Brodie in her mother's diary. Could a man with such a sickness in his head be judged fairly? Her father had been like a wounded animal, growling and snapping because he was in pain but could not heal himself. Who knew, maybe in one lucid moment of his insanity, he had thought about what was best for his daughter. Maybe he had known he would hurt her physically, as he had done to her half-brother Clay.

She tried to imagine his face, worn and weathered by the harsh elements in which he lived, his wild red hair and amber-colored eyes. There had been sadness there, she recalled. Maybe it was sadness for all of his sins against those he should have loved most. It was hard for her to feel sorry for the man. It was harder for her to forgive him for all the wrongs committed against her family. Clay had been able to forgive their mother for her cold treatment of him. Maybe Rachel could find it in her heart to do the same for her father.

"Yes," she finally answered. "I forgive him."

Just saying the words made her feel as if a weight had been lifted from her shoulders. What good had it done her to carry the hurt and the hate around inside her for so long? It had changed nothing—nothing but her own chances of finding her place, and her happiness. Happiness she deserved, Rachel realized. When she looked into Swift Buck's eyes, his gentle expression soothed her heart. So much time had been wasted for them. She would not waste this night. But first, she needed to hear him say what she had seen in his eyes so long ago.

"And what about you?" she whispered. "Can you forgive me?"

"For what?" he asked.

"For the pain I have caused you. For being white. For being part of a race that has devastated your people, and who even now will continue to try to take your way of life from you. Can you forgive me for that?"

He glanced away from her, and she knew that,

like her, he still fought his ghosts, the pain and the hatred in his heart.

"For any pain that you have caused me, you have made up for a hundred times by saving my daughter's life. I understand now why you could not show me your feelings. I understand why you were afraid to give your heart, and you cannot ask for forgiveness when the fault did not lie within you. But you must understand that I will fight for my people, for my daughter, for my way of life. It is one issue that will separate us—but I will not allow the fact that your skin is white and mine is not to stand between us again.

"When I first saw you as a woman, when I first knew that my feelings for you were not those of a brother toward a sister, I did not see that your skin was white. I saw you as one of us, and now I see you that way again. You have shown me that I cannot hate all whites. Somewhere among them, there are those like you, who do not wish for war, who are sickened by the slaughter of our people. Who want to help, even if they do not know how. When a man can fight with words and be heard, it is better. But when he cannot be heard, he must fight with his fists, with his heart."

She understood. Even if she hated war and violence, she understood that sometimes there was no other way. Rachel hoped that she could change the outcome of this particular war, if only for a little while. But she did not want to think of war, and killing tonight.

"I need something from you," she said.

"You know you can ask for anything within my power to grant you."

Could she? Rachel gathered her courage. "I need for you to say the words to me."

His dark brows drew together. "What words?"

"The words in your heart. The words you dared not speak to me when you thought that your feelings were wrong. The words your eyes have spoken but your lips have not."

To her surprise, his face darkened. She had rarely seen a grown man blush. "You know what is in my heart. All know what is in my heart for you."

"But I need to hear the words," she insisted.

He glanced away and ran a hand through his hair. She thought he might refuse her. She wasn't sure she would blame him if he did. She knew that he had been the brunt of many jokes among the Mescaleros for caring for her as he had. She knew that her refusal to face her own fears had hurt him. She knew that he had counted her actions as a rejection of him. Maybe she asked too much and gave too little. She reached out and pulled his face around to look at her.

"Whether it is right or wrong, whether it is too late for us, know that I love you," she said. "Know that I have loved you for a very long time."

His dark eyes were intense as he stared into hers,

as if he were trying to make certain she spoke words that were true, and not simply words that she thought he wanted to hear.

"I should not have to speak words that I have proven to you a hundred times over, but if you must hear them, then I will." Again he cupped her face gently. "I love you. I have loved you even when the inside of me said I should not. I have loved you when you gave me no reason to, and I love you still, now that you have. I loved you even when my heart should have belonged to someone else. I will *always love you.*"

She had not known the power of words until he spoke what she needed most to hear. They filled her heart with joy. They made her tremble. They chopped away the vine that had held her heart prisoner for so long. She could give herself now. She could give her whole heart.

"I ask one other thing of you," she said.

He lifted a brow.

"The day I saved Amoke's life you asked me what you could give me to repay you. You know, in truth there is no price I would place upon Amoke's life. You know that I love her as if she were my own. I did not ask for my freedom, but asked you to bring Mesa back to your lodge so that she would not have to be alone. Now I ask for only one thing more from you."

As he continued to stare at her, she grappled with her courage. It was harder to be brave than she imagined. She drew a deep breath. "I ask that for one night, you become my captive."

His brows rose higher. "Your captive?"

She nodded because she didn't trust her shaky voice.

He rubbed the back of his neck as if considering. "What would you have me do? Cook for you? Would you send me to the stream to fill the skins? Would—"

To halt his questions, she placed her fingers over his lips. "Do you agree?"

Removing her hand from his mouth, he answered, "If it pleases you, yes. I am your captive for the night. What do you ask of me?"

Her heart hammering in her chest, she rose. "Stand."

When he obeyed, she stared up into his eyes. "Now," she breathed. "Undress me."

Swift Buck thought he hadn't heard her correctly . . . maybe he hadn't understood what she meant for him to do. His heart lurched inside his chest.

"What . . . ?" He paused to clear the huskiness from his voice. "What did you ask?"

Rather than answer immediately, she reached out and ran her fingertip down his chest. Again he shuddered.

"I told you to undress me."

His fingers itched to comply, and hurriedly before she regained her senses. Then a thought occurred to him as to why she would ask him to undress her. "To punish me for the way I have treated you, do you plan to torture me?"

She smiled as if the prospect pleased her. "I have changed my mind," she said then.

Balling his fists at his sides, he tried to ignore the disappointment spreading through him. "Too late. You have already tortured me. But you are right, now is not the time for . . . for whatever you have in your mind."

Her smile grew. "I meant that I have changed my mind about having you undress me. Instead, I would like for you to stand very still while *I* undress *you*."

Again his heart did strange things. Silent Wind's hand reached for the belt holding his breechclout into place. His fingers closed over hers. "Silent Wind. What are you doing? What do you want from me?"

"I thought it was obvious."

For a maiden, she acted very brave. Swift Buck did not mind her aggression. In fact, it excited him, but he wanted to make certain that she wanted what he thought she wanted. "I need to hear you speak the words," he said.

Although he felt her hands tremble, they ran up his chest and she placed her arms around his neck, pulling his face down to hers.

"Walk into the flame with me," she whispered. "You are mine. You have always been mine . . . and I have always been yours. It is time."

Fire rushed to the already hardened member between his legs. He had wanted her for so long, had dreamed of having her, of belonging to her, and her to him . . . but she was wrong. The time for them was not yet right.

"Know that I want you more than I have ever wanted anything," he said, their lips only a breath apart. "But it is not time. Soon we will make war on the soldiers. Many Rivers has not returned and brought others with him, so we must now take matters into our own hands. We will tell our women and children to hide before we strike. If I do not return, I want you to take Amoke and raise her as your own."

Silent Wind's beautiful face drained of color. "But you said she did not belong in my world."

"She will not be raised on one of those reservations. Promise me this."

Silent Wind's lashes drifted downward. "When? When will you make war on the soldiers."

Swift Buck ran his thumb over her full lips. "In a week's time. The soldiers draw closer to our camp. Already they are five miles to the north. But we must give our women and children time to move from this area, to flee. The soldiers will know that we have a camp and will seek to destroy it. You must go into hiding with our women, Silent Wind. If I do not return, take Amoke and go. Return to the reservation and do what you can for our people; then you must take Amoke away from there. Do you promise to do this thing for me? For her?"

She nodded, but she would not look at him. He trusted her to keep her word. He tried to move away, but her arms tightened around his neck, and she looked up at him, tears shimmering in the blue pools of her eyes.

"You said that our time is not right, but then you speak of war and death. What if we never have another chance? Would you deny me what I ask of you? Would you deny me what I might never again have the chance to experience with you?"

"We should be joined," he told her. "But our future is uncertain. I would not disrespect you by taking you as if you were only a woman I wished to enjoy for one night."

Her arms tightened around his neck when he tried to pull away from her. The longer she stood so close, looked up at him with desire in her eyes, the harder it was for him to resist.

"I know your heart," she said. "You have spoken it to me. You know mine. Our destinies were joined long ago. If tomorrow our worlds must collide, why is it wrong to take what we can from each other tonight?"

She was right. To think that he might never hold her, never love her in all ways, was much worse than the threat of death and an uncertain future. He would savor her tonight, while he still had the chance. Surrendering, he lowered his lips to hers.

CHAPTER TWENTY-SIX

Rachel was relieved that he had told her about the planned attack, and that she didn't have to be deceitful to get the information from him. But then, she did plan to deceive him . . . tomorrow.

Thoughts of tomorrow quickly faded beneath his mouth's hungry demands. As the fire of passion leapt to life between them, and their love for one another had been revealed with words, she understood what it truly meant to walk into the flame. Finally, they came together with nothing else between them—only her heart and his heart, committed to one another. She felt no fear of giving herself, only joy that time had granted them this moment. She would not waste it, nor let the past come between them again.

Swift Buck gently untied the straps that held her dress in place. He peeled the garment from her skin, kissing each inch of flesh he exposed. He worshiped her breasts. His tongue laved her nipples until they hardened; then he gently suckled her, his hands moving over her flesh. His fingers found her woman's core, and he teased her with gentle strokes.

"I must make you ready for me," he said; then his finger slipped inside her.

He didn't poke or pry, but stretched her gently. He used his thumb to rub the sensitive nub hidden between the folds of her womanhood. Heat flooded her lower regions, and her thighs trembled. As he continued to stimulate her, she caught his rhythm and moved against his hand. The trembling in her thighs almost caused her knees to buckle, and he lowered her to the soft robes spread upon the ground.

He kissed her, and she moaned against his lips. His fingers were magic as they worked their spell, massaging her swollen nub until she strained against him. Her insides felt coiled, and with each steady stroke he pulled the rope tighter. All sensation centered in that once place where his fingers made love to her. She spiraled ever higher, finally bursting, shattering into tiny pieces while her nails dug into his shoulders, until at last she released a sound that sounded more animal than human.

As she floated back to earth, a languid feeling

washed over Rachel. Her arms and legs felt like limp rags tied to her body. She hadn't known, could never have guessed, that anyone could make her feel like this.

"Silent Wind," he said, and his voice sounded a long way off. "Touch me as I have touched you."

She willed her arm to lift, her hand to seek out the warmth of his body. His chest was smooth and hot beneath her fingertips. She moved lower, surprised to find that he had somehow shed his clothing without her being aware of it. She was more surprised when her hand brushed his sex. She'd known he was big, but he felt even bigger than she'd thought. She wrapped her hand around him, and his breath exploded next to her ear. Afraid she'd done something wrong, she tried to snatch her hand away, but his was on hers before she could, and he showed her how to please him.

As she had done, he moved with her movements, and his soft groans of pleasure stirred her body back to life. She thought she was getting pretty good at pleasing him with her hand when he made her stop.

"I want you," he said simply, and the next thing she knew, he had rolled on top of her.

He spread her legs with his knees and nestled his body between them. She tried not to tense, worried that what he had would not fit into what she had. But he only rubbed his sex against hers, and she relaxed. He kept rubbing and she could not stay relaxed. He was hot and slick against her, and his movements started the fire below all over again. She writhed with him and against him, and suddenly he slipped a little way inside her. She gasped. He pulled out and rubbed her until she felt that wonderful pressure building up inside her again.

"Silent Wind," he rasped, his teeth tugging at her earlobe. "I must hurt you for a moment, but the pain will go quickly, and then I will give you pleasure again."

Just the word made her tense. *Pain?* She'd heard nothing about pain. Swift Buck did not rush to bring her this pain he spoke of, but kept stroking her until her muscles relaxed again. Then suddenly he thrust into her, and deep enough that she felt a sharp, stabbing pain. She sucked in her breath; then his lips were against hers.

"I am sorry," he said, kissing her cheeks, her eyes, then her mouth. "I will not hurt you again. There is no gentle way to penetrate the barrier that made you a maiden. But now it is gone, and you are free to be a woman."

He moved deeper and she squeezed her eyes shut, expecting more pain despite his assurances. She did not experience it, though, just the feel of him filling her—and to be filled so completely was strange to her body. He moved deeper, and she wondered how she could possibly accommodate him, but somehow she seemed to be managing.

His breathing became ragged, and she felt him

trembling. "You cannot know how good you feel to me," he said. "See how we fit together? Our bodies were made for one another."

She would argue that maybe the fit was too tight, but he started to move inside her, in and out, slowly, and she could not think, much less argue. He kissed her and his tongue mimicked the penetration and withdrawal of his lower body. She tingled where they were joined together. He kept stroking her, and her muscles tightened and squeezed around him until she could not control of the answering press of her hips against his. Soon they were moving together, their bodies slick with sweat, their breathing ragged gasps for air. The tingling grew stronger, and she felt the gathering sensation his fingers had made her feel earlier.

He had not lied to her. She knew that soon, very soon, he would give her the same explosive pleasure that he had given her earlier.

Swift Buck sensed that silent Wind was close to finding release. He was glad, because he himself was about to burst. Even in his imagination, he would never have dreamed she would feel this way, hot and tight around him. There was nothing cold about her. He struggled to wait for her, pushing himself to keep up the wild rhythm they created so she could find her pleasure.

He thought he could not wait, but then he felt her tighten around him, felt her back arch and heard her low moans of release. He pumped harder into her, increasing her pleasure, drawing it out before his body betrayed him. His own release ripped through him like a thousand arrows. He thrust deep, held himself there, and called her name while his seed flowed into her. The force of his climax left him trembling. He did not want to crush her beneath his weight, so he rolled to the side and pulled her with him. She snuggled close to him, and for a while neither could speak.

"My dreams of you seem foolish now," she said. "In my innocence, I could never have imagined what it would be like to love you, to be loved by you."

He kissed her forehead. "And now that you know, what are you thinking?"

She sighed, a contented sound a man liked to hear from the woman in his arms. "I'm thinking dreams will never be enough again."

Gently he rolled her onto her back. "Because you are innocent, I will tell you that I have not yet loved you in all the ways I can and will. It will take several times of being together to show them all to you."

Her brows rose; then she smiled at him. "The night is still young."

CHAPTER TWENTY-SEVEN

Rachel stole quietly from the tepee. Morning had not yet bathed the mountains in light, and she had trouble seeing in the darkness. She would catch one of the horses that Swift Buck had taken from the reservation; otherwise, Franklin might question how she had come by a different horse. Since men were scarce, she knew where the camp's night guards were posted. Avoiding them would not be difficult.

The pull toward Jageitci's lodge nearly overpowered her. She wanted to see Amoke one last time, hold her close and tell the child that she didn't want to leave her, but for her safety, for all the Mescaleros' safety, Rachel knew she had to abandon them. Maybe she couldn't stop the war that would continue between soldiers and Apaches, but she would try to at least postpone this bloodbath.

Franklin, she hoped, still thought that he hunted only one renegade Apache, a small child, and a white woman. She prayed that she could talk him into giving up the search and returning to the fort. The soldiers would avoid an ambush by a handful of Apache warriors, and the man she loved, along with his Apache brothers, would avoid what she could only believe would be a suicide mission.

Rachel might not stop the inevitable, but maybe she could buy the Apaches more time to gather forces. Or maybe they would come to their senses and simply remain hidden in the mountains. Knowing what she did about the Apaches, she doubted that they would leave the others behind on the reservation forever. She couldn't blame them. Swift Buck knew the horrid conditions there, and Rachel knew them as well.

There was still not a simple solution to her dilemma, and Rachel had to admit that there probably would never be one. All she could do was try to help the Apaches at the moment and worry about how the situation between army and Indian played out at a later date.

Maybe Clay would know what to do. Her brother had surely found a way to win his release from a jail cell by now. Rachel had known her brother could take care of himself—otherwise she would never have left when she did. With her testimony about conditions on the reservation, maybe changes would be made . . . but Rachel doubted it. First of all, she was a woman, and men in politics seldom listened to women. In fact, most thought a woman should have no say in such matters.

The thought of returning to Washington, to the white world, was not particularly pleasing to Rachel. She once thought that she could make a place for herself there, but she had not. She loved her brother, his wife, and their children, but they had their own lives, and Rachel very much wanted her own life, too. Still, by doing what she did now, Rachel understood that there would be no coming back here for her.

Swift Buck and the others would view what she did as a betrayal. She didn't want to think about that . . . how Swift Buck would react when he found her missing, when he realized that she had run off. Would he think that what they had shared through this night had only been a ploy on her part to lower his guard so that she could run away?

That fear nearly made her physically ill. She loved him so much, and for him to think less of her, to believe that her declarations of love to him, and the sharing of their bodies, their hearts, their souls, had only been a devious trick that she had concocted to deceive him, was the worst kind of torture. But better he should hate her than she live with the torture of knowing he would be killed in an unnecessary hopeless battle.

Knowing that what she did was crucial—that it was the right thing to do—spurred her courage. Of course, she did not want to think about what might happen if she could not persuade Franklin to take his soldiers and return to the fort. She did not want to think about the possibility that he would not believe whatever story she came up with between now and the time she found his camp.

The white world would look upon her actions as traitorous. So would the Apaches. Again she was trapped in the middle. But she had made her decision, and she truly believed it was the right one, so Rachel continued down the path that would take her forever away from all the people she loved.

Swift Buck reached for Silent Wind, seeking her warmth, the soft curves of her body; he wanted her again before their privacy was interrupted. He found only an empty place beside him. He sat up, glancing around the tepee. He did not see Silent Wind. She had not started a cooking fire, and there was no evidence that she had risen to prepare a meal. Where was she?

Deciding that she had probably gone to the stream to wash their night of lovemaking from her body, or that she had gone to Jageitci's lodge to bring the rest of their family home, he threw back the heavy buffalo robes and prepared for the day. He left the tepee, his gaze searching the stream in the distance for signs of her, but he saw nothing.

Gray Wolf's lodge was the next logical place to look for her. Swift Buck stopped before the tepee entrance and called for permission to enter. Jageitci sat before her cooking fire preparing her family's— and he supposed his family's, judging by the amount of food—morning meal. Gray Wolf sat close to his wife, and Mesa and the children were still sleeping.

"I am surprised to see you here so early," Jageitci said, smiling at him. "I thought you might still be busy this morning, or sleeping because you had not had much of a chance to sleep throughout the night."

Her husband glanced at her, frowning, then glanced back up at Swift Buck. "Sit," he invited. "Share our morning meal."

Swift Buck did not want to sit. Silent Wind was not here, and a feeling of unease began to steal over him. "I am looking for Silent Wind," he admitted. "Has she been here? Have you sent her out to gather wood or bring water?"

Jageitci glanced up at him, a confused expression crossing her lovely features. "She is not inside your tepee?"

He shook his head.

"Then she must have gone to the stream to wash, or to fetch water to heat over her cooking fire so she could have a warm bath."

"Her cooking fire is not lit," he said. "I did not see her at the stream. I do not see her anywhere."

311

Mesa suddenly rose, stretched, and joined them at the cooking fire. "What is going on?" she asked. "Why is Swift Buck here when he should be busy elsewhere?"

Mesa and Jageitci shared a smile. Swift Buck would have wondered over their sly looks had he not been more worried about Silent Wind's whereabouts.

"He is looking for Silent Wind," Gray Wolf explained, and the Mescalero chief eyed the two women suspiciously.

"She might have gone for a moment of privacy," Mesa suggested. "That must be why you do not see her."

At Mesa's suggestion, Swift Buck tried to relax.

"A captive should not be allowed to roam around our camp freely," Gray Wolf scolded. "Nor should one be able to slip away from you so easily, Swift Buck."

"Silent Wind is not a captive," Mesa said. "Silent Wind is our sister, and Swift Buck is more than her captor. Besides, he was probably very tired this morning, and that is why he did not wake when she slipped outside."

Mesa and Jageitci shared another look. Both of them giggled behind their hands.

"Why do you both act strangely?" Gray Wolf demanded. "What do you know that I do not?"

Swift Buck was beginning to understand what the women knew that they should not. Silent Wind had evidently confided her plans about lovemaking to them. "I will go look again," he declared, wanting to get away from their sly looks and giggles.

"I will go with you," Gray Wolf said. The man rose and followed Swift Buck from the lodge.

Once outside, Swift Buck first went back to his own lodge to make certain that Silent Wind had not returned. She had not, but he noticed more this time than he had earlier. One of the canteens they had taken from the soldiers' horses was missing . . . that and a bridle.

The horses' tack belonged to him, since he had stolen the animals. The two saddles were still stacked in one corner—but they were heavy and would be difficult for her to carry. He did not like where his thoughts led.

He left his tepee and rejoined Gray Wolf outside. He did not want to tell the man what he suspected—he did not want to believe it himself—until he had no choice. He headed toward where the horses were corralled. On occasion his tribe allowed the animals to graze freely, but they did not have enough men to guard the pack, so corralling them at night made more sense.

There were few horses. The men could not raid or they would call attention to themselves, and they had tried to remain hidden these past two years while they waited for other bands to join them. It took him only a moment to see that one of the horses was missing—the horse that Silent Wind had ridden on their flight from the reservation.

Gray Wolf did not speak beside him. Swift Buck knew that the leader also realized the horse was gone. They stood there for a time, Swift Buck hoping the horse and Silent Wind would mysteriously appear from thin air. He was in shock that she would do this—escape him, especially after the night they had spent together, the confessions they had made to one another.

"You did not help her escape, did you?" Gray Wolf finally asked. "I know that only yesterday you asked that she be set free to return to her people."

"No," he answered, but he had to clear his throat before he could continue. "I respect your decisions as our leader. I would not go against you."

"Not even for her?" Gray Wolf pressed.

Swift Buck did not know. He might have gone against Gray Wolf if Silent Wind had begged him. But she had not begged . . . instead, she had seduced him.

"I did not go against you," he repeated.

Another short silence stretched between them.

"She does not know of our plans, does she?"

Running a hand through his hair, Swift Buck answered, "Yes. She does know. I told her last night."

The leader's face darkened. "And why did you think this information should be shared with a captive, a white woman?"

His heart began to understand that he had been deceived, tricked, made a fool of. Still, Swift Buck would not hang his head in shame. He had pride.

"I did not see her as a captive," he explained. "I did not see her as a white woman. To me, she had become Silent Wind again. And last night"—he paused, wondering if he could admit all of the ways she had tricked him—"last night she became my woman."

Gray Wolf shook his head. "No. Last night you became her fool! What do you think she plans to do now?"

Swift Buck was not certain, but there were some things he knew about her that he trusted. "She would not use the information she has against us," he said. "She would not tell the soldiers of our plans to ambush them, or of our location. She might have tricked me to escape, but she only wishes to return to her world. Silent Wind would not place us in danger."

"She already has," Gray Wolf hissed. "She has only a few hours' lead. You will go after her, and when you find her, you must silence her forever!"

Swift Buck's gaze snapped to his leader's face. "No. I will not. Do you think that my heart does not burn for revenge because she has tricked me? It does, but something else burns brighter. I love her. No matter what she has done, or will do, I will always love her."

Gray Wolf snorted. "You were always weak where she was concerned. But I do understand the consequences of loving the wrong woman," he admitted. "I will do this for you. My trust in her is not as strong as my concern for our people. I will quickly tell our people to move the camp; then, I will go after Silent Wind."

Gray Wolf started for the camp. Swift Buck did not follow. Now, more than anger churned his belly. "You will not kill her!" he called to Gray Wolf's back. "I will not let you. You will have to kill me first."

The leader stopped. He stood very straight; then his shoulders relaxed and he turned to face his longtime friend. "There are too few of us to kill one another. I will not kill Silent Wind. But I will cut out her tongue so that she cannot speak. I will blind her so that she cannot see. I will cut off her hands so that she cannot write. Then she can go back to her people and live with the crime of deceiving you—deceiving all of us."

Swift Buck received no comfort from Gray Wolf's leniency. Cut out her tongue? He enjoyed her tongue. Blind her? Her beautiful sky-colored eyes forever sightless? Cut off her hands? The hands that had touched him last night?

Once, not too long ago, his bitter heart would have whispered that she deserved this punishment for deceiving him again. For running from him again. But she had changed his heart, and deep inside he knew that he had changed hers, too. Whatever her reasons were for leaving, he knew they were for The People's sake, for his sake. And for her sake, he would defy Gray Wolf.

He would go himself and bring Silent Wind back. And whatever punishment his people demanded be given to her, he would take in her stead, as her brother Cougar had once done for his own woman. He would keep Silent Wind safe until this war between the Apaches and the soldiers had ended. Then he would set her free if she wished to go—if he was still alive to do so.

CHAPTER TWENTY-EIGHT

Rachel was not foolish enough to think the Mescaleros would not come after her. They would send someone, and in all likelihood, that someone would be Swift Buck. She must call on the Apache in her now to outsmart him, and to outdistance him. Once she reached Franklin's campsite, no one, not even Swift Buck, would dare pursue her. *He did so once,* a tiny voice inside her head reminded. Still, he had been after Amoke and not her when he had dared it the last time.

Riding bareback was not the most comfortable form of transportation, and certainly not when her body was sore from her night of lovemaking with Swift Buck, but she pushed herself and the horse relentlessly. Her old shredded petticoat and torn chemise looked horrible, but she'd worn them because Franklin would question where she'd gotten a doeskin dress. She'd wrapped a blanket around her to give her a measure of modesty when she reached the soldiers' camp.

She wondered what The People were thinking about her. Mostly, she wondered what Swift Buck was thinking.

Rachel gritted her teeth when her horse jumped over a fallen log, and she tried to keep her thoughts away from Swift Buck. Everything inside her screamed for her to turn the horse around and return to him. She could not listen to the voice of her heart now, though. Lives were at stake.

Night would soon be upon her and even then she would not stop. Apaches could go for several days without sleep, without food, without water, without even stopping to rest. If she couldn't see to guide the horse, she would walk and lead the animal.

If she did not embrace her Apache upbringing now, she stood no chance of escaping Swift Buck. He held all the advantages. He was taller, he was stronger, he was swifter, he was tougher. He knew these mountains, but then, so did she. As a young girl, she had often left their summer camps and gone alone to the cabin where her mother had died, and where her father had lived with her half-brother. She would spy on them, and sometimes she would sit beside her mother's grave.

Wolves had befriended her, and often ran alongside her as she slipped like a shadow through the woods. She was still that girl. Her white words and her white clothes could not change who she really was inside. Her determination renewed, Rachel picked up her pace before darkness slowed her progress.

Swift Buck was impressed. He thought he would have caught her by now, but she had managed to stay ahead of him, to elude him. She had become an Apache again, he realized, and could not help the smile that curled his lips. He could smile because he would catch her this day. She had forgotten to hide the hoof marks of her horse for the past day and a half, and he could tell by the tracks that she was only a short distance ahead of him. If he pushed himself, he would find her before nightfall.

He looked forward to finding her. This time, he would be the seducer. She would be frightened, not knowing what he thought, what he would do. For deceiving him, she deserved some type of punishment. He thought of all the ways he had not yet loved her, and, despite his exhaustion, his hunger, and his thirst, one need grew stronger than the rest. He rode onward, envisioning ways to torture her with his tongue, with his fingers, with all parts of his body. Soon he realized he was torturing himself more than he could ever torture her.

His thoughts turned to serious matters. Many Rivers had finally returned to the camp. He had brought fifteen warriors with him. It was not many, not enough to be certain of victory over the whites, but Swift Buck supposed it was better than nothing. During the excitement of Many Rivers's return, Swift Buck had taken a horse and escaped. Gray Wolf, he suspected, would still come after him and Silent Wind—but Swift Buck would worry about that confrontation when it happened. Now, all he must worry about was finding Silent Wind before she reached the soldiers' camp.

He did not want to have to face so many soldiers again in order to recapture her, but he would. If he had thought there was no danger there for her, he would have let her return to the reservation, where she could hide behind the wooden walls when his people attacked, but he knew she was in danger. She might say the wrong thing, do something that would make the pale leader suspicious of her. It was inevitable. And Swift Buck refused to consider what might happen to Silent Wind if the man realized she had lived among the Mescaleros, had been one of them, and how some of them hoped she would be one of them again.

Lost in his thoughts, he almost stumbled over her horse. The beast stood grazing. Swift Buck looked around for Silent Wind, expecting to see her running from him. He did not see her. A moment later he looked at the horse again. There was no bridle on the animal. He cursed. She had tricked him again. She had let the animal go, knowing he would follow the prints. He whipped his horse around and kneed the weary animal into a run. He was no longer smiling.

The cool water ran down her throat and Rachel drank, gulping loudly and uncaring that to do so was not ladylike or that she had an audience. Her feet stung from blisters, her hair was tangled, and her face was scratched and sunburned. Her clothes were filthy and ragged. She looked like an escaped captive who'd been on the run for several days, and that was exactly what she was, so she needn't feel any qualms about the concern etched on Franklin Peterson's sharp features.

"I still can't believe it," he said, his eyes wide and dazed. "I thought you must surely be dead by now."

Rachel wiped a hand across her mouth. "As you can plainly see, I am not." She realized that she sounded too calm, and tried to summon tears. "But I desperately wish to return to the fort, where I might feel safe again. Please, Franklin, forget your obsession to capture or kill this one Apache and take me back."

His gaze swept over her ragged appearance, and when his eyes met hers again, she didn't see the compassion there that she had hoped to see.

"Your attitude in the matter confuses me." He rose and began pacing inside his tent. "One would think that above all else you would want to see this savage captured. That would be more in line with your ordeal, to want him killed so that you would never have to worry about him coming after you again. Yet you plead for his life to be spared."

Her throat felt suddenly dry. "I did not plead for his life," she argued. "I only asked you to take me back to the fort. How can I feel safe here, Franklin, when the man managed to recapture me while under your very protection?"

Her reminder made his posture more erect, if that were possible since he always carried himself so straight. "Yes, I am still unclear about that night. Since Truitt was dead when we found him, there were no witnesses to explain what had happened . . . but I am wondering, Miss Morgan, why you didn't scream. Why you did not call out so my men could be alerted to the situation quicker. Not only would we have caught the savage then, but we would have spared you further humiliation at his hands."

His questions took her by surprise. Rachel hadn't thought about the fact that she hadn't screamed or called out that night. "Are you certain that I didn't?" she asked. She put a hand to her forehead and rubbed. "That night is a blur to me. I was shocked that the Apache would have the daring to steal inside your camp and take me and the child under your very noses. All I can recall is being terrified and thinking that I couldn't believe it was happening. I thought that I must surely be having a nightmare."

She glanced at him from beneath her lashes, trying to judge his reaction. Rachel hadn't missed the fact that he was back to calling her Miss Morgan rather than by her first name. Maybe Franklin wouldn't be as easy to dupe as she had thought. Perhaps some outrage was called for. She lowered her hand and narrowed her eyes at him.

"I've just realized that you are questioning me as if I have done something wrong, when in fact I am the victim. I will not take the blame for your own inadequacies, Franklin. Or the inadequacies of your men."

He pursed his lips, but he did not blush or lower his gaze in a show of shame. "Perhaps I have trouble seeing you as a victim, Miss Morgan. I have on occasion witnessed the return of a survivor of an Indian capture. It is a rare occurrence, since most white women captured are molested and killed shortly afterward. The survivors of such an ordeal, I can assure you, Miss Morgan, are totally insane. They are incapable of simple speech, much less of berating their rescuers for being incompetent. Yet, on two separate occasions you have been taken by this savage, and on both returns you seem hardly affected by the ordeal."

Hardly affected? She was very affected at the moment. Rachel had not witnessed what the captain had witnessed, and she supposed her behavior was totally unfitting. Still, to break down now and become a babbling idiot would only cast her in a more suspicious light.

"I am a strong woman," she told him. "I'm sorry

if I'm not reacting as you think I should. The savage was much more interested in escaping the soldiers and in the plight of his child than he was in me. I was a hostage to him and nothing more."

His blue eyes swept over her from tangled head to dirty feet. "I find that also difficult to believe, Miss Morgan. Maybe you have forgotten that this same savage showed an interest in you on more than one occasion at the reservation. I'm a man, Miss Morgan, and I know how a man looks at a woman he has taken an interest in. I don't believe for one moment that he held you all this time and did not take advantage of you. Therefore, judging by your demeanor toward the man, and your lack of desire to see him punished for his crimes, I can only believe that perhaps you were a willing partner to him."

He gave her no choice but to do what she did next. Rachel rose and walked to him. She slapped his face. "How dare you?" Rachel tamped down the guilt of striking a man for merely telling the truth. She knew she was in trouble. "I am insulted, and I will not stand here and listen to your filthy suggestions. If you will not take me back to the fort, I will go by myself." She started for the tent exit, but Franklin grabbed her arm.

"You are going nowhere at the moment, Miss Morgan. Since you are filthy and very much resemble a savage yourself, I have taken the liberty of having one of my men boil water for you. You will bathe, and I still have the dress you were wearing last time you were with us. Do not leave the safety of my tent, Miss Morgan. If *I* have gone to speculating, you can assume my men have done so also. You aren't safe with them."

He escorted her back to the cot she had been sitting on and indicated that she do so again. Rachel sat. Franklin then moved toward the exit. He paused. "Another thing I find curious. Just now you were willing to leave the protection of an armed military unit and venture out on your own. It doesn't seem the reaction of a woman who should be terrified of being recaptured by a savage who has misused her, and might again misuse her were she to fall into his hands. I'm thinking we should stay put for a couple of days. See if this savage has the nerve to come for you again."

"He's not an idiot," Rachel snapped. She was terrified suddenly, but not of Swift Buck.

Franklin looked over his shoulder, raising a brow. "Now praise for him. This does get more interesting by the minute."

He left, and Rachel realized that she should have kept her mouth shut. She'd been so busy for the past few days trying to outwit Swift Buck, she hadn't given much thought to what she would say or how she should act when she finally managed to find the soldiers' camp and confronted Franklin Peterson again. That had been a mistake. Franklin Peterson wasn't an idiot, either.

CHAPTER TWENTY-NINE

Franklin was a strange man. Rachel couldn't believe he traveled with a tent, much less with a hip tub for bathing. Since she was clean now, though, she wouldn't complain about his eccentricities. She wore the drab, heavy gown she'd worn on the day of her capture, minus underclothes, and she'd dug into the items Mrs. Stark had sent her and washed and brushed the tangles from her hair. Better to look as white as possible, she reasoned, steeling herself for the next confrontation with the captain.

There was a small dining table and chairs inside the tent. He hadn't had these pieces before, and she could only assume he'd left word of what he wanted brought to the wilderness, and someone had supplied his requested amenities. His table was even draped with a white linen tablecloth. His men must consider him insane, and Rachel wasn't too sure he wasn't.

He entered, looking clean and crisp despite their rugged surroundings. She sat at the table, deciding she'd do better if she didn't have to control her shaky legs. He carried two plates and set one down before her. At least he didn't eat high on the hog— the fare was beans and cornbread. Rachel was starving and didn't care what the food was as long as it was edible. Odd, how one could so easily slip into old habits. Rachel forwent her silverware and dug into the beans using a piece of cornbread as a spoon. She hadn't even waited for Franklin to be seated.

Realizing her error too late, she glanced up at him, her mouth full. He smiled indulgently and took his seat. Rachel forced herself to chew slowly. She wiped her fingers on a napkin and dutifully picked up a spoon.

"I haven't eaten in a few days," she said to explain her lack of manners.

"I'm sure you are starving," he commented. "But I am surprised that you aren't thinner than you are. I understand that most Indians' captives are only fed scraps. If they are lucky."

She didn't know what to say. "Since there was only him and the child, the scraps were sufficient," she decided.

He said nothing in response, just picked at his

food while Rachel forced herself not to shovel her own in. Even though she'd decided she would give as little information as possible, she found the silence between them almost more damning.

"Before," she ventured, "when I said that the Apache was not a idiot, I did not mean that statement to be praise. I would think his intelligence is fairly obvious, since he managed to elude you and take me hostage again even after you rescued me. I would prefer that you don't try to put words in my mouth."

"You are defensive," he pointed out.

"Only because you have forced me to be," she countered. "The truth is, Captain, if I had enjoyed being his hostage, why on earth would I escape and return to you?"

"A valid point," he agreed. "Do you mind if I enjoy a cigar? I find I can hardly force this bland meal down again. I do miss my quarters, and my cook."

Rachel was surprised that he hadn't brought his cook along, and his request to smoke in her presence was clearly a snub, because according to proper etiquette, which her sister-in-law had stuffed down Rachel's throat for the past five years, gentlemen did not smoke in the presence of ladies.

"I do mind," she said dutifully.

He lit a cigar anyway, and even blew a puff of smoke in her direction. "Are you by chance related to Clay Morgan?"

She suddenly choked, then made a pretense of waving away his smoke as if that had caused her startled reaction. Why was he asking about Clay? In her current circumstances, admitting an affiliation with her "Indian-loving" brother didn't seem like a wise idea. "I don't believe so," she answered. "Why do you ask?"

Franklin took another long draw on his cigar before answering, "I've been thinking—and frankly, I don't know why it didn't occur to me before now. Clay Morgan is also from Washington, and it is rumored that he once ran wild with the Apaches. He's quite a thorn in the military's side. He's always fighting for Indian rights, causing trouble, making accusations that the Indians are being treated unfairly and deserve this or that. I have never met the man, but I do recall hearing that he had a wife and children . . . and a sister."

He purposely let the end of his statement float in the air like his thick cigar smoke. Rachel knew that to admit she was Clay's sister now would not only place the Mescaleros in further danger, but herself too.

"I do not know the man," she lied. "I suppose if we are both from Washington that we could be distantly related. I have many relations in Washington."

"But you said you were originally from Texas," he reminded. "You said that your father moved the family to Washington because he took an interest in politics, not because he had relations there."

She was starting to get angry, and she knew the emotion wouldn't help her maintain any sense of calm. "We moved for both reasons." She changed the subject. "Do you or do you not plan to take me back to the fort? I'm sure the Starks are worried sick about me."

He sighed, blowing a stream of smoke into the already airless tent. "I said that I would in due time. You've survived worse hardships this long, Miss Morgan. I trust that you can survive a couple of days longer."

"That is where we differ in opinion," she said. Her tone was as cold as she could make it. "I cannot trust any such thing, which has already been proven once before." Frustrated, Rachel felt real tears gather in her eyes. "Please, Franklin. I thought you were a gentleman, and a gentleman would never put a lady in this sort of distress—not to mention danger."

He did not buckle beneath the onslaught of her tears. His eyes did soften, but only for a moment. "I'm afraid we might have both misjudged one another. Why don't you just tell me the truth?"

Her tactics were clearly not working on him. Rachel felt forced to switch to a new plan, although she didn't want to. "I am afraid to tell you the truth," she admitted, which wasn't a lie.

He snuffed out his cigar and leaned across the table. "Why? What are you hiding? I sense that you are lying to me, and I want to know the reason."

As much as it sickened her to do so, she reached across the table and placed her hand over his. "I'm afraid for your life."

He glanced down at her hand resting on his, but he did not remove it. "Afraid? For me? Please explain why."

She swallowed, gathering courage. "There isn't just one Apache," she said.

His brows shot up. "What are you saying?"

"H-he took me to a camp," Rachel stammered. She stopped, gently squeezing his hand before she continued. "There are hundreds of them, Franklin. Hundreds of Apache warriors. I feared that if I told you, you would do something foolish like wait for them to attack your soldiers and be massacred—or worse, you would try to meet them head-on in a battle where they held the advantage. I knew that, no matter if I died trying, I had to escape and warn you, had to convince you to leave these mountains and return to the fort where you at least stood a fighting chance."

"Hundreds," he whispered. "But how could that be possible? I tell you, the campaign launched against the savages was very thorough. Maybe a handful could have escaped, but hundreds?"

"I'm only telling you what I saw," Rachel said. "I was terrified by my ordeal, and then to see so many of them . . . and I knew that if I came in here screaming, crying, and babbling hysterically, you would feel even more honor-bound to risk your life for me, even if the odds are so clearly against you. I cannot have your death on my conscience, and I shudder to think what the warriors will do to me for escaping and warning you when they probably hoped to have the advantage of surprise."

He wasn't persuaded yet; Rachel felt it in the serious way he studied her, in the tense set of his shoulders. "Where is this camp?" he asked.

She shook her head. "I've been wandering around lost for days. I have no sense of direction, and even if I did, I don't know these mountains. I couldn't begin to tell you how to find them. I only know that if we don't flee, and soon, you and your men won't have to find them—they will find you."

"And explain again why you didn't simply tell me all of this to begin with."

This was the trickiest part of changing strategies. Rachel sighed. "Because I have come to know you, Franklin. I know that your duty and your honor would make you do something foolish. Even now, I see that spark of excitement in your eyes to do battle with these savages and prevail. But I fear that this time, you will not prevail."

What she did next she hated most of all. Again she squeezed his cold hand. "I have come to care for you during our short time together. Although I know now that you think of me as being dirty, used, and unworthy of your affections, I do owe you a debt. You have stayed and searched for me when it would have been easier for you and your men to return to that fort and leave me to whatever my fate might have been. I did not want to tempt you into doing battle with the Apaches. I wanted you safely at the fort before I told you the truth."

He pulled his hand from beneath hers and rose. He was clearly torn between believing her and the consequences of dismissing her claims. He paced back and forth while she watched him, hoping her expression reflected sincerity rather than her true riotous emotions. Rachel had never lied so much in her life. She was ashamed that she'd been given the gift of her missing voice only to use it in this manner. But she must lie for Swift Buck, for her people. Her people. She did not bother to mentally correct herself this time.

Rachel realized that beneath her white skin, behind her blue eyes, she would always be an Apache. Never had she felt more at home anywhere than among them. And never had she felt more miserable than she did right now, knowing that she would probably never see them again.

Franklin suddenly stopped before her. "You do realize that if you are lying to me, this would constitute treason. Treason is punishable by death, Rachel."

He'd called her Rachel, so she knew she was getting somewhere. "It was duty that brought me here, Franklin, but now my feelings have changed. I see things more clearly than I did before. I am forced to choose sides, and I have."

Reaching out, Franklin took her hand and pulled her to her feet. "You are a courageous woman, Rachel. I knew that about you from the beginning when you did not balk at the duties you had taken on. I am also that kind of person, and besides your beauty, our similarities in that area drew me to you. As for your ordeal among the Apaches, I am the sort of man who can overlook such a thing. My commission does not pay much—"

"I have a lot of money," she interrupted, noting the hoped-for spark of renewed interest in his eyes. "Once we put this behind us, there will be no need for you to serve in the army. You could do whatever you wish. Live wherever you choose. Maybe we could even restore your old plantation."

Now his eyes swam with greed, and Rachel began to relax—for a moment anyway. He suddenly pulled her close to him. "We must prove to one another that neither of us has been false in our claims of affection. Kiss me, Rachel."

She hoped her expression did not display the sudden repulsion she felt. Kiss him? How could she love one man and kiss another, for any reason? Rachel tried to calm her racing heart. Of course she could kiss him if she must. She'd already told him so many lies, she wasn't even sure what the truth was any longer. She had gone this far to further her plans; she could go a little further. But only a little.

She leaned forward and pressed her lips to his. Again the smell of his tonic water nearly over-powered her. She thought he must bathe in it every time he broke into a sweat. He pulled her closer and nudged her lips apart. He kissed her with an open mouth, but he did not use his tongue. Thank goodness. She wondered how long she must submit, and was struck again by her lack of a reaction. It was if she were kissing a cold fish.

"Captain! Captain!"

Luckily, a soldier burst into the tent and interrupted their intimacy. Still wrapped in Franklin's arms, she glanced at the man.

"I hate to interrupt, sir, but I thought you'd want to see this right away."

The "this" the guard had hauled inside was an Apache. An Apache named Swift Buck. Rachel gasped and tried to disentangle herself from Franklin. Instead of releasing her, he pulled her closer.

"Do not fear, Rachel," Franklin said. "I will protect you from this savage."

CHAPTER THIRTY

Why! Why! Why! Rachel screamed the words inside her head, since she could not express them aloud. Why had Swift Buck been captured, and why did he have to see her in Franklin's arms? Once Franklin released her, she staggered to the cot and collapsed. Now Swift Buck was at Franklin's mercy, and she could do nothing but sit and watch in helpless horror.

Two soldiers were standing at the tent's exit with rifles drawn. Swift Buck's hands were tied in front of him, and Franklin had a gun at the ready. The officer paced in front of Swift Buck, but the movement of Swift Buck's eyes did not follow him. Instead, Swift Buck stared straight ahead, seemingly at nothing. He wouldn't even look at Rachel. She hoped he would know that whatever she'd been doing with Franklin had been a necessary evil.

"I know that you can speak and understand English," Franklin said. "The woman has told me about the others, and about the Apaches' plan for a surprise attack."

Swift Buck's eyes still did not seek her out, but Rachel saw the slight clenching of his jaw muscle. She prayed Franklin would say something to indicate she hadn't told him the entire truth of the matter; otherwise, she would look like a traitor in Swift Buck's eyes—not that she didn't already.

"I want you to tell me where the camp is located."

Swift Buck of course said nothing. Rachel knew he wasn't about to tell Franklin anything. Suddenly Franklin rushed Swift Buck and stuck a pistol barrel against his throat. Rachel had to bite her tongue to keep from screaming.

"Tell me or die," he warned.

Her gentle warrior never flinched. He stayed perfectly still, staring at the same nothingness he'd been staring at since he'd been shoved into the tent. Franklin jerked the gun away and resumed his pacing. As he passed Rachel, he suddenly grabbed her and shoved the gun against her throat.

"Maybe this will work. Tell me or *she* dies."

Heart slamming against her chest, Rachel was so shocked she couldn't even issue a gasp. She hoped

Swift Buck wouldn't do anything foolish. Again his expression never changed, but she thought his jaw muscle jumped again.

After a tense moment, Franklin lowered the gun. He pushed Rachel back down upon the cot and said to her, "You know that I had to make certain."

She tried not to glare at him. Again Franklin took up his pacing. "I'll only ask you one more time," he said to Swift Buck. "After that, I will assume you will continue with this stubbornness and I will simply shoot you, thus ending your bothersome presence here both for me and for Miss Morgan." He took a deep breath. "*Where* is the camp?"

Rachel didn't bother to watch or listen. She knew that Swift Buck would say nothing, and he would continue to stare at nothing, aggravating Franklin all the more. He would die right here, before her very eyes. She couldn't stand to see that happen, but what could she do?

"All right, have it your way," Franklin snapped. Then he marched over and stood directly in front of Swift Buck, pointing the gun at his forehead. Rachel came up off the bed, and Franklin wheeled around to stand at eye level with her.

"But where are my manners? I should let Miss Morgan kill you. I know that deep down she wants to, regardless of her brave act for me." He walked to her and placed his gun in her hand. "Think of all the nights and days he has made you suffer. Think of the ways that he has humiliated you. It will give you the strength to do what you know you want to do."

Rachel glanced numbly at the gun in her hand. She walked to where Swift Buck stood. His eyes finally touched hers. There was no pleading there, but more of a supportive expression. As if he were telling her it was all right for her to shoot him. She raised the gun and pointed it at his forehead. Of course she would not kill him. She loved him. Rachel whipped around, pointing the gun at Franklin.

"Release him," she ordered. One of the guards moved forward, and she warned, "Don't come any closer or I will shoot your captain."

Franklin waved a hand. "It's all right, men." He moved toward Rachel, and she steadied the gun on him. He kept coming, and she had no choice but to pull the trigger. An empty click sounded in the silence. Franklin reached out and snatched the gun from her hand, smiling sadly at her. "It isn't loaded. I had to make certain."

Swift Buck wanted to fight against his bonds. He wanted to place his hands around the pale leader's throat and squeeze the life out of him. The men had deceived her, just as Swift Buck now felt certain that Rachel had deceived the man she called Franklin. But what had she told him? Swift Buck watched as the leader shoved her back down to sit again.

"Now, Rachel, let's begin again, and this time don't lie to me."

"My name is not Rachel," she surprised Swift Buck by saying, and her tone could freeze a man, as he'd once claimed her touch could—before he knew that her touch was warmer than a thousand flames. "My name is *doo yafti da nyol*—Silent Wind."

Pride swelled inside Swift Buck at her courage. The pale leader looked taken aback, but then he sighed.

"And my guess is that you are indeed Clay Morgan's sister and that he was not the only one running wild as a child among the Apaches."

She smiled at him—a chilling smile, Swift Buck thought. The paleface leader actually shivered.

"Tell me the truth and I will try to make your suffering less," he told her. "How many are there? A handful? Hundreds? Or just this one?"

"Hundreds," she said, lifting her chin.

The white man stared at her for a long time, then said, "You're lying. It was just him. You were trying to get me to run back to the fort so I'd stop hunting for him."

She said nothing. It was the right response, Swift Buck thought. So, she had told them that hundreds of Apaches were waiting to attack them. She hadn't told them the truth. He also knew why she had done this: to save The People from warring with the soldiers. To prevent their deaths when they had so few and the soldiers were so many. She had thought she could stop a war, at least for a time.

341

Franklin bent before her. "And the kiss? Did you only pretend to like that as well?"

His face moved closer to her, and Swift Buck struggled against his ropes. He could not sit and watch a man defile his woman. But then Silent Wind spat in the pale leader's face.

"It would have never worked out," she said to him. "You see, I am a mustang, Franklin, and you are a jackass."

One of the guards snickered, and, rather than hit Silent Wind, the leader rose, marched to the guard, and struck him instead.

"Out!" he snapped. "Both of you get out! And tell the others to start packing up the camp. We return to the fort at daybreak."

The officer removed his hat and ran a hand through his yellow hair. He rolled his neck around on his shoulders, then returned to where Silent Wind sat.

"I warned you about the punishment if you were lying to me. Treason is an offense punishable by death. Your brother and his money are not here to save you. You and that Indian lover of yours have made a fool of me. You will both serve as examples. As soon as we reach the fort, I intend to have you both shot by a firing squad."

The man rose and tugged at his gloves. "Now I will have you bound and leave the two of you alone tonight so that you and your lover can say your good-byes." He strode toward the exit but stopped.

"What about the child?" he asked, his gaze inquiring of Swift Buck. "What did you do with her?"

Swift Buck would not answer.

"I'm sure he left her somewhere with food and water. Somewhere he thought she would be safe from the elements," Silent Wind said.

"If you tell me her location, I will have one of my men ride out and bring her back. She can be raised on the reservation."

"Why? So she can grow to womanhood and your soldiers can rape her?" Swift Buck asked. "I would rather she die free than see her living beneath the white man's thumb."

The captain shrugged. "So be it. One less mouth to feed."

He opened the tent flap and stepped outside, calling for a guard. Silent Wind rose and rushed to Swift Buck. She threw her arms around his neck.

"Why did you come? How could you let them capture you?"

"I had to see you again," he said. "It is easier to get in than it is to get out."

She held his face, kissed his cheeks, his eyes. "I thought I would never see you again, and I'm sorry that I see you like this. I have to know one thing: Did you come for me because you thought I betrayed you? Or did you come for me for another reason?"

He stared into her blue eyes. "I came because I love you. You might have tricked me to escape, but

343

I knew you would not purposely betray The People, or me. I was afraid the pale leader might be suspicious of you by now. I feared for you."

"And now you die along with me," she whispered, and her eyes filled with tears. "I would never ask you to do that for me."

"You would not have to ask. I would gladly die for you."

Their lips almost touched when Franklin and a guard returned. Silent Wind took a step back.

Peterson frowned. "Tie her hands together. Tie his feet to the chair so he cannot get up. I want a guard stationed around every inch of this tent tonight. Understand?"

"Yes, sir," the man agreed, saluting. He tied Swift Buck's feet to the chair first. Then he moved to Silent Wind, and she held out her hands. While he tied her, the man kept glancing up at her.

"Captain, the men and me were wondering . . . well, being she's a traitor and all. We were thinking maybe we could have some fun with her tonight."

"Any man who touches her will be shot right along with her—is that understood?"

The man nodded but looked disappointed.

"You see, Miss Morgan, I do still have a few gentlemanly traits left. I assume you knew this Apache before."

"Yes," she answered. "I have loved him for a long time."

The guard snorted and mumbled something under his breath. Peterson cuffed him and told him to leave.

"Was your intention all along to rescue these people?"

Silent Wind said nothing for a moment. "No. I thought I could help them. I thought food and medicine would heal them, but it will not. Freedom is the very air that they breathe. You cannot understand this. You are not of The People."

"We are all slaves to something, Miss Morgan," the officer said. "I am a slave to my duty. It is all I have left to take pride in. I hope you understand that and do not think too harshly of me. In truth, I wish I had not shot the mustang."

The pale man left. Swift Buck did not understand their conversation, but Silent Wind did. Tears gathered in her eyes, and her bottom lip trembled. They sat and said nothing until the candle flickered and went low.

They could see the shapes of men outside, all around the tent, guarding them. Finally the candle went out, and they sat in darkness. Swift Buck heard a soft noise; then he felt Silent Wind's breath against his ear.

"I thought I would only have one night with you," she whispered. "But we have been given another night together."

He smiled. "Our hands are tied," he reminded her softly.

"That is true." Her tongue darted out and

touched his ear. "But you are wearing little, and beneath this dress, I am wearing nothing. We do not need our hands."

Rachel loved the way he smelled: clean, like the air after a snowfall. She straddled his lap and placed her bound hands over his neck so her arms rested upon his shoulders. He did the same. She could not run her hands over his body, but she felt his heat. Their lips joined, and the kiss was a mixture of tenderness laced with urgency.

She was glad he knew she had not deceived him and The People. She was glad he had faith in her. Tonight, she would have shot Franklin if the gun had been loaded. She had stood and fought, because she understood now that it was different when you had something to fight for. She might die tomorrow, but tonight her heart was free.

"I am not sorry I came back," she whispered against his lips. "I found my place. I understand now who I am, and I know that it is all right to be that person. My heart is neither white nor Apache, but it belongs to you."

His hands, tied together draped around her neck, twisted in her long hair. "I am proud to love you," he said. "There is no shame for us any longer. I would have asked you to join with me. I would have asked you to come into my lodge and be my wife, raise my daughter with me, and the sons and daughters of our own flesh."

She pressed her forehead against his, and joy

filled her. "I would have said yes," she whispered. "My place has always been with you and The People. Not long ago, I was afraid that I was not strong enough to stay with you during these dark days, but now I know that I am."

Beneath his breechclout, she felt him harden for her. She rubbed against him, her dress wadded up around her hips but unencumbered by undergarments. The rubbing alone excited her, but she wanted to feel him inside her. She had an idea. Lifting her arms from around his neck, she slid out of his arms and went to her knees on the floor.

"Silent Wind," he said hoarsely. "What are you doing?"

Rather than answer, she showed him. She used her mouth to lift the corner of his breechclout and move it aside. His thighs were muscled and warm, and she couldn't resist running her tongue down the insides of them. He jerked and muttered an Apache curse word. His sex was long, hard, and throbbing when she took him into her mouth. Without the use of her hands, she could only please him a little. He was too big.

"Silent Wind," he whispered, his voice urgent. "I want to be inside you."

She rose and used her hands to bunch up the front of her dress; then she straddled him again. He slid into her smoothly, nearly taking her breath away with his size. Her arms went around his neck, and his around hers. Their mouths joined, and they moved slowly. It took all of her willpower not to moan against his lips.

His breath came in harsh gasps, and since she had leverage and he did not, she used her legs to lift and lower herself upon him. He curved his hips up, thrusting deep inside her. They were moist and hot against one another, and the friction between them started the gathering ecstasy inside her. Tighter and tighter she coiled as he thrust into her until finally she snapped. She dug her teeth into his shoulder to keep from crying out. He thrust deep, and she felt him tense against her, heard the soft sound he made in his throat.

They sat together, joined, both breathing hard and trying to keep silent. Then Rachel simply rested her head against his shoulder and enjoyed being next to him. Finally the awkward position of their bodies forced them apart. She settled upon the cot, trying to slow the wild pounding of her heart.

"Silent Wind," he whispered to her. "I would not like to be found by the guards in the morning with my . . . well, uncovered."

She might have smiled under any other circumstances. Instead she said, "I will take care of it, but later. I am not finished with you yet."

CHAPTER THIRTY-ONE

The ride back to the reservation was uneventful. Swift Buck kept watching the bluffs, hoping warriors would suddenly appear there—hundreds of warriors, but his dreams did not take the shape of reality. The white leader did not let them ride together, but made Silent Wind ride beside him. Swift Buck's hands were bound together and tied around the saddle horn of the horse he rode. He could not jump off and try to run.

For Amoke's sake, he would have wished to, but he would never abandon Silent Wind when she needed him. She rode with her back straight and her head held high, like a true Apache. He realized now that she had needed those five years she had spent in the white world. She had been nurtured by her brother's love, and she had learned that although it was a place where people wore the same skin color as she, her heart was different.

It was true what Cougar had said, that she must have a choice—otherwise, she might not have known to cherish the gift that she had been given by her abusive father. The gift of love. The gift of belonging. The gift of being a Mescalero.

He could see the fort ahead. Their party had been spotted, and soldiers and Indians alike had gathered to see what they would see. To give his brothers strength, Swift Buck would sit straight, be proud even until death took him.

No one spoke; no child even cried as they rode past the Apaches. The captured people's expressions of defeat nearly broke his heart. He was a hero to them, he suspected, for daring what he did, escaping this place, the white man's hell.

Suddenly a voice spoke to them, loud and strong, the voice of a woman. "People!" Silent Wind shouted in Apache. "Gather your pride around you! Ready yourself for the day! Your brothers are coming!"

A loud cheer went up among his brothers. Swift Buck smiled. He could not help himself. Such a woman, and she was his . . . at least for a little while longer. Their horses danced nervously over the noise, and the soldiers held their weapons tighter. The pale leader rode as straight and proud as Swift Buck and Silent Wind, and Swift Buck thought for a moment that the white man should have been an Apache. But Swift Buck also knew that a man who could not bend would someday break.

Rachel kept up a façade of courage. Inside, she was terrified. She didn't want to die, but then, without Swift Buck by her side, she really did not want to live either. She caught a glimpse of black and saw Roman and Nelda Stark staring at her, their mouths hanging open wide. The sight of Nelda clutching the hand of a small Apache girl comforted her. She guessed Nelda had faced her demons during her absence.

Rachel was surprised when the captain ordered that Swift Buck be taken to the stockade and guarded, but she was to be confined to his quarters.

"I would rather be with Swift Buck," she told him.

His jaw clenched. "You may call yourself a savage now, Miss Morgan, but you came to my fort a white woman, and I will show you proper respect . . . up until I have you shot for treason."

"You are too kind," she retorted. Dread filled her to ask the next question. "W-when?" was all she could manage.

"At sunrise tomorrow," he answered. "I will, of course, send the reverend and his good wife to you for religious purposes. You do believe in the Christian God, don't you, Miss Morgan?"

"Yes, I believe in God—but I also believe that He goes by many names. To the Apaches, he is Usen or The Great Spirit."

"Well, pray to whomever you must. I am sorry that it has all turned out this way. If examples are not set and rules adhered to, we would live in a world of chaos."

As she rode past the starving Indians lining the way to the fort, their faces drawn, their clothes ragged, she said, "We already do, Captain."

Why had they taken her away? Swift Buck could withstand any torture but the torture of being without Silent Wind. He stared up at a full moon, his hands and feet bound, alone in a place of high fences and utter loneliness. To battle despair, he thought about Amoke and Silent Wind, he saw them together, walking in the meadow, poised before the great falls, rainbows dancing around them.

He smiled, the bright moon above shining down upon him, and in his mind, he joined Amoke and Silent Wind, holding them tightly in his arms.

A loud screech brought him from his thoughts, and he glanced up. Two eagles cast a shadow against the moon.

"I don't understand," Nelda Stark whispered, "The captain says you are to be shot for treason. You return to us yelling in Apache as if you've spoken it all your life."

"I have," she said, then corrected herself. "I mean I have been listening to it most of my life. As a child, I was raised by the Mescaleros."

"You tricked us into coming here," the reverend said.

"No. I mean, yes, but no," Rachel answered. "I wanted to help my people. I didn't know any other way but the way I chose. Forgive me."

Nelda's eyes watered. "You poor child. Sentenced by the captain to be shot. I don't know what to say—what to do. These people of yours—I was afraid of them. Then one day this little child came up and took my hand as if she had known me all my life. Suddenly, I realized that what most people call savages are only people who live and think differently than us. We opened our hearts to these people, and they opened theirs to us. I can't thank you enough for bringing us on this mission with you."

Shocked, Rachel glanced at the reverend. He nodded his head and came to her, taking her hand. "I said once that I would try to be more like you, and I will. Can I pray for you tonight?" he asked.

Rachel clasped hands with Roman and Nelda. "Yes. And pray for Swift Buck, too. I love him so much."

"He's the mean one, isn't he?" Nelda asked.

Her eyes tearing, Rachel shook her head. "No. He is my gentle warrior. I want you both to do something for me," she said. "When you return to

Washington, I want you to find my brother, Clay Morgan. Please tell him that I finally found my place, and that I am happy."

The Starks teared up, and nodded. "Do you want us to stay with you through the night?" Nelda asked.

Rachel didn't want to be alone, but only Swift Buck would suffice, and that was not possible. "No, but thank you. I would rather be alone . . . to think. To reflect and pray."

"Is there anything else we can do?" the reverend asked.

"If Nelda can, I would like for her to slip out to the camp and borrow a doeskin dress from one of the women for me. I want to wear it tomorrow."

Pinching her lips together to control a sob, Nelda nodded, then hurried off. The reverend left the room, and Rachel found herself alone. It would be the longest night she would spend in her life.

CHAPTER THIRTY-TWO

The doeskin dress she wore was old and a little ragged, but Rachel did not mind. She'd braided her hair and said her farewells once again to the Starks. Captain Peterson frowned over her choice of clothing, but he said nothing as he tied her wrists together and escorted her outside. Dawn streaked the sky with vivid colors of red, pink, and purple. The sunrise nearly took her breath away, and she wondered if impending death made everything look sharper, brighter, and more beautiful.

Swift Buck stood surrounded by guards, his hands also bound. He had never looked more handsome. Rachel hurried to his side, staring up into his eyes. She would have touched his face if her hands were not bound.

"You said to me that you were happy that you had come back," he told her. "Today I cannot be happy about your return to us. If you had stayed away, you would not be here with me, facing death."

"It was my destiny to return," she said. "This must be my destiny as well."

"We cannot join together in this world, but we will join in the next."

She couldn't hold back the tears, but she did not want him to see her cry, so she tried. "It is a good day to die."

"I would have rather left fighting," he admitted. "Fighting for you, for Amoke, for my people."

Her escape had stolen that from him, she realized. She had hoped to stop a war, and she supposed she had succeeded . . . at least for a little while. But what she had prevented was, she supposed, inevitable at some point. Maybe Swift Buck was right and it would have been better to go out fighting.

"I am sorry," she whispered. "You should not die this way."

He straightened. "I am proud to die by your side. Together we will show our people Apache pride. We will show them that we do not fear death, and maybe give them their spirit back."

His words made her straighten as well. He was right. She had been afraid most of her life. She would not be afraid today.

"Let's get to it," Franklin snapped. "Move."

Spines straight, heads held high, she and Swift Buck walked to a place where a line of soldiers waited, rifles in hand. So many rifles, so many bullets to tear into their flesh. Rachel thought it was a bit ridiculous. One rifle would do the task easily enough. Franklin did like ceremony.

But the captain didn't look as smug as she would have thought. His eyes were red and he looked tired, as if maybe he had spent the night awake as well. He carried a blindfold in his hand. One, not two.

He approached her. "I would like you to wear this over your eyes," he said.

She would not give him the satisfaction. "No. I want to be looking at the man I love when you have your men kill me. That is really the reason I am dying today, isn't it, Franklin? Because I love the wrong man?"

His gaze slid away from her. "Miss Morgan—Rachel, I have done many hard things in the line of duty, but I must say that this is the hardest for me. I do have feelings for you, but my country must come first. You have become an Apache, by your choice, and you have lied on their behalf. You have chosen the enemy over your own kind, and for that you must face the penalty."

"We are only the enemy because we stand in the way of the white man's desire to own everything he sees. We are only the enemy because we will not give up the life that we love for the life that you would have us live. That life, one of suppression and humility, is no life at all."

Franklin glanced at Swift Buck. "Do you let your woman do your talking for you?"

Swift Buck smiled, which she knew would only aggravate Franklin more since they should both be cowed and begging for their lives. "Her words echo my thoughts. The Apache man does not find a wise wife a threat to him, but an asset. He takes pride in her spirit. You seek to make an example of us to our people, when what you show them is what they already know: What the white man cannot control, what he cannot understand, he destroys. Our deaths will not weaken their spirits but strengthen them, because today we die to honor them and the life they once knew. Today our pride becomes their pride. Today we set their hearts free, even if their bodies must remain prisoners."

Pride swelled inside Rachel—no, she would not think of herself as Rachel Brodie, or Rachel Morgan again. From this day forward, she was only Silent Wind, and maybe someday her name would be whispered around campfires along with Swift Buck's, and stories would be told of how their spirits lived on even if their bodies were gone.

Franklin glanced at the Indians he had ordered to watch their execution, and Rachel saw his self-doubt written on his features. Swift Buck had made Peterson wonder if what he did would crush the Apaches' spirits, or fuel their hatred with more reasons to despise the whites. She knew Franklin, though, and to back down now would make him look weak—and he would never admit to having weaknesses, especially over a woman.

"Take them," he said softly to the guards.

Silent Wind and Swift Buck were pushed forward. They were herded to where they must stand facing the soldiers with rifles, and then the guards left them there. They stood straight and proud.

"Look at me," Silent Wind said, and they turned to face one another, clasping hands even though their wrists were bound.

"I love you," Silent Wind said to him.

"You are my heart," he said to her.

"Ready!" the captain called.

She heard the rifles cock from the short distance that separated them from their executioners.

"Aim!" Franklin's voice wavered slightly.

There came the sounds of the rifles being raised.

"Captain!" someone shouted. "Look!"

Rachel's gaze had been locked with Swift Buck's, and it was difficult to break the contact but she glanced at the soldiers and saw them staring into the distance. Her gaze followed their direction. Twenty mounted Apaches moved toward them. She saw the paint glinting off their bodies and off the coats of their horses. They had come to fight.

The People let out a loud roar. The firing squad seemed confused about whom they should aim their rifles at, and then the captives of the reservation surrounded her and Swift Buck, shielding them with their bodies. She felt the ropes around her hands being cut, and wondered where The People had come by knives.

"Captain! What should we do?" a soldier shouted.

"There's only twenty or so of them!" he shouted back. "We fight!"

"But the prisoners!" another man shouted. "I think they are going to rebel!"

Silent Wind knew what Franklin's order would be, and she struggled to push through those crowding around her. Swift Buck was right beside her, a knife clutched in his hand. They both emerged at the same time to stand before the prisoners.

"No! Franklin!" she shouted, then ran to him. "They are not a herd of horses. They are people, and you can't just shoot them when they have no way of protecting themselves!"

The area surrounding them looked like chaos. Soldiers ran here and there, raising dust as they took up positions to defend themselves.

"I have no choice!" Peterson shouted back at her.

"Yes, you do!"

Through the dust and shuffle of feet a voice came to them. To Silent Wind, it seemed as if everyone froze. She froze, too. She knew that voice. The dust seemed to magically settle, and a man sat before them upon a horse. A pack mule stood beside his horse.

"Clay," she whispered.

He nudged the animal closer. "You have two choices, Captain," he said. Clay nodded toward the pack mule at his side. "The first one is this. Every one of these bags is filled with gold. I finally realized that talking wasn't doing any good. There's enough gold here to buy you and all of your men a better life."

Franklin sputtered beside her. "Do you think you can just ride in here and buy these Apaches?"

Clay shrugged. "That would be up to you and your men. It's an awful lot of gold just to look the other way."

Rachel knew Franklin coveted gold, and she tried to encourage that vice. "You can go anywhere you want, Franklin," she said softly. "You can go home and rebuild your plantation."

Franklin licked his lips. She could tell that he was tempted. The solders were also interested—not as many were hugging their rifles so tightly against them. Then Franklin straightened, and a sinking feeling settled in the pit of Silent Wind's stomach.

"I have my duty, Mr. Morgan." He frowned. "What is the other choice?"

Clay glanced behind him. Silent Wind realized that everyone had been distracted by Clay's sudden appearance. Her eyes widened. There were no longer just twenty Apache warriors gathered behind them. There were hundreds.

"Death," Clay answered. "I rounded up a few of

my friends on the way. You can fight, but as you can plainly see, you cannot win. Not this time."

Franklin's Adam's apple bobbed. "If you take up arms with these Apaches, you are committing treason against your country," he croaked.

Her brother shrugged again. "I imagine the Apaches can take care of this without my help. Besides, none of you will be left alive to accuse me of anything. And it's not just my country, Captain. It's their country, too."

"Let's take the gold, for Christ's sake!" one of the soldiers shouted. "We're outnumbered!"

The captain only took a moment to evaluate the situation. He pointed to one of his men. "You! Get the pack mule and take it inside the fort walls. The rest of us will follow and close the gates."

Silent Wind almost breathed a sigh of relief when an Apache yell shattered the quiet and Swift Buck lunged forward, knocking Franklin Peterson to the ground, his knife poised at the man's throat. The soldiers did not rush to their captain's aid.

"I will kill you now," Swift Buck hissed.

Silent Wind watched for a moment. Beads of sweat ran down Franklin's face. But to his credit, he did not cower. Instead, he lifted his head so that his throat would be exposed.

"Go ahead," he goaded.

Gently Silent Wind placed a hand on Swift Buck's shoulder. "No, Swift Buck. It has to begin somewhere. The healing instead of the killing.

Compassion instead of hatred. Let it begin with us."

His knife shook, and she knew how badly he fought himself. She could not really blame him. Captain Peterson had been responsible for much suffering and many crimes against their people.

With a groan, Swift Buck pulled the knife away. He leaned down close to Franklin's face. "If I see you again, if you or your soldiers do not leave us in peace, I *will* kill you."

Swift Buck rose, and Franklin scrambled up from the dirt. It was the first time she'd seen him dirty, Silent Wind realized. The captain rose and ran for the fort. The heavy gates closed with a resounding thud behind him. No one moved for a moment; then Swift Buck took control of the situation.

"Go!" he shouted to the prisoners. "Gather what you have. We leave this place."

Shouts of joy rose around them. The mounted warriors approached and stationed themselves between the fort and the prisoners who hurried away to gather their few belongings. Clay dismounted, and Silent Wind ran to him, throwing her arms around his neck.

"You saved us," she said, her voice breaking.

"I should wring your neck for this stunt you pulled," he scolded, but he hugged her to him. He released her and walked to Swift Buck.

"It is good to see you, brother," Clay said. "After

I heard about the massacre, I feared you would be dead."

"You should have come sooner," Swift Buck said, his tone cool.

Clay nodded. "Yes, I should have come sooner. I thought words would make a difference, but the whites are not ready to listen. Not to words anyway. But they still listen to gold. I have purchased the Sacred Mountains for you and The People. Bribe money, but it will keep you safe there until the government gives you full rights to your land."

"Do you mean that we can live in peace there?" Swift Buck asked. "That we will not be forced to fight to keep the land?"

"Not for a while anyway," Clay answered. "I can't promise you a lifetime there, Swift Buck. I know as well as you do that the white man does not always keep his word. But right now, they are tired of fighting."

Swift Buck nodded.

Clay turned to Rachel. "I have a horse for you. I'm taking you home."

She opened her mouth to speak, but Swift Buck spoke first.

"No," he said. "You will not take her from me again."

CHAPTER THIRTY-THREE

His blood brother frowned. "She doesn't belong here with you, Swift Buck. I almost had to fight you to let me take her the last time. I will fight you again if I must."

"So be it," Swift Buck told him, then stepped forward and threw down his knife. "We have fought over Silent Wind with words, but now we fight with fists."

Cougar raised his fists and stepped forward. Silent Wind got between them.

"I will not have the man I love and my brother smashing each other's faces." She turned to her brother. "I love him, Clay, and I won't run away this time."

"But, Rachel," he argued. "You heard me. I have

bought them peace for a time, but I may not be able to buy it for long. The life you choose will be one of hardship, danger. I can't let you stay."

Swift Buck pulled his woman aside and put his face in her brother's. "Do you not trust me to take care of Silent Wind? Do you not trust me to provide for her? Protect her?"

"You almost got her killed today!"

Silent Wind again wedged herself between them. "That is not true, Clay. I'm the one who almost got *him* killed today. What better proof can a man give a woman of his love than to risk his own life because he thought she had placed herself in danger? What greater proof of his love than to die beside her?"

Her brother frowned and stepped around her to face Swift Buck. "Think of everything you are asking her to give up," he said.

Swift Buck had not really thought of that. Her fine things, the fine home her brother lived in. Luxuries he could never give her. Silent Wind spoke before he could answer, though.

"I don't want those things you can give me, Clay. I appreciate them, but all I want is to be with Swift Buck. To help him raise his daughter, Amoke, and to raise our own children together. The place you have found for yourself is not my place. My place is with The People, Clay. My place has always been with them."

"Amoke is your daughter?" Clay asked Swift

Buck. He suddenly tensed. "I will not allow my sister to be just *one* of your wives."

Swift Buck gently pushed Silent Wind aside. "I took a wife when I thought that your sister would not return to me. The one we called White Dove died giving my daughter birth. I respected the one who is gone; I treated her kindly, but she is dead. Always your sister has had my heart, and I will not share it with another. She will be the only wife in my lodge."

Cougar glanced away from him and looked at his sister. "Is this what you really want, Rachel?"

She straightened her spine. "My name is Silent Wind. Rachel is gone. She died long ago, Clay. You said you wanted me to have a choice, remember? I have made my choice. I will make my life with Swift Buck, the man I have always loved. I will make my life with my people."

Swift Buck's heart swelled with love and pride. He'd thought he could never have her but he had always loved her, and now she would at last be his. And he hers. She had chased the bitterness from his heart and taught him to love again.

Cougar sighed. "I will miss you," he said to his sister.

Her eyes clouded with tears, and she hugged her brother. "If you have bought us peace for a time, it may be the right time to bring your wife back to visit The People. It may be time to introduce your children to those who accepted you when your own people would not."

Her brother smiled. "It took some talking and a few hundred warriors as a gift to get Gray Wolf to allow me inside his camp." He glanced at Swift Buck. "He's not too happy with you, either, by the way. He said he was going to follow you, but then Jageitci convinced him that Silent Wind would never deceive her people, and he decided to trust both you and my sister. Your devotion to her after your anger was enough to convince him."

Swift Buck was glad that The People trusted Silent Wind. He would have left them for her if they had not accepted her back among them, but now he was not forced to do so.

The People started moving past them, carrying their possessions.

"Will you come with us?" Silent Wind asked her brother.

He nodded toward the fort. "I have a little unfinished business inside. Documents I have to present to the captain to let him know he must not go snooping around the Sacred Mountains. Although I have a feeling this fort will soon be deserted," he added with a slight smile.

"Tell the Starks good-bye for me," Silent Wind said. "Tell them that The People left the reservation with all their most prized possessions, and that I saw many of them carrying Bibles. Maybe you can escort the two of them back to Washington," she suggested.

Her brother nodded agreement. He sighed, then hugged his sister again. To Swift Buck, he extended his hand. Swift Buck took it, and his blood brother, now his brother-in-law, pulled him closer.

"I'll be along shortly. I *will* see my sister married before I go back."

Swift Buck noted Cougar's warning and, together, he and Silent Wind watched Cougar lead his horse toward the fort. The gates cracked open and the white man slipped inside.

The gathered warriors started moving out. Swift Buck watched the line of Apaches moving away from the reservation. A shadow crossed overhead, and he glanced up to see the eagles that watched over him.

He took Silent Wind's hand, and together they began their long journey home.

In Trouble's Arms — Ronda Thompson

Loreen Matland is very clear. If the man who answers her ad for a husband is ugly as a mud fence, she'll keep him. If not, she'll fill his hide full of buckshot. Unfortunately, Jake Winslow is handsome. Lori knows that good-looking men are trouble, and Jake proves no exception. Of course, she hasn't been entirely honest with him, either. She has difficulties enough to make his flight from the law seem like a ride through the prairie. But the Texas Matlands don't give up, even to dangerous men with whiskey-smooth voices. And yet, in Jake's warm strong arms, Lori knows he is just what she needs—for her farm, her family, and her heart.

Lair of the Wolf

Also includes the sixth installment of *Lair of the Wolf*, a serialized romance set in medieval Wales. Be sure to look for future chapters of this exciting story featured in Leisure books and written by the industry's top authors.

___4716-0 $5.99 US/$6.99 CAN

PRICKLY PEAR

RONDA THOMPSON

Daddy's little girl is no angel. Heck, she hasn't earned the nickname Prickly Pear by being a wallflower. Everyone on the Circle C knows that Camile Cordell can rope her way out of Hell itself—and most of the town thinks the willful beauty will end up there sooner or later. Now, Cam knows that her father is looking for a new foreman for their ranch—and the blond firebrand is pretty sure she knows where to find one. Wade Langtry has just arrived in Texas, but he seems darn sure of himself in trying to take a job that is hers. Cam has to admit, though, that he has what it takes to break stallions. In her braver moments, she even imagines what it might feel like to have the roughrider break her to the saddle—or she him. And she fears that in the days to follow, it won't much matter if she looses her father's ranch—she's already lost her heart.

___4624-5 $4.99 US/$5.99 CAN